He had never made a bigger fool of himself in his entire life.

And that was saying something.

Michael Lafferty sighed. What a mess. It was his job to help the district attorney convict Alicia Walker, and yet every time he saw the accused murderess, all he wanted to do was get her into bed. He had to put a stop to it. And worse than his personal interest in the murder suspect was his overwhelming desire to help her, which was going to make him about as popular with his superiors as a lion at a lamb picnic. This was all wrong in every way—he knew that, but he had to force himself to stay where he was and not run back into the house and pick up where they had left off.

Dear Reader,

Welcome to another month of fabulous reading from Silhouette Intimate Moments, the line that brings you excitement along with your romance every month. As I'm sure you've already noticed, the month begins with a return to CONARD COUNTY, in *Involuntary Daddy*, by bestselling author Rachel Lee. As always, her hero and heroine will live in your heart long after you've turned the last page, along with an irresistible baby boy nicknamed Peanut. You'll wish you could take him home yourself.

Award winner Marie Ferrarella completes her CHILDFINDERS, INC. trilogy with *Hero in the Nick of Time*, about a fake marriage that's destined to become real, and not one, but *two*, safely recovered children. Marilyn Pappano offers the second installment of her HEARTBREAK CANYON miniseries, *The Horseman's Bride*. This Oklahoma native certainly has a way with a Western man! After too long away, Doreen Owens Malek returns with our MEN IN BLUE title, *An Officer and a Gentle Woman*, about a cop falling in love with his prime suspect. Kylie Brant brings us the third of THE SULLIVAN BROTHERS in *Falling Hard and Fast*, a steamy read that will have your heart racing. Finally, welcome RaeAnne Thayne, whose debut book for the line, *The Wrangler and the Runaway Mom*, is also a WAY OUT WEST title. You'll be happy to know that her second book is already scheduled.

Enjoy them all—and then come back again next month, when once again Silhouette Intimate Moments brings you six of the best and most exciting romances around.

Yours,

Leslie J. Wainger

Leslie J. Wainger
Executive Senior Editor

Please address questions and book requests to:
Silhouette Reader Service
U.S.: 3010 Walden Ave., P.O. Box 1325, Buffalo, NY 14269
Canadian: P.O. Box 609, Fort Erie, Ont. L2A 5X3

AN OFFICER AND A GENTLE WOMAN

DOREEN OWENS MALEK

Published by Silhouette Books

America's Publisher of Contemporary Romance

SILHOUETTE BOOKS

ISBN 0-373-07958-3

AN OFFICER AND A GENTLE WOMAN

This edition published by arrangement with Harlequin Books S.A.

® and TM are trademarks of Harlequin Books S.A., used under license.
Trademarks indicated with ® are registered in the United States Patent
and Trademark Office, the Canadian Trade Marks Office and in other
countries.

Visit us at www.romance.net

Printed in U.S.A.

Books by Doreen Owens Malek

Silhouette Intimate Moments

The Eden Tree #88
Devil's Deception #105
Montega's Mistress #169
Danger Zone #204
A Marriage of Convenience #282
An Officer and a
  Gentle Woman #958

Silhouette Special Edition

A Ruling Passion #154

Silhouette Romance

The Crystal Unicorn #363

Silhouette Desire

Native Season #86
Reckless Moon #222
Winter Meeting #240
Desperado #260
Firestorm #290
Bright River #343
Roughneck #450
Arrow in the Snow #747
The Harder They Fall #778
Above the Law #869
Daddy's Choice #983
Big Sky Drifter #1097

DOREEN OWENS MALEK

is a former attorney who decided on her current career when she sold her fledgling novel to the first editor who read it. Since then, she has gained recognition for her writing, winning honors from *Romantic Times Magazine* and the coveted Golden Medallion Award from the Romance Writers of America. She has traveled extensively throughout Europe, but it was in her home state of New Jersey that she met and married her college sweetheart. They now live in Pennsylvania.

For my Monica, the karate kid.

Chapter 1

The security guard, whose name was Moresby, lounged against the wall near the entrance to the stage of the Plaza Hotel ballroom, straightening when he saw Alicia Walker come in by the back door.

"Mrs. Walker," he said deferentially, touching the brim of his cap. "We were told you were ill. The Chairman will be so glad you were able to make it after all, even just for the end."

The woman smiled briefly and glanced at the steps leading to the podium.

"He's still onstage—he'll be departing from the green-room on the other side," Moresby said.

She nodded.

"You still have time to slip in and leave with him, if you like," he added helpfully.

She nodded again and brushed past him, leaving a drift of expensive scent in her wake, clutching her bag to her side. The guard watched her go, his eyes skimming her slim figure in the beige silk Adolfo suit, dropping to the exquisite legs sheathed in sheer hose and the narrow feet shod in calfskin pumps. He sighed mentally. What a looker. If he had that waiting for him at home *and* two hundred million dollars he wouldn't be spending all his time stumping for a stressful political job no sane man would want in the first place.

But who ever knew what Joseph Walker, called The Chairman by his friends and associates, was thinking?

The woman stopped at the stage's entrance, nodding to the press secretary, Drew Smithson, who glanced up at her in surprise. He was gesturing for her to join them when Walker swept off the stage, beaming at the burst of applause that accompanied his departure. As the members of the press rattled their papers and recorders, and the flash cameras whirred, she stepped into the shadows, waiting until Walker had left the stage. He trotted down the steps, leaving the press gathering behind as he was enclosed by several of his advisors.

The crowd noise faded as the auditorium emptied, and the Walker group progressed along a hall, heading for the kitchen exit. Suddenly the woman stepped forward, reaching for her bag in the same motion. A pistol appeared in her hand as Smithson, the only one in the small group not looking at his boss, saw what she was doing and his mouth fell open in horror.

She took aim with practiced ease as Smithson frantically shouted a warning. Walker, still high from the crowd's approval, glanced at his aide in confusion as a bullet entered the side of his head and effectively ended his life. Those closest to him, alerted by the muffled *thup* of the silencer, stopped and stared, trying to understand what was happening. Walker reeled, and in the second before he collapsed, the woman saw that she had found her target, shoved the gun into her purse and ran.

Smithson dashed after her as two others rushed to Walker's side. Two more aides scrambled frantically for cover as realization of the tragedy dawned. The departing press conference crowd, chattering and shuffling in ignorance of the drama taking place nearby, flooded into an area near the other end of the hall, thwarting Smithson's efforts to catch the assailant. He bellowed in helpless frustration as the police, summoned by Smithson's shouts and focused on the wounded man, let Walker's wife rush by them and make her escape handily.

"Grab her!" Smithson screamed at a New York City patrolman, who looked at the woman's departing form, then back at him in puzzlement.

"She shot him, dammit, grab her!" Smithson shouted, pointing, but it was too late. She had fled through the emerging crowd and was gone.

"Mrs. Walker, what happened?" Moresby gasped in alarm, as she almost knocked him down on her way past him. "Are you all right?"

She didn't meet his eyes and didn't answer, flying through the door just as the call came from the interior of the building, "Seal all the exits, Mr. Walker's been shot."

The guard charged after her, gun drawn, but she had vanished into the street.

"Where's Mrs. Walker?" Moresby yelled to another guard, who was shoving his way through the swarm of people.

"I didn't see her."

Moresby scanned the crowd once again and then ran back inside to use the police radio. It was possible that a patrol car could catch her on the road.

Inside, Smithson turned back to Walker, who was

sprawled on the floor surrounded by the small group. Most of the reporters and photographers had left, unaware that anything had happened behind the scenes, and the few who had realized something was wrong were held back from the scene by the police. A figure detached itself from Walker's side and hurried over to Smithson. It was Chuck Weiss, a Walker administrative assistant. His face was the color of cream and his crisp tailored shirt was stained with blood.

"How is he?" Smithson gasped.

Weiss shook his head and closed his eyes, his lips trembling. "There's a doctor with him, but...his head—" He stopped and swallowed. "I'm sure he's dead."

Smithson sighed deeply, glancing over at the prone figure, visible only from the knees down. His expression was tinged with sadness and regret. Then it hardened.

"Did you see her?" he asked sharply.

"Who?" Weiss replied, pushing his disordered hair back with a shaking hand.

"Alicia. After Joe was shot, she darted out of here."

Weiss stared at him blankly for a moment, then recovered his wits. "What the hell are you saying?"

"I'm saying," Smithson replied flatly, "that Joseph Walker was murdered by his wife, and I saw her do it."

When Alicia Walker's doorbell rang an hour later in Scarsdale, the sound awakened her from a light sleep. She blinked groggily at the clock, remembered that she had sent Maizie home at three in the afternoon, and reached for her robe. She was belting it around her waist and padding softly down the wide, winding stairwell when the doorbell rang again.

"All right, all right, I'm coming," she muttered, crossing the flowered Aubusson rug on the parquet floor.

She switched on the overhead light and the brass chandelier flooded the foyer with a warm glow. She pulled open the door.

Two policemen with badges on display stood on the brick pediment between the polished brass tubs of flaming geraniums. Their expressions were grave. The first was an older man of about sixty, and the second one, much taller, was a handsome man close to her own age, with thick black hair and a steady blue-gray gaze that made her feel somewhat breathless and disconcerted. Beyond the colonnade of her front porch three police cars crowded the circular drive, their blue lights pulsating silently, ominously.

Her hand went to her throat. "Has something happened?" she said quickly. "My children?"

"Mrs. Alicia Walker?"

"Yes, yes, what is it? What's happened?"

"I'm Lieutenant Chandler of the Twenty-First Precinct, Manhattan," the older man said flatly, and added, gesturing to his partner, "And this is Detective Lafferty. Mrs. Walker, your husband is dead."

Alicia gasped and the younger man stepped across the threshold to take her arm, leading her to the brocade love seat at the base of the staircase. As she sat, her hand brushed the Lalique vase on a stand next to the chair, and the delicate crystal crashed to the floor, shattering and spilling roses and water everywhere.

Alicia glanced at it automatically. "Don't worry, Maizie will get it," she said, and then shook her head, annoyed. "No, she's gone. I'll clean it up myself." She made as if to rise, and the policeman pushed her gently but firmly back into her seat.

"Mrs. Walker," Lafferty said, "sit down."

Alicia glanced at him sharply and then obeyed, her eyes

wide and watchful. Lafferty sat facing her, trying not to be affected by her ethereal loveliness. She had lush maple-blond hair just touching her shoulders, the color of honey in a glass jar, and clear hazel eyes—not green or brown but something in between—fringed by thick lashes much darker than her hair. Her skin was pale and flawless without makeup; there was no lipstick on her heart-shaped mouth and no color in her cheeks. She was slim, almost thin, with prominent bones showing above the collar of her robe and at her wrists. The overall effect was one of priceless fragility, exquisitely and expensively maintained. She looked like the wife of a millionaire, all right, but she didn't look happy. There were dark shadows under her eyes, and the faint lines bracketing her lips indicated a mouth that frowned more often than smiled.

"Are you all right, Mrs. Walker?" Chandler asked, advancing into the hall, glancing around as he pulled the door closed behind him. Chandler's wife worked for an interior decorator and he recognized everything in the room as top of the line. To his left was a formal dining room with a massive Waterford chandelier and a Hepplewhite breakfront; to his right, through a set of French doors, was a living room dominated by a Baldwin grand piano and a lavish fireplace with an elaborate mantel. He had seen the rest of the house from the road; there was a den and a study and some sort of solarium filled with plants and flowers at the back of the first floor. Some setup.

Alicia nodded mutely, responding to his question.

Lafferty cleared his throat. "Your children are away at school, Mrs. Walker?" he asked.

"Yes."

"Is anyone else here?"

"No, I told you, my housekeeper went to her sister's

house in Yonkers this afternoon, and the rest of the staff are all day workers. Please, how did my husband die, Detective…Lafferty, is it?''

''Yes, ma'am.''

''You haven't told me anything. How and when did it happen?''

''He was shot about eight o'clock tonight. After delivering his speech at the Plaza Hotel.''

''Then why did no one call me? I've been here this whole time.''

Lafferty exchanged a glance with his colleague.

''Detective, I have asked you why no one called me.''

''Mrs. Alicia Walker?'' Chandler said again sternly, moving briskly closer to her.

''Yes, of course,'' she said warily, looking from one man to the other. ''What's going on?''

Lafferty looked away.

''We're here to arrest you for the murder of your husband, Joseph Walker.''

Alicia's ivory complexion became almost ghostly. ''Wha-what?'' she whispered.

''You have the right to remain silent,'' Chandler said, beginning the drone of the Miranda warning as he unclipped a pair of handcuffs from his belt.

''Lieutenant Chandler, this is preposterous!'' Alicia said indignantly, regaining her wits as the policeman talked. ''I didn't shoot my husband, I was here all night, asleep!''

''I would advise you not to say anything else, Mrs. Walker,'' Lafferty interjected warningly.

''You have the right to an attorney. If you cannot afford an attorney,'' Chandler went on, looking around the spacious hall at the antique furniture, the gold framed paintings, the china figurines in a cherry cabinet against the wall, "one will be provided for you by the court."

"Who says I killed my husband?" Alicia demanded in an outraged tone. "Who says so?"

"There are several eyewitnesses, ma'am," Chandler said flatly, gesturing with the handcuffs for her to extend her wrists.

"Eyewitnesses? That's ridiculous, there's been a mistake! I was here! I wasn't feeling well, I have a cold, so I let Maizie go early. She had gotten a message that her son was sent home sick from school and she was concerned about getting home to him. I went to bed early and fell asleep until the doorbell woke me."

"Mrs. Walker, be quiet!" Lafferty said, more urgently this time. Chandler threw him an exasperated look.

"Why should I be quiet? I have nothing to hide, I'm telling you the truth," Alicia countered heatedly.

"Do you understand these rights as I have explained them to you?" Chandler concluded. He held out the handcuffs impatiently.

"Don't you think we should let her get dressed first?" Lafferty asked quietly.

Chandler registered the satin negligee and matching lace collared robe Alicia was wearing.

"Take her to her room and let her change her clothes and pack a bag," Chandler said gruffly. "Make it quick. Five minutes."

Lafferty gave him a look.

"Okay, ten," Chandler amended.

"I have no plans to escape, Lieutenant," Alicia said with as much dignity as she could muster. "I'm sure this misunderstanding will be cleared up very quickly."

Chandler nodded toward the staircase. "Bedroom up there?" he asked flatly.

"Yes."

Chandler gestured and Alicia rose, climbing the stairs with Lafferty following in her wake. He passed an overhanging balcony filled with lush exotic plants and then reached the landing, turning left along a wide hall carpeted in peach plush and hung with striped peach wallpaper. A large basket of apricot-hued tulips sat on a cherry table under a brass-framed mirror.

"This way," Alicia Walker said, glancing over her shoulder at him. He followed her into the master bedroom suite and stopped. The king bed was draped with the same chintz fabric as the spread, the pale pastel colors blending with the huge circular Kirman rug on the floor. In the dressing room beyond he could see a wall of closets flanking a triple-mirrored dressing table cluttered with bottles and jars. To his immediate right was a gleaming tiled bathroom with an elevated Jacuzzi tub and separate stall shower, its anteroom lined on one side with double sinks and a marble vanity, on the other with a cedar storage closet.

Lafferty made a show of taking it all in since he didn't want the lady to know the effect she was having on him. A trail of delicious scent wafted behind her and the silk negligee she was wearing whispered about her legs like a caress. Her hair shone with golden highlights. He could see the outline of her slim shoulders and the faint shadow of her nipples against the thin material when she turned to him.

He looked away.

"You can wait there, detective, it's three floors down from any of these windows. I am not planning to jump, and my high-wire act is somewhat rusty." She seemed to be using sarcasm as a weapon, trying to distance herself from what must be, to her, a surreal experience. She stepped into the dressing room and pulled the door closed, leaving it slightly ajar.

"I'll keep talking anyway so you'll know I'm here," she called. He could hear her opening drawers and rustling fabrics. "Will I be allowed to call my lawyer, like in the movies?" she asked dryly.

"Of course."

"I'm afraid I don't know any criminal attorneys, not personally anyway. I've never been arrested on a murder charge before tonight. May I call Judge Reynolds? Perhaps he can recommend someone."

"You can call anyone you like." He waited, studying the framed photographs of a boy and a girl on the bedside table. The boy was about nine and the girl about twelve, obviously a future beauty like her mother. He was reading the titles on a shelf of books next to the bed when she emerged, dressed in a tan skirt and ivory blouse, an overnight bag in her hand.

"I'm ready," she said flatly.

They descended the stairs together, Lafferty acutely conscious of her feminine presence just in front of him. Chandler was waiting for them, a folded sheaf of papers in his hand.

"We have a warrant to search your house for evidence, Mrs. Walker," he said to her, proffering the document. It was several pages of computer generated typeset with SEARCH WARRANT stamped across the lead page in large red capitals.

"Not losing any time, are you, Lieutenant?" Alicia said witheringly.

"In murder cases it's best not to lose any time, Mrs. Walker." Chandler whipped a pen out of his breast pocket and handed it to her. "Please read it and sign on the last page."

Alicia glanced through the pages, flipping them methodically, then took the pen from him and signed her name neatly on the last sheet.

"Thank you. While we're taking you down to the station my men will be going over the house and grounds."

"You're welcome to the task, Lieutenant."

Chandler extended his hand for her bag, and she gave it to him.

"May I make my call now?" she asked, eyeing him narrowly.

Both men stood back as she called Justice Hector Reynolds of the New York State Supreme Court. They listened as she accepted his condolences and then stood silently as tones of outrage poured from the other end of the line after she had explained her situation.

"Thank you, Hector, I'm sure it's all a mistake, too," Alicia said. "But in the meantime I *am* being arrested and I need someone to come to the Precinct House in Manhattan and see about bail. Can you help me?"

There was a short discussion, during which Reynolds seemingly promised to come straight to the jail to meet her. When she hung up the phone she squared her shoulders and waited silently.

Chandler opened the front door and signaled to one of the waiting cars. Alicia watched as a female police officer came up onto the porch and into the hall.

"This is Sergeant Garcia, she's going to search you now."

Alicia flushed faintly, whether with embarrassment or anger it was difficult to say.

"Here?" she said shortly.

"Bring her into the parlor, Garcia," Chandler said gruffly.

The policewoman took Alicia by the arm and led her into the adjoining room, closing the French doors.

Chandler went through Alicia's bag quickly, shoving aside toiletries and a change of underwear, looking for a weapon. When he found nothing the two men waited in tense silence until the women returned.

Garcia nodded. "She's clean."

Alicia, looking grim but calm, glanced at Chandler as if to determine what fresh indignity he was about to inflict. She didn't have to wait long. He stepped forward with the handcuffs.

"Is that necessary, Charlie?" Lafferty asked quietly. "She's not armed, and it's unlikely she could overpower both of us on the way to the station."

Chandler thought about it, then shrugged. Alicia shot Lafferty a grateful look as Chandler clapped a large hand on her shoulder and steered her out the door. Alicia stopped short as Lafferty opened the back door of the cruiser and held it for her.

"Get in, Mrs. Walker," he said.

She looked at him. A current flowed between them as if a switch had been turned on, and Lafferty had the irrational desire to take her in his arms. She gazed up at him a moment longer, then pressed her lips together and obeyed.

Alicia Walker was booked, fingerprinted and photographed as Chandler and Lafferty sipped coffee in the squad room and completed the arrest report. Reporters screamed questions from the hallway and flashbulbs went off like fireworks when she was led to the holding room. The station sergeant shut the connecting doors after she had moved on, cutting off the cacophony generated by the press.

Alicia looked over her shoulder at Lafferty as she passed.

"Why, Mike, I think she likes you," Chandler said, chuckling and digging his elbow into Lafferty's ribs.

"She's going to be right at home in the tank with all the hookers and crackheads," Lafferty said dryly, putting down his cup.

"Mike, she's been accused of murder, not cheating at bingo. Where do you think she belongs? Should we put her up at the Ritz, maybe get her an appointment at Elizabeth Arden while we're at it? What the hell is wrong with you?"

"I'm just saying she'll be a target for the other prisoners, that's all," Lafferty replied uncomfortably.

Chandler snorted. "She won't be in there five minutes before her high-priced mouthpiece bails her out."

"Not if she isn't arraigned until the morning. She'll have to spend the night here."

"Don't count on it. Anybody who can get the Honorable Hector Reynolds on his home phone will be in and out like a roll of film at the Photomart."

"The DA will keep her overnight," Lafferty said flatly. "You'll see."

"So what? She'll live. Come on, we should get back out to the Walker house."

They got up together and left the squad room.

"Some classy dame, huh?" Chandler ventured, once they were in the car. "She sure brought out the Sir Galahad in you."

"I don't know what you mean," Lafferty said.

"You don't? 'Let her take her time to get dressed.' 'Don't handcuff her.' I thought you were about to roll out the red carpet all the way back to the city."

"I didn't think it was a good idea to arrest her in her

nightgown, Charlie, what with all the photographers sure to be waiting for us when we brought her into the station. And since each of us outweighs her at about two to one, I didn't feel that she was very likely to escape, did you?''

Chandler snorted, and Lafferty restrained himself from saying anything further. It was obvious that Chandler could not see Alicia Walker in a sympathetic light, while he himself had no trouble doing so. She was a fragile, beautiful woman whose world had suddenly jumped out of orbit and gone flying off into space. Chandler wanted her convicted yesterday because she had money and had been married to a powerful man. Lafferty saw just the woman—frightened, vulnerable and achingly lovely.

He already knew that he could not be impartial about her.

''What did you think of that perfume?'' Chandler said, ignoring the logic of Lafferty's earlier reply. ''Three hundred bucks an ounce if it's a nickel, my boy. She'll have some trouble getting hold of that fancy stuff in the clink. No fresh flowers, either. What an inconvenience that will be for her ladyship.''

Lafferty stared out the window. The older man had an irritating habit of talking like a flatfoot in a Mickey Spillane potboiler. Lafferty found it best to ignore his tirades.

''Well, she won't be the first broad I've come across with the face of an angel and a heart of stone,'' Chandler added.

Lafferty said nothing.

''You didn't see her crying her eyes out when we told her that her husband was dead. She was more concerned about breaking that pretty vase and making a mess on her expensive floor.'' Chandler had the working-class cop's disdain for the concerns of the wealthy, and the finely tuned resentment to go along with it.

"She was in shock, Charlie. You don't need me to tell you about the strange things people do when they're in shock. Not everyone washes away on a river of tears like a B-movie actress."

"Shock, no way. She wasn't in shock if she plugged him, and my money says she did. The kids were conveniently gone, she sent the servant home so she wouldn't be around. She had plenty of time to get into the city and back home and pretend she was in Scarsdale all along."

Lafferty shook his head. "She doesn't *seem* stupid. Why would she shoot him in front of witnesses? And if you were planning a murder wouldn't you prepare a better alibi than 'I was sleeping at my house by myself'? It just doesn't make sense."

Chandler shrugged. "Maybe she's crazy, one of them whatchamacallits—schizos, multiple personalities. I don't know, I'm no shrink. The inside word on her old man is that he was a great hand with the ladies. Maybe she finally got fed up with it. Maybe knowing that she would have to put on a big show of the happy family for his political campaign finally drove her around the bend. All I know is that the DA's got about five witnesses, including Walker's press secretary and one of Walker's private security guards from FlameTree Publishing, who are going to stand up in court and swear on an FTGold edition of the Good Book that the lady did it."

Lafferty pursed his lips thoughtfully but didn't answer.

"You think those people were having a shared hallucination?" Chandler asked, grinning as he popped a stick of gum in his mouth. He was trying to quit smoking and chewed gum constantly. "The press aide, some guy named Smithson, is a direct eyewitness. He was Walker's friend of twenty years, his college roommate and an usher at the wedding, for heaven's sake. Do you think he could be wrong?''

Lafferty shook his head, unable to answer.

Chandler hit the turn signal just as a radio call came in saying that the search of the Walker house had turned up some relevant evidence. Chandler reached for the radio handset.

''What have you got, Red?'' Chandler asked his patrolman at the Walker mansion.

''Found a woman's two-piece dress, a suit I guess, stuffed behind the water heater in the basement,'' Red Jenkins replied.

Chandler glanced at Lafferty, who was leaning forward, listening intently.

''Is it Alicia Walker's?'' Chandler asked.

Jenkins's reply was lost in a burst of static.

''Say again?'' Chandler directed curtly.

''Must be hers, it's got some kind of label sewn into the collar, looks like a signature,'' Jenkins replied.

''Bag it and tape it, we'll be there in half an hour,'' Chandler said crisply then dropped the handset onto the seat beside him. He cast a sidelong glance in Lafferty's direction. ''Now why, do you suppose, has the lady of the house been hiding her little duds in her cellar? Want to bet it matches the description of the suit she was wearing when she nailed her beloved with a .32? If Santa is good to us it might even have some gunpowder residue on it.''

Lafferty was looking unconvinced.

''What?'' Chandler said.

''She has to know that her house is the first place we'd look for anything like that. Would she stash the stuff right on the property? It wasn't even hidden that well, it couldn't have been if Red Jenkins found it. You know

Red, Charlie. He's a stand-up guy, but not exactly Sherlock Holmes.''

"So what? I'm not looking a gift horse in the mouth, and neither will the DA. I know the lady has nice legs, kid, but she did her husband. Get used to it."

Lafferty mentally shook his head. It didn't feel right, it was too easy. It felt to him like Alicia Walker had been framed, like somebody had set her up and planted the evidence in her house to implicate her.

Or maybe he just wanted to think that, because his whole body had responded to the Walker woman in a gut-wrenching visceral way the instant he saw her.

Lafferty glanced at his partner as Chandler changed lanes.

Then he trained his gaze out the window again.

Alicia sat on the edge of the cot in the holding cell, her hands folded in her lap, studiously avoiding the eyes of the prostitute who was staring her down from across the room. A drunk was throwing up in a corner, the sound of her retching permeating the narrow space, and the smell of urine and vomit and stale cigarette smoke was overwhelming.

Alicia shifted her weight and sighed, finally looking directly at the prostitute and holding her gaze levelly. To Alicia's surprise the woman shrugged slightly in response and looked away.

It seemed an eternity before Hector arrived. When the guard came to take her out to the visitors' room she ignored the catcalls that followed her into the hall and smiled at Hector with a confidence she didn't feel.

"You have ten minutes," the guard said, and then left, taking a position outside, which allowed them to see his head through the glass at the top of the door.

"My dear, I'm so sorry to find you in such a dreadful situation," Reynolds said, taking a chair across from Alicia once she sat. An old golfing buddy of her father's, he was a dignified gray-haired man in his sixties about to complete his current term on the bench. Alicia noticed that his manner was entirely different from the bluster he had exhibited on the telephone: he now seemed subdued, worried.

"I've talked to your grandmother on the phone. She is attempting to engage Harry Landau for your defense," he announced.

Alicia was too stunned to speak. Harry Landau was a flamboyant media figure, a ruinously expensive lawyer who was usually brought in to perform his magic in support of wealthy—and clearly guilty—clients. Like Saint Jude, he was the patron of hopeless cases.

"Hector, is it really that bad?" Alicia asked quietly.

He sighed, his expression grim. "Alicia, I have spoken to the police and read the arresting officers' statement. Your defense attorney will have to convince the jury that the several witnesses District Attorney Woods intends to call are all mistaken about what they saw. One person, yes. But four? Or five?" He shook his head. "And the search of your home revealed a dress like the one the assailant was wearing, hidden in your cellar."

Alicia stared at him. "In my cellar?"

"Yes."

"What dress?"

He passed a hand over his brow. "Beige, I think. A top and bottom, silk. Adolfo."

"That suit is in my closet!" Alicia said decisively.

"Are you sure? Have you checked?"

"Why would I check, I haven't worn it in months!" she retorted in exasperation.

"Maybe it isn't there any longer."

"You mean someone took the suit?"

"It's possible, isn't it?"

"I suppose," she said thoughtfully. "Or copied it."

"I'm afraid there's more. Woods is attempting to have your assets frozen if you are released on bail. He's claiming that you're a flight risk."

"Oh, for heaven's sake, Hector, where would I go? My children are here."

"It's more or less standard procedure with defendants of great wealth."

Alicia couldn't reply. How could this nightmare be happening so fast? A few hours ago she was asleep in her bed, and now this disaster, in a twinkling, had overtaken her life.

"And you'll have to spend the night here. You're being arraigned in the morning. I think Woods is determined to make an example of you. He might even try to hold you without bail."

"I see."

"In all likelihood Landau will be here by tomorrow, but if he can't come himself he will probably send a member of his staff to handle the bail hearing."

"So I'm stuck here."

"I guarantee you'll be out after the arraignment. We'll meet whatever bail is set, or I'll get it reduced. The district attorney is powerful, but I'm not without friends myself."

He stopped, and Alicia waited.

He folded his hands on the scarred table before him. "Alicia, I was your father's friend for thirty years, and as far as bail is concerned I will do what I can to help you. But after that I will not be able to involve myself in this matter any longer. I'm coming up for re-election in the fall and this sort of thing, the scandal…"

"I understand," Alicia said shortly. She was sure he wouldn't be the only old friend to abandon her when apprised of her plight.

He looked relieved. He stood up and offered his hand.

"Good luck, my dear. I wish I might do more, but..."

"Thank you, Hector," she said expressionlessly.

He looked at her for a long moment, then said, "Alicia, I know that Joe wasn't easy to live with. If you did—"

"I didn't," she replied distantly. "Thank you for coming, Hector. Good night."

Back at the precinct at eight-thirty the next morning, after working a double shift supervising the search of the Walker mansion, Charlie Chandler sent a parting glance toward Lafferty as he paused at the door on his way home to his wife of thirty-two years.

"We're getting warrants for the Walker town house on Lex and the country house in Maine this afternoon."

Lafferty groaned. He'd had enough of sifting through drawers of lingerie and taking apart exercise equipment.

"She couldn't possibly have made it to Maine and back, Charlie, give me a break. Does she own a Concorde?"

"Woods wants us to check it, we check it."

"Isn't there enough of a case with the witnesses? Why do we have to go through all this?" he asked wearily.

"Captain Cramer wants it wrapped tight as a drum," Chandler said, turning back to him. "He's got my vote. Aren't you tired of assembling cases that go south for lack of evidence once they get before a jury?"

Lafferty didn't reply, looking around restlessly for a clean foam cup.

"See you tonight, kid," Chandler called, and vanished from the doorway.

Lafferty located a cup that was only slightly stained and filled it with coffee smelling strongly of afterburn. The first sip confirmed that it was as old as Chandler's jokes, but he drank it anyway, hoping to remain conscious long enough to make it back to his apartment. He was leaning against the chipped tile counter, contemplating whether he should have breakfast before signing out, when he saw Alicia Walker go past the glass door and into the visitors' room, followed closely by a nervous-looking patrolman and Captain Cramer.

Lafferty leaned back out of visual range and waited until Cramer had left the kid posted outside the door. Then he set his half-empty cup on the counter and went out into the hall. He didn't even think about what he was doing; he was acting instinctively, responding to an autonomic directive as natural as the urge to breathe. He nodded to the patrolman as he passed, moving quickly before the boy could ask him what he was doing.

Alicia looked up as he entered and her expression cleared.

"Oh, Officer Lafferty," she said.

"Detective," he said, correcting her.

"Oh, yes, I'm sorry. That's important, isn't it?" she said, seemingly annoyed with herself for underranking him.

"It was to me," he said lightly. They gazed at each other. She looked as if she'd spent a sleepless night, but was still beautiful, her irises so clear that he was sure a side view would make them seem transparent. He was trying not to stare, but her features exerted a force on him, like the moon drawing the tides. He could not look away.

"Is there something else I need to do?" she said sharply.

He blinked. "I beg your pardon?"

"I was told they would bring my lawyer in here to see me. I'm to be arraigned at nine, whatever that means."

"It's just a preliminary hearing for the judge to set bail."

"Will they let me out on bail?" she asked. "Hector, Judge Reynolds, said the district attorney might be trying to make an example of me and would argue to keep me confined." She smiled thinly. "I understand the DA wants to land in the mayor's office, and my misfortune may help him get there."

The fear underlying her bantering tone made him wait a long moment before answering. "You're not a career criminal, Mrs. Walker. I feel sure they'll let you out."

"I seem to be convicted already," she said.

"I can't discuss your specific case outside the presence of your counsel, but I can tell you that in my experience people in your situation are usually released on bail. A high bail, but they get out."

"People in my situation," she murmured thoughtfully. Then her brow furrowed. "I don't understand, Detective. Why are you here to see me?"

Good question, Lafferty thought. "I just wanted to see if there was anything you needed," he said.

She gazed at him warily. "How thoughtful," she said, her words belying her expression.

"Is there anything I can do for you?" he said.

She looked blank. Then, "Oh, yes. I forgot to mention this to Hector and it's been worrying me. It's morning now and news of all this will have reached the schools where my children are staying. I don't want them to hear…" Her voice trailed off and she bit her lip.

"Yes, of course. I understand completely. What do you want me to do?"

"If you could contact my grandmother, Hannah Green,

Hector has the number, and make sure she has called my children, I would appreciate it very much. To learn that their father is dead and their mother has been arrested for his murder—'' She stopped abruptly. After a moment she began again. ''Hannah would find some easier way of breaking it to them than letting them hear it from an announcer on the morning programs. And I'd like her to bring them back from school—children can be so unkind, and they should be spared as much commentary from their classmates as possible. Can you do that for me, call her? Would it be permitted? My grandmother may have talked to Hector about this already, but I won't rest easy until I know for sure.''

''I'll take care of it,'' he said quietly.

''Are you sure you can?'' she asked, her gaze measuring.

''Yes.''

She sighed and nodded, satisfed. He appreciated the way she took his word for it, which made him determined to scale fortress walls to complete the errand.

They both looked up as Captain Cramer paused outside the door and looked in through the glass.

''I have to go, Mrs. Walker,'' Lafferty said.

She laid her hand on his arm, touching his coat sleeve. ''You've been very kind,'' she said, her gaze direct and full of feeling. ''No matter what happens to me, I will remember your kindness when I needed it most.''

Lafferty found himself speechless, then turned away quickly before she could see his expression. He brushed past Cramer, who called his name sharply.

''Later, Cap, I'm headed for the john,'' he called over his shoulder, and kept going. He would figure out some excuse to give Cramer later, justifying his visit to Alicia Walker.

First, he had to get in touch with Hannah Green.

* * *

When the search team entered the Walker town house at Seventy-eight Street and Lexington Avenue, Chandler and Lafferty paused in the entry hall and looked up at the Lucite staircase ascending regally to the second floor. There was a moment of reverential silence.

"I'll be damned," Chandler said, breaking it. "This looks like Joan Crawford's house in *Mommie Dearest.*"

Lafferty had to smile. It did. The whole place was done in a gray-and-ivory, Art Deco style reminiscent of the thirties, as cold and impersonal as a magazine illustration. Chandler led the way inside, and as they looked around Lafferty could see that this place was as different from the Scarsdale house as two dwellings could be. There were no pictures or flowers or personal touches, no indications that human beings actually lived here. Chandler placed a gloved finger on a counter and lifted a line of dust.

"Maid comes in tomorrow," he said.

"What about Mrs. Walker?" Lafferty asked. "I gather her old man used this place when he was in town and she rarely ever came here."

"It looks it." Chandler smiled. "Did you hear she's out? Two million cash bail, what did I tell you? She's probably on her way to Tripoli right now. First class."

"She's not going anywhere, Charlie. Her kids are in school in Massachusetts and she won't leave them."

"How do you know where her kids are?" Chandler asked suspiciously.

"You should read the data sheets more often, Charlie," Lafferty replied lightly, opening a drawer.

"I leave that to you college boys," Chandler replied. He sighed. "Let's get to it," he said.

They had been searching for half an hour when Chandler, prying the grate off a heating duct, said, "Bingo."

Lafferty looked over at him, a sinking feeling in his chest.

"What?" he said warily.

Chandler extracted a package wrapped in canvas from inside the vent, handling it gingerly. He climbed down from the chair he was standing on and loosened the canvas as the other cops crowded around him. Inside the package was a .32 revolver with a snub nose and a rubber pistol grip.

Chandler picked it up with one gloved finger and left it dangling free for all to see.

"Belong to anyone we know?" he asked, and grinned.

Sandler Woods closed the Walker file on the desk in front of him and glanced out his window at the just-budding trees. With luck he would wrap this one up before the end of the summer.

Sandy Woods had no qualms about shuttling Alicia Walker straight into a conviction for capital murder. He was a liberal democrat who had detested Joe Walker. The wife, smiling like a mannequin by Walker's side and riding his questionable coattails into a luxurious life-style, he found little better. Good riddance to both of them, and if the publicity from prosecuting the case could carry him into Gracie Mansion, so much the better. He was salivating at the prospect of exposing Joe Walker as a sham and convicting his lovely widow as quickly as possible.

He looked up as his assistant showed Drew Smithson through his door. Joe Walker's press secretary looked gray around the gills and distinctly uncomfortable, but impeccably dressed, as usual.

"Have a seat, Smithson," Sandy said coolly.

Smithson sat.

"I've been reading the deposition you gave my assistant prosecutor," Sandy said.

Smithson said nothing.

"It says in here that you can absolutely identify the shooter as Mrs. Walker, is that correct?"

"Yes."

"How can you be so sure?"

Smithson sighed. "I knew the woman for fifteen years. I saw her almost everyday. It was Alicia."

Sandy nodded. "That brings me to my next question. What reason would she have to kill her husband?"

Smithson was silent.

"Can you think of any? My prosecutor didn't really pin you down on this, but you'll find I'm a lot more persistent."

Smithson wet his lips.

"You'll be subpoenaed, Smithson," Sandy said quietly. "You might as well tell me now, because I guarantee I'll get it out of you in court. You wouldn't want to be charged with obstructing justice and hindering this investigation, would you?"

Smithson looked down at his lap. "Joe played around. A lot. I don't think he ever touched Alicia after their boy was born."

Sandy made a note in the file, feeling a stab of satisfaction. "Any particular woman?" he asked.

Smitshon shrugged. "He liked prostitutes, escort services, you know. No muss, no fuss, no loose ends. There may have been one call girl he saw more than others, but nobody he was attached to emotionally."

"What about his wife?"

"She made her life the kids, charities, cultural activities. The typical thing."

"No boyfriends?"

"Joe made it clear that she would never see the kids again if she even thought about it, that she would be the big loser in a divorce. He could have done it, too. She knew that."

"So how did the wife take it? Was she ever treated for emotional problems, mental illness?"

"Not that I heard."

"So he had other women, in fact he never slept with her at all. She was ignored, restless, unhappy. Then with the additional pressure of his new involvement in politics, could she have flipped out?"

"Isn't counsel leading the witness?"

"Would you say she was unstable?" Woods persisted.

"I don't know. She always seemed pretty tightly wound, like she had it all under control, but there had to be a lot of suppressed anger, had to be."

"Was there any physical abuse? Did Walker hit her, for example?"

Smithson shifted uncomfortably in his seat.

"Well?"

"I saw him swat her a couple of times."

"Swat?"

"Slap, you know. Not hard. Just enough to…"

"Show her who was boss?" Woods supplied sarcastically.

Smithson looked away.

"He sounds like a prince, your pal," Woods observed. "What were they fighting about? The bimbos?"

"Nah, after a while she just tolerated that. It was the kids. Joe wanted them sent away to boarding school, and she wanted to keep them with her and have them attend day classes. There was a lot of static about that."

"But he won."

"Joe always won," Smithson said flatly.

"Who else would want him dead?"

"Wealthy people often have enemies."

"But his wife was the one who shot him in front of you," Woods supplied.

Smithson hung his head. "Maybe they weren't Jane Wyman and Robert Young from *Father Knows Best,* but nobody deserves to go the way Joe did."

"So he had good qualities?"

"Sure."

"Like keeping you employed for twenty years?"

"I don't think you're donating your services to the city here, are you, Woods?" Smithson said, bristling.

Sandy smiled slightly. "I think that will be all for today. If I need you again before the prelim I'll let you know."

Smithson left the office in a great hurry, as if he were fleeing a burning building.

Sandy grinned to himself as he slipped the Walker folder into place in the stand on his desk. He disdained computers; he liked to see everything written out before him in black-and-white. What he saw here was that he had motive, means, opportunity, eyewitnesses and evidence: Alicia Walker's fingerprints were all over the gun.

Even Harry Landau would not be able to save her.

Chapter 2

A middle-aged black woman with a lively, intelligent expression answered the door at the Walker house in Scarsdale.

"Detective Lafferty, NYPD," he said, flashing his badge. "Is Mrs. Walker in?"

"She's in the living room with Miss Fisher," the woman said uncertainly.

"Please tell her I'm here. I'll wait."

The woman went inside and returned in seconds.

"Mrs. Walker will see you," she said.

Lafferty was shown into the parlor. Alicia Walker was seated on one of the twin couches that faced the showy fireplace, across from a woman her age, a meticulously groomed redhead with a frank, observant face. The latter stared openly as Lafferty was led to the seated women.

"Thank you, Maizie," Alicia said. As the housekeeper left, she added, "Hello, Detective Lafferty. This is my friend, Helen Fisher. What can I do for you?"

As Lafferty opened his mouth to answer, the beeper in his pocket went off loudly. He reached inside his jacket to silence it and then said, "I'm sorry. Is there a phone I could use?"

Alicia gestured to the den across the hall. "Press the top button for an outside line. You can close the door for privacy."

As soon as Lafferty left, Helen said to Alicia, "Alicia Green Walker, you've been holding out on me."

"What do you mean?"

"What do I mean? Who is that gorgeous creature?"

"That," Alicia said with exquisite irony, "is the policeman who arrested me."

Helen shook her head in amazement. "I must be doing something wrong. All the policemen I meet look like that actor from the old TV cop show, Broderick Crawford. Fat old guy with a fedora? He resembled a bulldog, if I recall correctly."

"It was hardly a romantic moment, Helen. He was taking me off to jail," Alicia replied tartly.

"You can't tell me you didn't notice him!"

"I had just heard that Joe was dead and they were arresting me for his murder!" Alicia countered incredulously, at the same time thinking that she *had* noticed Lafferty. But she was not about to say that to Helen, who would seize upon the admission to pry further into Alicia's confused and contradictory feelings.

Helen's expression changed. "You didn't say anything to those policemen about you and Joe," she said, lowering her voice and glancing toward the door.

Alicia shook her head. "No, but they're going to find out anyway, Helen. It's only a matter of time."

Lafferty returned, looking from one woman to the other as he entered the room.

"I appreciate the use of the phone," he said.

"Detective Lafferty, would you like something to drink?" Alicia asked.

"No, thank you. I'm on duty."

"Something soft? Cola?"

"All right."

Alicia glanced into the hall. "I think Maizie went upstairs. I'll get it."

She slipped out of the room and the minute she left, her friend said to Lafferty, "She's up the creek, isn't she?"

Lafferty didn't answer.

"I know everybody thinks she did it," Helen continued, "but I'm certain she couldn't. Joe Walker was a louse and a phony and a damn hypocrite, but Alicia doesn't have it in her to shoot anybody."

"If you want to help her you should call her defense attorney, Mr. Landau, and volunteer as a character witness."

"I'm not sure how long Mr. Landau will last. Alicia wants to replace him."

"That's an idea that deserves close consideration, Ms. Fisher," Lafferty said feelingly.

Helen nodded. "Gotcha," she said.

Alicia returned with an iced drink for Lafferty, and Helen took that as her cue to go. She kissed Alicia goodbye, took another long look at Lafferty and left.

"So, Detective, what brings you out here again?" Alicia said levelly, sitting once more.

"You left your overnight bag in the property room at the station," he said. "I brought it back for you. It's in the hall."

"That's very nice of Captain Cramer to send it out here. I'm afraid I was in such a hurry to leave that I never missed it.'' She raised her brows delicately. ''Is it usual to send a detective on such a minor mission?''

He looked sheepish. ''No, it's not. The captain is, uh, anxious that the department—'' He stopped.

''Crosses all its *T*s on this one?'' she suggested archly.

He nodded resignedly, then took a sip of his soda.

''It's almost lunchtime, would you like a sandwich to go with that?'' she asked him. ''My son will be coming back home shortly, and Maizie will be fixing him something.''

Lafferty stared at her. How could she be so detached, acting the suburban hostess with such aplomb? Did she really have no idea that she was sinking slowly in quicksand?

Alicia looked back at him and could see exactly what he was thinking. He watched her draw a deep breath and pass a slim hand lightly over her hair.

''Yes, Detective, I have a complete understanding of my situation,'' she said flatly, answering the question in his eyes. ''If I didn't before, Mr. Landau, the attorney my grandmother engaged, explained it to me very thoroughly this morning. What you see before you is reliance on form, falling back on ritual when you can't think what else to do. Though I must confess I don't know how much longer I can maintain this act. It's beginning to wear on me.''

''That's understandable,'' Lafferty said.

Alicia sighed, her expression grim. ''Would you like to hear what my famous attorney told me, Detective Lafferty?''

Lafferty opened his mouth to reply negatively, but she went ahead before he could speak.

''He told me that he doesn't care if I'm guilty, that it doesn't matter to him.''

Lafferty didn't comment. That sounded like Landau, a high-priced mouthpiece with a florid face, snow-white iridescent hair and the genial benevolence of a carnival showman.

"He said that if I plead innocent and the judgment goes against me, as it surely will in his opinion, I could receive the maximum penalty," Alicia went on. "If I plead guilty with special circumstances, a good choice according to him, I could get off with the minimum at a white-collar jail, tennis everyday, library privileges, movies every week, early probation, the works. You will not be surprised to learn that pleading guilty is what he advised."

Lafferty met her gaze slowly.

"It did not seem to interest him that I didn't do it," Alicia added dryly. "In fact, my insistence that I didn't kill Joe seemed to annoy him a great deal, as if I were dragging in irrelevant information that would just muck up the works."

Lafferty looked away from her. He didn't want to tell her his opinion of Landau, whom he had last seen on television wearing a double-breasted sharkskin suit with spectator shoes and a flowered tie, holding forth on the protections afforded criminal defendants by the fifth amendment. Lafferty detested celebrity lawyers, and he thought Landau was among the worst of them.

Alicia closed her eyes, recalling the interview. "He kept calling me *little lady* and acting like I was some feeble-minded female who had gotten her silly self into a big bad mess and now had to be bailed out of it by good old Uncle Harry. But when I resisted his wisdom about my case and expressed dismay at the idea of pleading guilty to something I had not done, Uncle Harry became flinty fairly quickly."

"So the choice was to do what he told you or go elsewhere?'' Lafferty asked quietly, getting drawn into the conversation despite his resolve to remain detached.

"Pretty much. I think I will be going elsewhere.'' She laughed shortly. "Not that I have a clue where else to go,'' she said.

"Mrs. Walker...'' Lafferty began.

"He kept referring to what 'we' were going to do, as if we were both facing a criminal indictment,'' Alicia murmured, not looking at Lafferty as she relived it, talking to herself. "*He* is not charged with murder, *I* am. And what kind of attorney doesn't care if his client is guilty? He didn't even consider the possibility that someone was setting me up.''

"Who would do that, and why?'' Lafferty asked.

Alicia glanced at him. "You sound like Uncle Harry. That's exactly what he said. And when I couldn't supply a list of alternative suspects he said that 'we'd' better take a long look at reality and prepare my case accordingly. By that time I was already firing him in my mind.''

"Mrs. Walker, I really shouldn't be talking about your case with you,'' Lafferty said flatly, falling back on correct procedure to stem the flow of her discourse. He was distressed by the lifeless, hopeless tone of her voice.

"According to Mr. Landau,'' Alicia continued, "all of this means that I had better take whatever deal is offered and be thankful for it.''

"That's usually the approach of an attorney who feels there is no case to argue in favor of his client.''

Alicia shook her head. "I know it doesn't look good for me, Detective Lafferty, but I refuse to believe that my only recourse is the jaded representation of Harry Landau, the last refuge of the guilty defendant.''

Lafferty didn't comment. He agreed with her about Landau, but it was not his place to say so.

Alicia met his gaze, and she seemed to realize suddenly that she had been rambling. "I'm sorry," she said. "Of course I shouldn't be burdening you with this. Please excuse me. I don't know quite how to act under these circumstances. I have never been a murder suspect before, and the protocol is new to me."

"No problem," he answered shortly, relieved that she would now stop confiding in him. He wanted to know what was happening with her, more than he should, but at the same time he was aware that he was pushing the limits of professional behavior by conversing with her on this subject.

"Well," she said briskly, rising, "let me see about some lunch for you." She took a step, then faltered, her hand clutching at the back of the sofa.

He was at her side in an instant, setting his drink down on an end table and catching her as she fell. She felt like a bundle of sticks in his arms, her bones as light as air. He went to put her on the sofa and then remembered about the boy coming home for lunch. He didn't want the kid to see his mother passed out on the couch. He carried her into the hall, looking around for the servant, then took her up the staircase to her room.

Her lashes fluttered as he set her down on the bed. He let her go reluctantly, cradling her slim shoulders in the silken blouse an instant longer than he had to, inhaling the clean scent of her skin, her hair. As he released her she stirred and murmured, "Oh, no. Did I faint?"

"I think so," he replied, sitting next to her.

"I haven't done that in years," she said, blinking and struggling into a sitting position. "I used to do it all the time, low blood sugar or stress or something. Did you catch me?"

"I had to, or you would have hit the floor."

She flushed deeply. "How awful for you to be caught in such a situation. I really have been a problem since you first met me, haven't I?"

They looked at one another, Lafferty studying the fine, flawless quality of her skin, Alicia noticing the row of lashes that gave depth and character to his eyes. They stood frozen in place when they heard Maizie's voice from the intercom on the wall.

"Mrs. Walker?" the housekeeper called.

They started guiltily, like clandestine lovers caught in a stolen embrace.

"I'm up here, Maizie, in the bedroom," Alicia called, thumbing back her hair and slipping her legs over the edge of the bed. Lafferty moved to assist her, and as she rose she turned against him. His arm came around her tightly, and she allowed herself the luxury of accepting it, shocked by how much she suddenly seemed to need his support. Her head fell against his shoulder and she felt his answering movement, the muscles tensing in his arm, his back. He smelled of soap and starch and the tropical wool of his suit jacket, and she had an irrational impulse to fling her arms around him and bury her face in his chest. Here was the strength she'd sought in Joe and never found, here was the basic decency she'd yearned for when she discovered her husband didn't know the meaning of the word. She sighed and clutched him, her eyes closing, and she felt the hardness of his response against her thighs.

They both heard the housekeeper's footfall in the hall and she stepped away from him just as Maizie came through the door.

"Mrs. Walker, what's wrong?" Maizie asked, glancing from one to the other in concern.

"Nothing, Maizie. I felt a little faint and Detective Lafferty brought me up here, that's all." Alicia avoided looking at him as he made his way to the door.

"It's no wonder you're fainting, you don't eat enough to keep a bird alive," Maizie said. "Do you want me to call Dr. Gleason?"

"No, no, I'll be fine. Is Joey home yet?"

"That's why I was looking for you, he just got here. You're having some lunch with him, if I have to force feed you."

"I'll be going now, Mrs. Walker, if you're sure you're all right," Lafferty said from the doorway, his expression unreadable.

"Yes, thank you, Detective. Goodbye."

"I'll show you out," Maizie said.

"Please send Joey up to me," Alicia said to Maizie, and watched as the two of them left. She sat on the edge of the bed and lay back against the pillows, staring at the ceiling.

The incident with Lafferty was not significant, she knew that. It only seemed that way because a man had not touched her with longing in so many years that she had almost forgotten what it was like. Some of Joe's aides had looked at her, sure, but they had been far too intimidated by him to try anything. It was a heady experience to feel the tension of desire in a man's body after so long, even if he would have responded that way to any woman.

She closed her eyes and put the back of her arm across her forehead. Joe had just died, and here she was lusting after the cop who had arrested her for his murder. Of course she'd had no relationship with Joe, so it was not exactly disloyal to think about someone else. Of course nothing would happen with Lafferty, because she'd be in jail. The fates were surely standing in the wings jeering at her, as they had been for years. All that time playing the loving wife, covering up the emptiness and the loneliness—maybe it had driven her crazy and she just didn't know it. Her behavior lately was not exactly the hallmark of stability; an attractive man assists her when she's fainting and she's ready to fling herself into his arms. She had to calm down and concentrate on the main problem at hand: defending herself against the murder charge. Everything else was secondary.

"Hi, Mom," Joey said from the doorway.

She smiled at her son.

Well, not everything.

Lafferty came in from a game of handball that night and headed straight for the refrigerator, popping the tab on a can of beer. Leaning against the counter of his kitchenette, he took a long drink. The exercise had not accomplished its objective, it hadn't eradicated his visit to Scarsdale from his mind. It was not exactly his practice to play clutch and grab with murder suspects, but then again, most of them had few teeth and reptilian tattoos and bore no resemblance to Alicia Walker.

He sighed heavily and looked around the room. The apartment was a mess, but then, folded stacks of underwear and neatly hung suit pants made him nervous, anyway. His ex-wife had marveled at the chaos that traveled with him, from which he always emerged as spotless as tennis whites. She had loved him madly, but divorced him anyway when he wouldn't quit the police force and go to law school.

Lafferty rubbed his hair, still damp from his shower, and took a long pull of his beer. He glanced out the window idly, then more intently as a limo pulled to a stop at the curb in front of his building. Limousines were not a common sight in his area of Queens, and especially not on his street, which was lined with brick tenements inhabited by moderate-income types. He watched as a chauffeur got out of the front seat and opened the back door for an elderly lady who emerged slowly, walking stick in hand. He looked on for a moment longer and then remembered his cheeseburger. He unwrapped it and put it into the microwave. When his doorbell rang, he looked at the door in surprise, as if it had spoken. Had he forgotten to pay the paperboy? He strolled barefoot across his sister's cast-off carpet and yanked open the door.

The old lady from the limo was standing in the hall.

"Detective Lafferty?" she said.

"Yes?"

"I'm Hannah Green, Alicia Walker's grandmother. We spoke on the telephone regarding Alicia's children. May I come in?"

Dumbfounded, Lafferty stood aside as she proceeded into his living room, looking around at the barbells stacked in a corner, the books piled randomly on the coffee table, the discarded shoes on the floor. She watched him, boyish in his college gym shorts and NYPD T-shirt, as he shoved a stack of papers onto the floor to make room for her in the most comfortable chair. She sat, leaning her stick against the arm, and waited as Lafferty cleared a space for himself on the couch. When he looked at her, his forearms resting on his knees, she smiled.

"My sources tell me you're the only one on the police force who is questioning this frame that's been constructed around my granddaughter," she said.

Lafferty stared at her, a slight old woman dressed in black taffeta with a fichu of lace at her throat fastened by an ivory cameo. Her sources? What did she have—ESP? The only one he had talked to was Chandler, and Chandler would rather spit out his tongue than give away inside information, especially to somebody like Hannah Green. Who was she paying?

Mrs. Green read his mind. "I haven't bribed anyone, Detective, nor do I intend to do so. If District Attorney Woods got wind of it, my granddaughter would be sacrificed." She waved her hand dismissively at his stare. "Rich people have means, that's how we stay rich."

"I can't discuss your granddaughter's case with you, Mrs. Green," he said, finding his voice at last.

"I understand that."

"I'm sorry you came all the way out here for nothing, but—"

The buzzer on the microwave went off loudly.

"What's that?" she asked.

"Dinner," he said.

"Oh, am I interrupting you?" she asked politely.

"It can wait."

"May I go on?"

"Mrs. Green, as I said, I don't think—"

She held up her hand. "Please, indulge me. Just give me a few minutes of your time."

He hesitated, then nodded.

She linked her gnarled hands in her lap, a huge diamond winking on her ring finger like a pier light.

"Alicia was a very sheltered child, an innocent, which contributed, I think, to her infatuation with Joe Walker. She was twenty when she met him, twenty-one when they married, and she thought he was Adonis and Jack Kennedy and Andrew Carnegie rolled into one. I had misgivings but finally gave my blessing to the match. He could offer security and stability and she had a family that went back to the Mayflower. If our name was older than Joe's, well, this is America, is it not? The marriage seemed a fair bargain."

Lafferty said nothing.

She sighed. She brought her stick round in front of her and folded her hands on top of it.

"Things degenerated rapidly. She found Joe with some woman two weeks after they came back from their honeymoon. At the end of a year Alicia wore the expression of a survivor of a plane crash, but she was already pregnant and determined to make a go of it. After the second child was born they led separate lives. She ignored the absences, the affairs, what have you, but her tolerance took a terrible toll on her nerves. She became distant, reserved, even withdrawn—the woman you see today. I told her to divorce that bastard six years ago, but she wouldn't do anything to harm the children or expose them to scandal. Joe made it clear that he didn't want a divorce—very bad for the image of a public figure—and that if she filed it would be a bitter battle and the children would suffer. And then, of course, with his entry into politics the intact family became even more important, and she went along with it, again for the sake of her kids."

Lafferty waited.

"District Attorney Woods would now like us to believe that this same woman would shoot her husband in front of several reliable witnesses and expose her children to a hundred times more ridicule and abuse than a divorce would cause. Does that reasoning make sense to you, Detective?"

"She's been positively identified by Walker's press aide, a man who knew her for years."

"It could have been an actress selected for the resemblance, dressed and coiffed and prepped to impersonate Alicia," she said, watching his reaction.

"I doubt if such a performance would fool a man who saw her so frequently," Lafferty said.

"Why not? At a time when everyone is shocked and horrified there is mass confusion and mistakes are made."

"Your granddaughter's fingerprints were found on the gun, which was hidden in her town house."

"It was her gun! Joe bought it and kept it for prowlers, I'm sure she told you that."

"Nobody else's prints were on it."

"Then the murderer wore gloves."

"Mrs. Green," Lafferty said, rising, "I can't be drawn into this discussion."

"Why would she kill him?" Hannah Green persisted. "After putting up with him all these years? Do you think she had a psychotic episode? Talk to her doctor, she's as sane as I am." She leaned forward intently. "I understand District Attorney Woods. I understand that he has earned everything he has by himself and must make political hay out of this case to get ahead. He doesn't have private means and so must pursue those avenues which open up to him. Under other circumstances I would find his determination admirable, but he is not going to climb over my granddaughter's body to get what he wants."

"Woods doesn't have to manufacture a case, Mrs. Green. It's already there."

"Don't you care that you're about to participate in a miscarriage of justice?" she demanded.

"You could be wrong about this, Mrs. Green."

"You sense it, too, don't you?" she said. "You feel that something is wrong."

"My job is to go with the available evidence, not with my feelings."

She sat back in his chair and fixed him with a gimlet stare. "Detective Lafferty, I am eighty-two years old, and

I have seen a lot of things and known a great many people. I am not wrong about this. Alicia is innocent.''

Lafferty faced her down, feeling as if he were back in elementary school, on the carpet before a principal who was deciding whether or not to suspend him.

"I have said what I came to say. Please feel free to call on me if you need anything," Hannah Green concluded, rising. "I can always be reached at the number Alicia gave you. Leave your name."

He didn't move, his gaze locked with hers.

"My granddaughter is a very pretty girl, isn't she, Detective?" the old lady said slyly, and then walked quietly out the door.

Chapter 3

"**Y**ou mean that Daddy is not coming back?" Joey said, tears sounding in his voice before they appeared in his eyes.

Alicia had promised herself that she would be strong, but the sight of Joey crying over the father who hadn't even known his own son was on a Little League team almost broke her heart. She enfolded her son in her arms and looked over his shoulder at Claire, who was three years older than her brother and had guessed a lot more about her parents' marriage. She looked stonily back at Alicia. Claire had her father's eyes.

"Come here, honey," Alicia said.

The girl obeyed silently, sitting next to her mother on the sofa, her shoulders stiffening when Alicia put her hand on her arm.

"Claire," Alicia began, but the girl shook her head and looked away from her.

Joey pulled back and stared at his sister. "Won't you miss Daddy?" he asked, sniffling.

"No," Claire said. "He didn't even care about us. I'm glad he's...gone."

Joey broke into fresh sobs as Alicia said quietly, "You mustn't talk that way about your father."

"Why not?" Claire said, shrugging off Alicia's touch and standing again. "It's the truth." The girl bolted from the room, and Alicia heard her footsteps as she ran up the carpeted staircase to the second floor.

"But what about this summer?" Joey wailed, misery on his tear-streaked face. "Daddy was going to take us on a camping trip in the mountains...."

Alicia hugged him again, her own eyes filling. The way Joe continually promised the boy things and then disappointed him was one of the cruelest aspects of her late husband's character. He must have thought there would always be time in the future to fix at least some of the damage. But now, of course, his time had run out forever.

"We'll go camping, Joey, just as you planned," she said softly, kissing the top of her son's head, wondering how she was going to handle him, and his sister, during the rest of the nightmare they were about to live.

At present the children knew only that their father had been killed; before long they would also know that their mother had been accused of his murder. Once they began to watch television and interact with the rest of the world, Alicia would have to deal with the worst part of the problem: explaining to them that she did not shoot their father when everybody else thought she had.

"The chemistry set just arrived for Joey," Maizie announced from the doorway, favoring Alicia with a significant look. "It's in the kitchen."

"Oh, Joey, your science kit is here," Alicia said, feigning an enthusiasm she didn't feel. "Why don't you go with Maizie and take a look at it?"

The boy obeyed, wiping his eyes with the back of his hand and looking at his mother once uncertainly before he left the living room. When he was gone Maizie said to Alicia, "It was delivered to the back door by messenger."

"Don't look at me that way," Alicia said to Maizie. "I admit I took the coward's way out and ordered it this morning. I want to keep Joey occupied."

"Oh, he'll be occupied," Maizie said darkly. "I just hope he doesn't blow up the house."

"It's a kiddie set. It's perfectly safe, the concoctions just fizz and turn colors. The salesman said so," Alicia replied.

"Hmmph," Maizie said, indicating what she thought of the representations of salesmen.

"Keep an eye on him, will you?" Alicia said to Maizie. "Dealing with Claire will be enough for the moment."

Maizie nodded and then turned her head when the doorbell sounded.

"Oh, no," Alicia moaned. "I can't bear the thought of anymore reporters."

"The extra security people Mr. Landau hired will keep the reporters out," Maizie said.

"Are they still here? I fired Landau."

"He paid them for a month," Maizie said archly as she walked into the hall.

"You mean I paid them for a month," Alicia mumbled, aware that she would receive the bill from the dismissed lawyer. She sighed and ran her hand through her hair distractedly as Maizie answered the door and then returned with a visitor.

"Detective Lafferty to see you, Mrs. Walker," Maizie

said, raising her eyebrows behind the policeman's back as she folded her hands and waited for direction.

"Thank you, Maizie," Alicia said. "Detective, how nice to see you once more. You're becoming a regular visitor. Would you like some coffee, or anything else?"

Lafferty shook his head. "No, thanks."

Alicia nodded at Maizie, who left. Slowly.

The policeman stood looking at Alicia, and she felt her face grow warm under his scrutiny as she remembered their last encounter. The sense that she could easily make a fool of herself with this man returned with a sharp stab of fear, and she deliberately hardened her gaze.

Lafferty was wearing jeans with boat shoes and a navy V-neck sweater. The effect was to make him look younger, almost college age, an impression enhanced by the clarity of his gray-blue eyes looking back at her.

"I take it this is not an official visit, Detective," Alicia said, gesturing for him to sit when she sat herself.

"No." He waited for her to settle back in her chair, then sat on the edge of the brocade sofa gingerly, leaning forward with his elbows resting on his knees.

Alicia waited politely.

Lafferty cleared his throat. "I had a visit from your grandmother," he said bluntly. "Actually, I had a visit and then a phone conversation with her. She talked with me in person and then called me again from her car a few minutes later."

Alicia stared at him for a moment, then closed her eyes.

"I'm sorry," she finally said.

Lafferty said nothing.

"Did she…threaten you?" Alicia asked faintly.

"No, no, she's not that—" He stopped.

"Stupid?" Alicia suggested.

He met her eyes, then looked away.

"Did you report her visit to your superiors?"

He paused, then shook his head.

"Why not?" Alicia asked, watching him.

"I thought it would be better to handle it without an official record," he said.

Alicia understood. He didn't want to come right out and say as much, but he was doing her a favor. Yet he could have accomplished his mission over the telephone; why had he come to her house in person to say this?

Was it possible he wanted to see her again, without his caustic partner? Meeting his candid gaze, Alicia could almost believe it.

Then she realized that she was being idiotic and sighed. Conducting adolescent fantasies about the policeman who had arrested her was not the way to solve the worst problem she had ever encountered in her life. She was accused of murder, and this detective was, in effect, her enemy. It would be a lot wiser to treat the man as the adversary he certainly was.

"Thank you," Alicia said abruptly, snapping out of her reverie when she realized that Lafferty was staring at her.

He cleared his throat.

"I think I should warn you, Mrs. Walker, that if the old lady runs around town trying to intimidate the investigating officers on your case it is really not going to help you."

Alicia nodded. "I understand that." She bit her lip. "Detective, I beg you to believe me. I did not send her to see you."

"I believe you," Lafferty said flatly.

Alicia looked at him quickly.

"She told me she was acting on her own and she's... pretty convincing," he added.

"She is that," Alicia replied, sighing.

He smiled slightly, and Alicia found herself smiling along with him.

"I can see that she's a great person to have in your corner, but any help she wants to give you is best administered privately," Lafferty said. "Moral support is okay, but the police have a tendency to resent—"

"Interfering old broads with tons of money?" Alicia suggested.

"You could put it that way," he replied dryly.

"Did she give you a bad time?" Alicia asked, almost wincing.

"No. She talked about you mostly, and your past with Joe Walker."

"I wish she hadn't done that," Alicia said in a low tone. "Anything else I should know? Did she tell you about the time I played a camel in my fourth-grade Christmas pageant?"

"She said that you can be your own worst enemy, using sarcasm to keep people at a distance and avoid being hurt."

"I seem to be proving her point, don't I?" Alicia murmured, avoiding his direct gaze.

"She also described you as a failed romantic."

"Then she definitely said too much," Alicia answered, flushing deeply.

"She was right. A brittle attitude won't help your defense. It will alienate the media first, and then of course a jury when you come to trial."

"Thanks for the tip, Detective. I'll bear it in mind."

"She also let me know that she had done a background check on me. She had all the details on my life, my undergrad degree and my Master's in criminology from John Jay College. In her estimation I am not the, uh, typical policeman."

Alicia groaned. "Did she put a private detective on you?"

"She may have. She thinks your fate is in my hands, which in her mind produced an obligation on her part to find out about me."

Alicia shook her head wordlessly.

"I told her that in placing your fate in the hands of Harry Landau, she couldn't have made a more unfortunate choice, because the common perception is that anyone who hires him is guilty. And Landau himself thinks you are."

Alicia almost choked. "I can just imagine what Hannah said to that," she observed.

"Actually she seemed pleased to have finally gotten a reaction out of me."

"Yes, she would be."

Lafferty met her eyes directly. "Your grandmother is under the impression that I gave you special treatment."

"I never told her that," Alicia interjected quickly, vowing to throttle Hannah at the earliest opportunity.

Lafferty nodded. "I explained to her that I had merely followed procedure and hadn't exceeded my authority. And it doesn't necessarily mean that I think you are innocent."

Alicia felt an icy finger trace her spine. Was he telling her that he thought she was guilty? For reasons she didn't understand she found that idea more alarming than the prospect of ten more conversations with the odious Harry Landau.

"I hope she didn't ask you to tamper with evidence," Alicia whispered, barely able to look at Lafferty now, imagining the worst. This policeman probably thought that she and her grandmother were *both* criminals.

"No. She said she wanted me to look beyond the obvious to find the real killer."

"And?"

"I told her that once the criminal investigation is over it's out of my hands entirely. She asked me to keep the investigation open, and I told her that is not my decision. The prosecuting attorney is satisfied that he already has located the guilty party."

Alicia didn't reply. If Lafferty agreed with the DA there was nothing else to say.

"Woods is not looking for anybody else," Lafferty added, as if to clarify. "He thinks you killed your husband."

And do you think so, too, Detective Lafferty? Alicia wondered, wishing she could ask him aloud.

Lafferty waited.

"I understand," Alicia said smoothly a moment later, trying to keep her misery out of her voice. "And I appreciate your candor about my grandmother's actions. I'm sure you know she was trying to help me but she can be a trifle...overbearing."

He nodded.

"Thank you for coming here on your own time to tell me about it," Alicia said, rising.

"You're welcome," he responded, and, taking her cue, stood up to go.

Alicia extended her hand to him and he took it. Her small fingers were lost in his large, calloused ones and as before, a physical connection with Lafferty made Alicia feel small and feminine. She wanted to reach up and put her arms around his neck, bury her face on his capacious chest and let him take her troubles on his broad shoulders. She wanted to feel his hands in her hair, his breath against her cheek, his lips against her mouth. She looked into his eyes and wanted to take him upstairs and ask him to make love to her.

But that, of course, was not possible.

"Mrs. Walker, are you all right?" he asked, his hand still gripping hers.

At that moment Maizie entered the room with a tray.

They both turned and looked at her inquiringly.

"I thought I'd bring the coffee, anyway," she said brightly, striding past Alicia and setting the tray on a table.

Lafferty looked at Alicia, who had no recourse but to say, "Won't you have a cup, Detective?"

Lafferty looked trapped but sat down again.

Alicia shot Maizie a meaningful, exasperated glance. The housekeeper ignored her, gliding from the room with a smug expression on her face.

Alicia poured coffee into two cups and then handed Lafferty one of them.

"Cream or sugar?" she asked.

Lafferty shook his head, taking a careful sip. "Black is fine for me."

Alicia sat facing her guest, her hands cradling her cup.

"What are you going to do about a lawyer?" Lafferty asked, eyeing Alicia measuringly.

"You mean now that I've fired the fairgrounds huckster?" Alicia retorted.

He didn't smile. "Yes."

"I'm interviewing several over the next couple of days," Alicia said. "I suppose I'll find somebody."

"No doubt." He set his cup in its saucer.

"What does that mean?" Alicia asked crisply.

He glanced at her sharply, then shrugged. "Just that I agree with you."

"You agree that I have the cash to command the attention of a legion of lawyers?" Alicia suggested.

He said nothing, merely watched her, nonplussed.

Alicia sat forward to put her cup back on the table, her face flaming once again.

"Please forgive me for snapping at you," she said. "You've been nothing but kind, and my manners have deserted me."

Lafferty stood. "Don't worry about it. I've heard a lot worse in this job."

Alicia looked down, then up at him again. "Thank you." She paused and then added, "Why did you ask about my lawyer?"

He pulled a set of keys out of his pocket. "I just wanted to make sure you were looking at some other people," he said mildly.

"Some excellent people, supposedly." Alicia paused and pushed a strand of hair behind her ear. "I'm afraid I don't know very much about criminal lawyers. I never thought I would need one." She tried to smile but failed. When she felt her lower lip begin to tremble, she bit it, hard, turning her head to hide her struggle for control.

Lafferty rattled his keys and coughed. "I'll be off, then," he said, striding past her as Alicia stood and turned to follow him into the hall.

"I'll walk you out," Alicia called.

"That's not necessary, Mrs. Walker," Lafferty said quickly, and when he stopped to turn and face her, Alicia, right on his heels, crashed into him.

They were very close for several seconds as he steadied her, holding her forearms with his big hands. Alicia looked up into his deep blue eyes and saw a longing there that mirrored her own.

He wants me, too! Alicia thought. The idea flashed like lightning through her consciousness.

As if he could read her mind, Lafferty released her and stepped back.

"Sorry," he said.

"Don't apologize. I can't seem to stand on my own two feet these days, as you must have noticed." Alicia took a deep breath and looked back at him.

The hunger she had seen in his face a moment before had vanished.

She must have imagined it. Alicia tried not to let this disappointing knowledge show in her face as she gathered her resources and moved toward the hall.

"I appreciate your letting me know about this incident with my grandmother privately," Alicia said, and she heard the quaver in her own voice.

"I thought it would be easier this way," Lafferty said shortly. "I didn't want your grandmother to be cited for interfering with the judicial process."

"Hannah has yet to realize that even a person with a great deal of money can't control everything," Alicia said resignedly. "She's over eighty and still trying to do that."

"I'd say that the delusion of control is pretty common among the wealthy people I've seen," Lafferty replied, not looking at her and edging toward the door.

Alicia realized he anticipated that she was going to cry and was trying to get away from her before the tears started to fall.

"Thank you for stopping by," she said faintly.

"It was no trouble. Goodbye," he said, already in the front hall. She heard his footsteps and then the sound of the door closing behind him.

Alicia put her head in her hands and allowed herself to

give way to despairing thoughts for a few minutes. When she looked up again Maizie was standing in front of her.

"What?" Alicia said wearily.

"Is he gone?" Maizie asked.

"Yes. How is Joey?"

"Probably setting fire to the kitchen," Maizie replied equably. "That detective didn't stay very long."

"Despite your best efforts to prolong his visit," Alicia suggested wryly.

"I don't know what you're talking about," Maizie replied, bending down to pick up the tray.

"Oh, please, don't give me that innocent look. The man said he didn't want any refreshments and five minutes later you brought them anyway. It wasn't a party, Maizie. He was here to tell me that my grandmother is acting up, as usual."

"He likes you."

Alicia closed her eyes.

"Well, he does."

"Maizie, my husband is just dead."

"He was never a husband to you."

"That's not the point. He was murdered and everyone thinks I killed him!"

"Not everyone," Maizie said primly, sitting on the sofa next to Alicia. "Not Mrs. Green, not me, and not that detective."

"He's investigating me, and something tells me he is very good at his job," Alicia said flatly.

"What could he possibly find to implicate you, since you didn't do it?"

"What could he find?" Alicia demanded, rising and throwing her hands into the air. "Clothes, a gun, not to mention an impersonator dressed like me who shot Joe in front of several of his closest aides? Who could possibly believe my claim of innocence? I can hardly believe it myself!''

''I think Detective Lafferty knows you didn't kill Joe.''

Alicia shook her head. ''He just wanted to warn me that Grandma Green came to his apartment to have a talk with him. Oh, and they had a phone chat, too.''

Maizie was stunned into silence.

Alicia nodded.

''You'll have to stop her from doing things like that,'' Maizie finally said quietly.

Alicia snorted. ''I plan to speak to her, of course, but you know Grandma.''

''Was she trying to intimidate him?''

''I don't think he intimidates easily.''

''I wish I'd been able to listen in on those conversations,'' Maizie remarked. ''Something tells me that policeman and your grandma might be an even match.''

Alicia sighed. ''I don't want to find out, so I'm going to have to give Hannah a piece of my mind.''

''How about some lunch?'' Maizie asked.

Alicia shook her head and closed her eyes.

''I'll bring you a tuna sandwich, anyway,'' Maizie announced, and went off on her errand.

Alicia opened her eyes and looked around the room, as if seeking aid among the fine appointments it contained.

But there was no help anywhere.

Lafferty slid into the chair behind his desk and picked up a sheaf of papers from the blotter. From ten feet away, he could feel Chandler's eyes on him, gazing over the rim of a cup of coffee, the older man's rumpled shirt and bleary eyes telling the tale of a long night on the street.

''What are you doing here?'' Chandler asked.

Lafferty glanced over at him casually, picking up a pen. "What do you mean?"

"Isn't this your day off, junior?"

"Yeah. So?"

"I take it that you feel an overwhelming desire to see all of our ugly mugs when you are away from this place?" his partner inquired sarcastically.

Lafferty shrugged. "I just wanted to see what was doing on the Walker murder."

Chandler smiled thinly. "I thought so."

"You thought so?"

"You're obsessed with Lady Macbeth," Chandler announced with satisfaction.

"Why don't you lay off the Jack Daniels bottle you have stashed in that drawer?" Lafferty inquired disgustedly.

Chandler put down his cup and swiveled around in his chair. "I may like a nip now and then, but that doesn't change the fact that you're here looking for a way to get Mrs. Walker off the hook."

"I just came in to see if you goofballs had made any progress on the case." Lafferty dropped his pen in resignation. "Doesn't look like it."

Chandler drained his cup and tossed it smartly into the trash can under his desk. "Not much of a case, Mike. She done it." He stood and picked up his coat from a chair. "I understand she's getting a new lawyer."

Lafferty looked at him.

Chandler winked. "She filed for a change in her attorney of record. But seems like you already knew that."

Lafferty said nothing.

Chandler slipped into his sleeves and shrugged the coat onto his shoulders. "Kid, she can hire herself Clarence Darrow back from the grave and she will still walk that long, lonesome highway.'' Chandler chuckled to himself and kicked the bottom drawer of his desk shut. ''Don't go sipping on any of my prime stuff while I'm away, I got the level marked on the bottle with invisible ink.''

Lafferty watched him walk out of the staff room, then began to punch the keyboard of the PC on his desk. He barely glanced at the screens as they went by, logging into the department information file and waiting for the Search space to appear. When it did he typed ''Alicia Green Walker'' into it, and then sat back as the Waiting for Page sign came up and the number of bytes flashed rhythmically at the top of his screen.

He was going to find out everything there was to know about the fragile little lady in the big house, her relatives, her friends, her mailman and her dog.

And then maybe he could be as objective as his jaded, world-weary partner.

Lafferty switched off the computer and rolled his chair back from his desk. He glanced at the clock and realized that the squad room was almost empty; it was nearing midnight.

He had been reading for six hours, and now knew more about the subject of the Walker murder investigation than he had ever dreamed possible. Newspaper articles had made up the bulk of his study, and from them he had formed a pretty good picture of the woman whose house he had visited earlier that day.

Alicia Walker had been raised in luxury, an only child, in posh Hunterdon County, New Jersey, by a millionaire businessman, Daniel Green, and his wife Margaret. Alicia had been given all the advantages money could buy, and up to the time of her marriage had led a sheltered, cultured existence. She had met Joe Walker, the eldest son of a

Midwestern publishing giant, at a college mixer between Radcliffe and Harvard and married him two weeks after graduation.

And right there, Lafferty reasoned, Alicia Walker's charmed life began to change. Lafferty had his own opinion of Walker, a prepackaged politico who had been groomed from toddlerhood to be a head of state, the ride to that goal cushioned for him by his family's money. Joseph Walker III, 42, Chairman of the Board of FlameTree Publishing, had been running the many-faceted company founded by his grandfather, a minister, to publish Bibles—called FTGolds for the gold edged pages and gold stamped lettering they featured—when his advisers decided the time was right to launch him into the political arena. Walker had used his family's history to form a "back-to-basics" campaign founded on religious values and right-wing politics, gaining his support from traditional conservatives as well as reactionary voters disgusted with drugs and crime.

But Lafferty knew that Walker's private life was nothing like the image he projected. Policemen have access to information the general population never learns, and Lafferty had heard stories for years about The Chairman, as he was known. The cops knew that Walker had been picked up more than once during raids on brothels and paid his way out of the charges, then switched to call girl services, which posed less risk and provided better cover. He was, in fact, a dissolute who ignored his family and yet expected his wife to play the role of loving spouse necessary for his image.

To all appearances, Alicia had complied. But Lafferty had noticed that in the file photos she looked more fragile and wan with each passing year, and now she was almost gaunt. The charade has taken its toll as her grandmother had said. Lafferty could only imagine why she hadn't divorced Walker—the usual story in such cases was the threat to cut off access to the children, and Lafferty knew the possibility was real. He had seen it happen. Alicia's family had serious money, but the Walkers had a lot more. Attorneys and judges could be bought, induced to repay favors or go into debt for future ones. A woman like the fragile wraith accused of the murder would have little chance against the Walker machine, and no one would have known that better than Alicia herself.

Lafferty rubbed his eyes and stretched, nodding at a detective who wandered past him, stubbing out a cigarette in a metal ashtray. Lafferty didn't want to consider the picture that was emerging, but it was unavoidable. The bottom line was that Alicia Walker had ample private reason to wish her husband dead. He had treated her, and her children, like props in a performance he was staging for himself. Had she finally snapped and shot him? But why would she do it in front of onlookers, with no hope of concealing the crime? Was she deranged, suicidal, detached from reality? Lafferty could not reconcile the rational woman he had met with the kind of complete insanity necessary to shoot a public figure in front of witnesses. Alicia was worn out, depressed and now fighting for her very life, but she certainly did not appear to be crazy.

The double doors to the squad room opened and Captain Cramer strode through them briskly, stopping short when he saw Lafferty sitting bleary-eyed in front of the computer.

"No extra pay for unscheduled overtime," he said to Lafferty, who smiled thinly.

"The Walker case?" the captain asked.

Lafferty nodded and looked away.

"What's the problem?" Cramer asked.

Lafferty shrugged. "Too easy, I guess. She goes berserk and plugs the unfaithful husband with a handful of his buddies watching at ringside? Why? She could have poisoned his coffee, for God's sake, she didn't have to sign her own death warrant at the same time. It just doesn't make sense to me."

"Maybe she flipped out. It certainly looks that way."

"She doesn't seem nuts."

"Neither did Ted Bundy. Go on, kid, go home. Get a life. Get a girlfriend."

"I don't want a girlfriend."

"Why not?"

"Because she might become my wife, and I had a wife," Lafferty said dryly, rising.

"All right, so marriage didn't work out for you the first time around. Is that any reason to become a monk?"

"I'm not a monk," Lafferty replied, smiling. "I'm just particular."

"You're too particular. Keep it up and you'll wind up alone, playing cards with the boys on Friday night and sporting an enormous beer gut."

Lafferty grinned. "Thanks for that inspiring vision of my future," he said.

"Hey, it's a warning. If you eat and sleep this job, it'll bury you." Cramer grabbed a stack of folders from a desk and went back out the way he had come, whistling.

Lafferty kicked his chair under his desk and sighed.

He had been divorced for three years and hadn't had a date in six months.

Maybe the captain was right.

Alicia stepped out of the car and looked warily at the imposing facade of the Peninsula Hotel.

"I'll call you on the cell phone when I'm ready," she said to the driver, who touched his cap and then pulled into the stream of traffic. The limo disappeared quickly amidst the yellow taxis, transit buses and other vehicles which quickly enclosed it, and Alicia turned to face the fate awaiting her.

During the two days since Lafferty had visited her she had spent most of her time on the phone, arranging the meeting she was about to have. She looked up as she went into the building using the employee entrance, wondering if when she came back out again it would be with the knowledge that her last hope had been exhausted.

A hostess was waiting for her just inside the door. With the aplomb displayed by the management of expensive hotels everywhere she smiled and greeted Alicia quietly and then led her through the employee lounge to a narrow hall. There was a small staff conference room at the back of the ground floor, with two windows facing a brick wall across an alley and a single table surrounded by six leather chairs. One of the chairs was occupied.

"Thank you for agreeing to host this meeting surreptitiously," Alicia said to her escort.

The woman smiled again. "A waiter will be with you shortly," she said, and left.

"How do you do, Mr. Kirby," Alicia said, walking into the room and shaking hands with the distinguished-looking older man who rose to his feet to greet her.

Oswald Kirby nodded and pulled out a chair for Alicia. When she was seated, Kirby sat also and said, "Mrs. Walker. I'm sorry that our introduction is happening under these most regrettable circumstances."

Alicia nodded. "Thank you for arranging to see me here, Mr. Kirby. I really did not want to go to your office and then see my arrival there featured on the evening news.''

Kirby gestured dismissively. "I often make these considerations for clients in, ah, special circumstances. Someone may have seen you come here, of course, but the likelihood of the media hounds tracking you to the employee wing of this restaurant is far less than if you showed up at my place of business. And I can offer my guarantee that the staff here is extremely discreet.''

"Yes." Alicia was sure he had done whatever was necessary to make them so. "You will understand that I have not yet made a decision about your representing me, and I didn't want to give the impression of trolling the waters for a compliant attorney.''

Kirby inclined his graying head. He understood.

"You are familiar with my previous representation?'' Alicia asked as the waiter arrived with long-stemmed water glasses and hovered anxiously.

"Come back in half an hour," Kirby said to the waiter. "We'll order then.''

The boy vanished.

Kirby made a small moue of distaste to Alicia. "Harry Landau. I know him, as does everyone who owns a television.''

"My grandmother's idea," Alicia said, sighing.

"I trust I will be dealing with just you, then?'' Kirby asked.

"Yes. I have instructed my grandmother to confine her future efforts on my behalf to prayer.''

Kirby smiled slightly. "Well, since we are sharing confidences, I should say that I was not an admirer of your husband's, or of his politics, Mrs. Walker," he said flatly.

"Neither was I, Mr. Kirby," Alicia replied wearily.

Kirby lifted his briefcase from the floor. Alicia examined the man sitting opposite her, who was removing a notebook and a small recorder from his bag.

Oswald Kirby was a well-proportioned man of medium height with graying dark hair and a thin, ascetic face. He was an old line Boston brahmin who practiced law because he loved the profession and was dedicated to its ideals. He was the antithesis of what her husband had been, the genuine article as opposed to the poseur, which was one of the reasons Alicia wanted him to represent her. He also had a reputation for absolute, faultless integrity, which was the other reason for her decision.

She realized that he was looking at her inquiringly.

"Yes?" she said.

"Perhaps you'll give me your version of the events in question, Mrs. Walker."

Alicia took a deep, cautious breath. "I didn't kill my husband, Mr. Kirby."

Kirby eyed her steadily. "I have never thought that you did, Mrs. Walker."

Alicia stared at him. He was the first person to say this to her since Joe was murdered.

Kirby shrugged. "My problem with your case is not that I don't believe you, Mrs. Walker. I do. My problem is to convince a jury that you didn't do it, and that is an entirely different matter."

Alica exhaled. "Why do you believe me? No one else seems to doubt that I shot Joe in cold blood."

"I opposed everything your husband stood for, Mrs. Walker. I can assure you that I know what he was really like."

"I'd think that would convince you I killed him," Alicia said despairingly.

Kirby shook his head. "No. It is apparent to me that you coped by adopting a stance of ignoring your husband's transgressions and keeping your life separate from his as much as possible. I assume there were threats of losing the children if you attempted to divorce him?''

Alicia nodded.

Kirby pressed his lips together. ''I would also guess that you had a long-range plan of divorcing Walker once the children were older, when he had achieved his political goals and no longer needed the window dressing of a smiling wife.''

''Yes.''

''So why would you suddenly rebel now and kill him in a manner which would remove *both* parents from your children's lives at the same time?''

Alicia looked back at him steadily. ''I wish other people accepted your reasoning,'' she said. ''I didn't think I would even make bail. The district attorney kept talking about how easy it would be for me to flee the country.''

''I read the transcript. Apparently the hearing judge was unpersuaded.''

''She felt that I would not go anywhere without my children, but DA Woods argued that I would do just about anything to save my own skin.''

Kirby sat back in his chair and took a sip of his drink. ''You have to understand that you will be taken at face value and resented by a certain proportion of the population just because you are young, beautiful and wealthy. They don't know what your personal life was like—you were seemingly living in the lap of luxury without a care in the world. They will want to fry you just because they saw you on the news walking into the Hotel Pierre wearing a Scaasi dress.''

Alicia looked away from him uncomfortably. She knew he was right. ''So your job will be to find jurors who don't feel that way?'' she asked weakly.

"I won't be able to find jurors who don't feel that way to some degree," Kirby replied. "My job will be to find jurors who aren't overwhelmingly prejudiced against you."

"And how will you convince them that I didn't kill Joe, when eyewitnesses 'saw' me do it?" Alicia asked.

"That's what we will discuss today," Kirby answered. "Do you know of anyone who looks enough like you to pass for you in a situation like that?"

"No."

"Relatives, even distant ones?"

"Nobody. Several of my husband's associates who knew both of us for years swear that it was me—I am just dumbfounded by the depth of their conviction about it."

"Any axes to grind there?"

"Oh, possibly some of them were not fond of me, but I can't think of anyone who hated me enough to want to see me convicted of a crime I didn't commit." Alicia took a sip of her water and added, "I suppose someone could have searched out an actress who looked like me, but *why,* and could the resemblance have been close enough to fool Joe's colleagues?" She shook her head.

"This is why we have our work cut out for us, Mrs. Walker," Kirby said gravely. "Your husband treated you badly, and enough people knew it to believe that you had a strong motive to kill him. And several witnesses *think* they saw you do it."

Alicia put down her glass and raised her hand to her forehead. "How could this be any worse?" she whispered.

Kirby surprised her by patting her free hand, which rested on the table between them.

"Do not despair. I'm on your side now. And I'm a formidable opponent."

Alicia sighed shakily and said, "Thank you."

He smiled. "Now shall we begin?"

Alicia focused on his questions, wondering if Oswald Kirby would be the only person to look beyond the obvious and see that she was innocent.

Chapter 4

"I still say you shouldn't be going to this thing," Maizie grumbled, her tone heavy with disapproval.

Alicia turned and surveyed the back of her gown in the full-length mirror. "I'm not hiding out here like the criminal the district attorney wants everyone to think I am," she said firmly, tugging at the base of her zipper.

"I don't understand you at all. You've got crazy people calling here saying they're going to kill you, and you want to parade into Manhattan and do a public appearance to give all the loonies a better target."

"I'm not a doing a public appearance. I chaired the committee to sell tickets to a benefit performance of *La Boheme,* and all the people who paid inflated prices for those tickets expect to see me, dressed appropriately, smiling and shaking hands. I will not disappoint them."

"And what about your children? Can they afford to lose both parents if somebody shoots you, too?"

"A police detective has been assigned to protect me for the whole night."

Maizie made a sound of disgust. "Policemen are assigned to protect a lot of people. Some of them still die."

"Maizie, please. This isn't easy for me, but I am determined to get through it." Alicia adjusted the halter top of her dress and patted her upswept hair.

"Why can't Helen handle it?"

"Helen is not the chairperson of this event." Helen Fisher had assisted with the benefit performance and would be attending with a date.

"I still say it's a bad idea. We got another one of those calls just today."

"I can't control every idiot out there who has access to a telephone," Alicia said with a bravado she didn't feel. She found the harassing calls a lot more unnerving than she cared to admit, to Maizie or anyone else.

"There. I'm as ready as I'll ever be," Alicia said.

A seamstress had taken in the dress she was wearing; she had lost weight since her arrest. It was still a stunning gown, with a criss-cross bodice that draped into a halter fastening at the back of her neck. It had a billowing sweep of chiffon skirt, and the pale apricot color flattered her skin and hair. Her grandmother's diamond earrings and a pair of ankle-strap pumps completed the picture.

Someone knocked on the bedroom door, and Maizie answered the summons.

"Your car is ready," Maizie said.

Alicia nodded and picked up her wrap.

Maizie followed her down the stairs, and they stopped in the foyer as a man turned to face them.

"Detective," Alicia said lightly to Lafferty, who nodded at her solemnly.

He was wearing a slim black tuxedo with a boiled white

shirt and a black satin tie matching the satin stripes on his pants. Studs gleamed in his cuffs and his shoes where polished to a high ebony sheen. The well-fitting clothes made the most of his broad shoulders and slim hips, and his wavy hair had been tamed somewhat by a recent trim.

He looked wonderful.

His gaze traveled swiftly over Alicia, then moved away from her.

"You didn't tell me the policeman was him!" Maizie hissed in Alicia's ear.

Alicia ignored her as she retrieved her bag from the hall stand.

"Please come into the kitchen for a second, Mrs. Walker, I need to talk to you," Maizie said firmly.

Alicia shot Maizie a look, but followed the older woman reluctantly down the hall.

"How did he get this job?" Maizie demanded.

Alicia shrugged. "The police department assigned him to escort me."

"Why?"

Alicia was silent.

"Did you ask for him?"

Alicia sighed. "Yes."

Maizie waited until Alicia met her eyes.

"So I'm right," Maizie said softly.

"Don't look at me that way, Maizie. He makes me feel safe and I need that tonight. It will be difficult enough to get through this event without worrying every minute of every hour. Detective Lafferty is capable and professional, and that's all."

"Are you sure that's all? That is one fine-looking man in there—and I have a feeling I'm not the only one who thinks so."

"Maizie, I have to go. We can continue this discussion later," Alicia said briskly, and fled.

Lafferty was waiting and fell into step with Alicia as the chauffeur opened the front door for both of them. Lafferty didn't look at her as she said, "Thank you for coming along with me, Detective."

"I was assigned the duty," he replied flatly.

"You had no choice about it, then?"

"None."

Something about the way he said the word made Alicia examine his profile closely.

"You don't want to be here?"

Lafferty paused as the chauffeur opened the door of the car and offered his hand to assist Alicia into the back seat. She waved the driver away and remained standing, facing Lafferty. Once the chauffeur was in the driver's seat, his car door closed, she added, "I take it I have inconvenienced you?"

"I do my job," Lafferty replied shortly, standing beside the open door.

Inexplicably, Alicia felt stung.

"But you didn't want to do it tonight?" she inquired.

"The captain said that you had asked for me," he answered flatly.

It took a few seconds for the import of his statement to register with Alicia.

"I see," she said softly. "So that's it. My request embarrassed you."

Lafferty didn't answer.

"I'm so sorry," Alicia said. "It was not my intention to put you in an awkward position with your superiors. After tonight I can assure you that you will not be involved in any extraneous duties concerning me or my case."

He still said nothing.

"Come on, Detective," Alicia said, annoyance creeping into her tone. "I am aware enough to realize that NYPD is providing an 'escort' for me with an ulterior motive in mind. I think your captain is less worried about protecting me from crazies with handmade signs than he is about my vanishing through the stage-door exit during the third act of the opera."

Lafferty looked down, his fingers closing on the handle of the door.

"How distressing for him if I disappeared from the jurisdiction on his watch," Alicia continued bitingly. "But you need not worry on that score. It was very difficult for me to get bail, I have already surrendered my passport, the court has frozen my assets and I came very close to being put under house arrest with one of those little beeping bracelets on my arm. So I am not going anywhere."

Lafferty met her eyes, and Alicia was surprised by his expression. He didn't look angry, but rather as if he were taken aback by her caustic speech.

"I'm surprised that your superior actually sent you and agreed to my request," she added. "They must suspect me of bribing you to spirit me away to some foreign country with no extradition treaty with the United States. Or would that be too obvious? I certainly wouldn't be stupid enough to draw you into my intrigues and at the same time advertise my predilection for your company, would I? Or maybe your captain thinks I am brazen enough to do that very thing? Are *you* being watched tonight, too, Detective Lafferty?"

Lafferty stared at her until her eyes filled with tears and she turned her head to hide them.

"Yes, Detective, I do have feelings, and what I have just described is peculiar treatment for an innocent person, in my book,'' she whispered as she gracefully slid into the massive back seat. ''But I guess you don't believe that I *am* innocent. So why am I even talking to you about it?''

The chauffeur turned, and Lafferty shut the door abruptly. Tears slipped from beneath Alicia's closed lids and ran down her face as she searched through her purse for a handkerchief.

She was making a fool of herself and she had to stop. This policeman didn't know or care about anything except that he was doing his work. She had been silly to ask for him to be assigned this duty, and she had made the situation worse with her outburst. How was she going to get through the rest of the evening now? Her eyes stinging and her face burning with humiliation, Alicia watched through a watery blur as Lafferty slid into the front seat next to the driver and signaled for him to go.

Alicia pressed the square of linen to her lips and resolved not to lose control again.

The fountain at Lincoln Center sprayed jets of water into the air as the limousine pulled up to the curb. Crowds of people pressed against the car, camera flashes went off like fireworks, and Lafferty sat forward, alert, as the driver put the car in park.

Alicia took one look at the chaotic scene and closed her eyes in despair. Maizie had been right—why hadn't she listened? No matter how much she wanted to follow through on her work for the charity, she should have stayed at home. She was an accused murderer, charged with killing her public-figure husband, and the media harpies were not going to let her forget it.

She turned to look at Lafferty, and he said quietly, ''Do you want to turn around and go back?''

Something about the "I told you so" tone of his question stiffened Alicia's spine.

"No," she said firmly. "I can handle it."

Lafferty nodded. "Wait until I open your door, then stay close to me," he said, and got out of the car.

The driver stood idly by as Lafferty handed Alicia out of the limousine. She was assaulted by a wall of noise and realized that the crowd had been screaming all along but the luxurious car had prevented her from hearing the sound.

Alicia was no stranger to crowds, her husband's career had forced her to deal with many of them. But those gatherings had been receptive and welcoming, since most were associated with his political ascent and filled with well-wishers. This was a mob: hostile, jeering, insulting. Lafferty took her arm firmly and steered her toward the center path of carpeting which led to the door. Whistles and catcalls split the crisp spring evening air, and people carrying signs held them high to be captured by the cameras. Alicia saw a sign with "Murderess" written in red with blood dripping from the letters and then looked away, resolved not to read anymore. As they stepped up from the curb, reporters converged on them and jammed their microphones into Alicia's face as a pair of uniformed policemen brought up the rear behind Alicia and her escort.

"No comment," Lafferty repeated to them, his expression grim, his strong body acting as a battering ram moving Alicia inexorably forward. The crowd followed them, the reporters yammering questions incessantly, her detractors yelling epithets and thrusting their signs into the air, the cameras whirring and flashing. Video cams wobbled as newsmen dodged through the melee to get a continous feed for their tapes. The Metropolitan Opera House seemed a hundred miles away as Alicia finally bent her head and shielded her eyes, unable to take the glare of the spotlight any longer.

The trip to the entrance was endless. Even with Lafferty looming next to her their progress was maddeningly slow, and the jostling came close to knocking Alicia down several times. Lafferty was almost carrying her by the time they stepped onto the red carpet which led to the reception room. Just as they entered the building Alicia felt a sudden wetness on her face and she realized with shock that someone had spit on her.

She stopped short, then saw the group assembled in the room to greet her, all the staring faces turned in her direction. She closed her eyes, unsure what to do. Lafferty noticed her hesitation and looked around desperately, spotting a ladies' room just a few feet across the marble-floored hall.

"Mrs. Walker will be with you shortly," he announced, steering Alicia in the direction of the rest room and bumping the padded door open with his shoulder.

The uniformed attendant inside glanced up at their entrance and then stared at Lafferty, who looked at her and said, "Out."

The sixtyish woman's mouth opened as she folded her hands over her net apron. "I'm sorry, sir," she began officiously, but Lafferty cut her off by removing his wallet and showing her his badge.

"Police business," he said. "Just step outside and wait, I won't need this room long."

The woman examined the badge, then his face, and decided to obey. Once she had left, Lafferty picked up an ornate stool in front of the vanity and jammed it against the closed door, preventing anyone from coming into the room until it was removed.

Then he took out his handkerchief and gently wiped the spittle from Alicia's face.

She stared at the floor, unable to meet his eyes.

Unsure what to do next, Lafferty touched Alicia's shoulder comfortingly, and she fell into his arms.

"Take it easy," he said soothingly, his mouth against her hair and his voice rumbling in his chest under her ear. "The bad part's over, it will get better now."

Alicia should have been ashamed of herself for clinging to this near stranger. She should have been self-possessed enough to care. But she wasn't. The mob's reception had been so ugly, and Lafferty's strength was so protective and reassuring by comparison that she let go and did what her body wanted her to do. Her arms slipped up around his neck and she felt his lips move against her brow.

"I'll take you home now if you want to go," he added quietly, his voice next to her ear. "I'll make your excuses and get you the hell out of here."

The prospect was so inviting her mouth almost watered at the thought. Just as appetizing was the idea of staying in this man's arms for the foreseeable future. She sighed and dug her fingers into his shoulders. She felt his grip tighten in response.

Alicia would never know what might have happened next, since a raised voice in the corridor outside caused Lafferty to pull away from her and listen at the door.

Alicia was leaning against the silk-covered wall, her eyes closed, when he turned back to her.

"Better now?" he asked.

Alicia's eyes opened. "Yes. Thank you," she whispered.

Lafferty said nothing, merely stood looking at her, waiting for her to make the next move.

"I guess you knew I wasn't prepared for this," she finally murmured grudgingly.

He turned to run some water into a paper cup provided by a dispenser and handed it to her. Alicia swallowed gratefully and said, "Why do they hate me so?"

"Well, probably a lot of them do think you killed your husband, and even the ones who aren't sure resent the fact that your money allows you to be out on bail when most others accused of a similar crime would be locked up in a cell. Your coming to this event, all dressed up, stepping out of a limo, is just flaunting in their faces the fact that you bought your way out of the jailhouse."

"You seem to understand mob mentality very well," Alicia replied sadly.

"It comes with the job."

Alicia shook her head. "These are probably the same people who were cheering me a month ago at one of Joe's rallies."

"They were cheering your husband. Now that they think you killed him, they have turned against you."

"And what if I didn't kill him?" Alicia demanded, crushing the cup and tossing it into the gilt wastebasket under the vanity. "Does anybody think about that? Whatever happened to 'innocent until proven guilty'?"

"It's more interesting to think you shot your husband. It's a much more sensational story."

"Oh, for heaven's sake! If I were going to kill Joe, why would I do it in front of witnesses? Do they all think I'm an idiot?"

"People believe what they want to believe," Lafferty replied flatly.

Alicia searched his face. "You think it's hopeless, don't you? Why am I even bothering with a defense?

Nothing I can do or say will ever convince anyone I didn't pull that trigger."

Somebody began pounding on the door.

"Open up," a voice called. "Security."

Lafferty studied Alicia's face. "Are you okay to go back out there?"

Alicia sighed and nodded.

Lafferty removed the stool and pulled open the gilded door. They saw a blue-suited guard standing in the hall with the rest room attendant.

Neither one of them looked happy.

"May I see your badge, Officer?" the guard demanded.

"Detective," Lafferty corrected him. "And there's no need for ID. We're done here." He took Alicia's arm and whisked her past the two staring people before they could object.

"Okay," he said as they paused at the entrance to the reception room for a second time that night. Inside the crowd was milling around, sampling the refreshments, glasses in hand.

"Showtime," he added, looking down at Alicia.

Alicia glanced up at him and then fixed a welcoming smile on her face.

"That's better," he said.

"Thanks for the save," she whispered.

"Part of the service," he replied briefly, and before Alicia could consider what he meant by that, Helen emerged from the crowd and came forward to take both her hands.

"Are you all right?" Helen asked, sotto voce, while beaming for the crowd and kissing Alicia's cheek.

"I am now," Alicia replied.

"That was quite a charming greeting you got from the hoi polloi outside," Helen said dryly.

"I guess I should have entered through the kitchen as the security director advised," Alicia replied. "For some insane reason I thought it was important to show my face and act as if I had done nothing wrong."

"You'd better exit through the kitchen. Or the basement, or the skylight. They are still lying in wait for you out there, believe me."

"I never realized that I was so popular."

"You have that dishy policeman in tow again," Helen whispered as she leaned in to link arms with Alicia. She led her friend forward to start greeting people. "What he does for that tux is scandalous. Is he here to protect you?"

"Something like that."

"Details. I want details."

"I'll tell you all about it later," Alicia retorted briefly, looking over her shoulder to make sure that Lafferty wasn't close enough to hear what they were saying. He was not far, scanning the crowd, his expression alert and speculative.

"You can bet on that," Helen said sweetly, and extended her hand to the pencil-slim wife of a captain of industry. "Mrs. Dilworthy, it was so kind of you to come."

Alicia assumed a similar gracious expression, casting a final glance in Lafferty's direction.

He was, as always, watching her.

The rest of the evening passed without incident. Lafferty sat behind Alicia during the performance and when she glanced back at him she found herself secretly amused by his attempts to look interested and appreciative; he was obviously not a fan of the opera. Helen and her date, a rising congressional aide with steel-rimmed glasses and a professorial air, made conversation with Alicia during the two intermissions, while Lafferty stood nearby and tried to appear unobtrusive. He didn't succeed. As Helen had commented while she was downing the first of several glasses of champagne, "No matter what he does, he looks like a cop."

Alicia exited through the kitchen and encountered only a few persistent hecklers who had anticipated her alternative route and stood waiting outside the service door.

"These people need a life," Lafferty muttered as he bustled Alicia past them and into the waiting limousine. "Don't they know what time it is?"

Alicia ignored their thin catcalls as she settled into her seat and kicked off her shoes with a sigh. It was over at last. She had done her duty but didn't think she would be venturing into public again anytime soon. If she had needed a reading on the popular opinion of her guilt or innocence she had gotten it tonight.

The ride back to her house was swift and silent. Lafferty didn't say a word the whole time, and the driver broke the silence to ask a question only twice. Alicia dozed and then sat up with a start when the long car came to a stop in the circular drive in front of her Scarsdale house, behind Lafferty's unmarked police car.

"I'll take over from here," she heard Lafferty say to the driver. He handed her out of the car, which then continued around the drive as Lafferty took her keys and opened the door.

The house was silent. Maizie had left the hall light on, but the children were in bed.

Lafferty looked around uncomfortably. "Well," he said, running his finger inside his collar, "I guess I should get the car back."

"Yes, Detective, I imagine that you are dismissed. Unless your mission extends to checking the closets for assassins. Weren't you instructed on that point?''

Lafferty reddened slightly, and Alicia regretted the thoughtless barb.

"I'm sorry," she said, sighing. "It's been a long night. Of course you want to go."

"I didn't say that," Lafferty replied, finally meeting her eyes. His were very blue.

"Then take off your coat and tie and I'll make some coffee," Alicia said. "Just let me have a minute to change."

She ran upstairs, aware that she had shamed Lafferty into staying, but unable to work up any guilt about it. She did not want to be alone.

Alicia took off her evening clothes rapidly and donned jeans and a sleeveless top, stepping into loafers. She pulled the pins from her hair as she walked across the room and dropped them in a tray on the dressing table by the door. She was fluffing her hair with her fingers as she descended the stairs, then stopped short as Lafferty looked up at her from the first-floor hallway.

"What?" she said, at the expression on his face.

"That's quite a transformation," he said quietly. "You look about fifteen."

Alicia laughed shortly.

"In dog years," she said wearily, and then realized that he was looking uncharacteristically abashed.

He had meant to pay her a compliment.

"Thank you," she added. "That's nice to hear."

His jacket and tie lay on the marble-topped table in the hall. He had opened his collar and rolled his sleeves up to the elbow; he looked as informal and relaxed as it was possible for a man still wearing a cummerbund and tuxedo pants to look.

"Follow me," Alicia announced, and led the way to the kitchen at the back of the house, its hanging copper-bottomed pots gleaming dully in the darkness.

Alicia flipped a switch, and the room was flooded with light, the polished tile floor reflecting the overhead glow like a mirror.

"You could field a soccer team in here," Lafferty said dryly. He glanced around at the separate dining area with hanging Tiffany lamp, large oak food preparation table and triple-glass doors leading out to a spacious redwood deck.

"Yes," Alicia answered dryly. "Joe did everything on a grand scale." She went to the oversize stainless steel refrigerator and removed a bottle of milk.

"Joe? Didn't you buy this house with him?"

"No. He bought it with a real estate agent. I never saw it until I moved into it."

"It is a beautiful house."

"The decorator has to take credit for that. Joe had it 'done' and presented it to me as a wedding gift."

Her tone was neutral.

"Didn't it occur to him that you might have found that a little…high-handed?" Lafferty asked, aware that he was overstepping his bounds but eager for a reading on her attitude about her husband's arrogance.

"You mean I killed him because he didn't let me decorate my house?" she asked, smiling slightly.

Lafferty was silent. Her ladylike manner belied an incisive wit, as her grandmother had pointed out to him. She was sharp and feisty under the gracious facade, something Joe Walker, preoccupied with himself and distracted by her undeniable loveliness, may have discovered too late.

Alicia took two mugs from a cabinet and set them on

the table. "You never met Joe, so you can't understand what he was like. If he was interested in you, there was nothing he would not do for you, and it would have seemed so ungrateful for me to quibble about the terms of such an extravagant present." She took two spoons from a drawer. "But once he lost interest in you, it was like you became invisible. You did not exist for him any longer." Her tone continued to be noncommittal; if her husband's dismissal of her had enraged her enough to shoot him, she was a very good actress.

"Would you like something to eat with the coffee?" she asked as she took a couple of checked napkins from a holder and placed them on the table.

Lafferty shook his head. "No, thanks."

"Have a seat, Detective," Alicia said, when she saw that he was standing awkwardly with his arms at his sides.

Lafferty pulled out a rustic dark pine chair and sat on the well-padded, leather-covered seat. He stretched his long legs under the table and sighed.

"Tired?" Alicia asked. "Opera fatigue?"

He looked at her and smiled. Alicia was glad she had already put down the box of coffee filter bags because otherwise she might have dropped it.

That was quite a smile.

"I gather that you are not an opera fan, either?" Lafferty asked slyly.

Alicia shrugged as she dropped a filter bag into the cup and locked the plastic basket into place. "I am a survivor of many performances. As Joey likes to say, it wouldn't be so bad except it has all that screaming in it."

Lafferty laughed. "For entertainment value, I'll take the Knicks any day."

"I'll bear that in mind next time I am planning a charity event," Alicia said dryly. She filled the well of the coffeepot with water and flipped the switch to start the brewing cycle. She sat across from Lafferty as the dark liquid spurted into the glass pot, and the delicious aroma of brewing coffee drifted into the room.

"So, Detective, is this what they call 'fraternization?'" she asked.

"I guess this must be it," he replied, sitting back and closing his eyes.

"No Kaffeeklatsches allowed?"

He opened his eyes. "Does all of this seem so ridiculous to you?" he asked tersely, not smiling.

She framed her mug with her hands, not looking at him. "No," she replied slowly, "not at all. It's just that I'm terrified and I always make jokes when I'm scared. I'm sorry."

He regretted challenging her—why did he always say the wrong thing to her? Why wasn't he driving back to the city right now, instead of sitting in this murder suspect's kitchen trying to make himself believe that she was as innocent as he wanted her to be?

"Why did you become a policeman?" she asked suddenly.

He didn't answer immediately, and she took his lack of response as a rebuke. "I guess everyone asks you that," she mumbled, rising. "Not very original, am I?"

"Actually, my wife wanted me to be a lawyer," he said, and she turned to stare at him.

"You're married?"

Was it his imagination, or did the idea seem to upset her?

"Divorced. She didn't want to be married to a cop."

"She's a fool," Alicia said crisply, then she blanched. She paused a long moment before adding quietly, "Forgive me again. I must have drunk too much champagne at that reception. I obviously need this." She filled two mugs with coffee and set one before him, resuming her position at the table and staring down at the cup.

"It's all right," Lafferty said quietly. "I'm over it by now. I removed the dart board with her picture on it six months ago." He inhaled a large swallow of his coffee.

She smiled and looked up at him.

"Good," he said, gesturing with the mug.

"Premixed, premeasured, prefab. My favorite type of consumable, I can't do a thing to ruin it."

"Not much of a cook, eh?"

"I could screw up a grilled cheese sandwich and have. My kids would starve without Maizie."

"Oh, somehow I think you would be resourceful enough to open a soup can if Maizie quit."

"I'd be resourceful enough to run an ad for another cook," she replied dryly, and he grinned.

"Don't those finishing schools teach proper young ladies all the homely arts?" he asked.

"I didn't go to finishing school," Alicia said crisply. "I went to college and majored in journalism, which came in handy every time I had to write a description of a flower show for the Congressional Women's Quarterly."

Lafferty was silent, unsure how to reply.

Alicia glanced at him and sighed, then laughed lightly. "My, don't I sound bitter? I'd say that I'm sorry again, but I know I'm beginning to sound redundant."

"Most people falsely accused of a murder would tend to be bitter."

Alicia studied his face and then looked down at her drink. "You and my new lawyer, Oswald Kirby, seem to be the only people who consider that a possibility."

"What?"

"That I might be falsely accused."

"Mrs. Walker, several people saw you shoot your husband. Those people might say that I was a fool for keeping an open mind."

"I didn't kill Joe. There were plenty of times when I was younger that I wanted to, but by the time he died I was over it."

"Over what?"

"The rejection, the disappointment, the misery. We just moved on and had separate lives. He had his career and his...women, I had the children. Except for official functions, when he needed me on hand as his armpiece, we barely saw each other."

"So you just didn't care anymore?"

"Oh, I cared, I was just numb. To love somebody as much as I loved Joe at the beginning and then to experience such an emptiness with the same person, that was hard. But I learned to shut it off, to disconnect and survive. The pain lessened as time went on and it became a condition of life, like a headache that would never quite end." Alicia met Lafferty's steady gaze and then looked away. "I should shut up, shouldn't I? All this babbling about my existential angst is making it sound even more like I shot him." She rose abruptly and dumped the rest of her coffee into the sink.

Lafferty got up and followed, looming at her shoulder, just standing silently behind her until she was forced to turn and look up at him.

"Existential angst?" he asked, and raised his brows.

Alicia smiled slightly, then wider as he smiled back. "My mother always did say that I dramatized myself," she replied, and he chuckled softly. At close range his eyes looked a deep blue, almost indigo, and the beard shadow on his cheeks was visible as stubble. He looked down shyly and his lashes swept his cheeks; when he looked up again they framed his eyes like fringe.

"I should go," he said, his voice low, a low rumble deep in his chest.

"I know," Alicia said softly.

"I don't want to," he added. He reached out to touch her, and she flinched. They both looked down and saw a large, purpling bruise on her upper arm.

"I never noticed that," Alicia said in a wondering tone, as if she had suddenly sprouted a tattoo. "I must have gotten it tonight."

"How?" he asked. Their gazes locked and they both had the same thought at the same moment.

"I did it," he said.

"No, of course not..."

"I had a death grip on you, getting us through that crowd. Look, you can see the imprint of my fingers. Oh, geez."

"Michael, it's nothing."

He blinked when she said his name.

"I hurt you."

She shook her head. He was very close. Her head came just to his chin level, and she could feel the warm exhalation of his breath.

"I never meant to do that," he added.

"Forget it," she said.

"I can't forget it," he replied, and bent his head, watching her face. He kissed the bruised flesh of her upper arm, and she gasped at the touch of his warm lips on her skin. She waited, her lips parting, and then he straightened up and looked at her.

"Better?" he whispered.

"A little. Not enough."

"You want more?" he said hoarsely.

"Much more," she murmured, and he kissed her.

His mouth was soft but firm, and he drew her in slowly with his arm so that she rested against his shoulder. It had been so long since a man had kissed her with passion that she'd thought she would forget how to react, but this was not the case. All her senses reawakened and responded with a rush to meet his desire. Her lips opened fully under the pressure of his like flower petals reacting to the sun; she felt his probing tongue and caressed it with hers. When he made a sound deep in his throat, tightening the pressure of his arms, she found herself moaning softly in return.

Lafferty was big, both taller and heavier than her late husband. Her memory of Joe's embrace was muted by the passage of time but not completely silent, and so she was conscious by comparison of feeling engulfed and very small in Lafferty's arms. He pulled her more closely against him and she stood on tiptoe to put her arms around his neck, but somehow her hands crept upward and sank into the wealth of hair at the back of his head. It felt surprisingly soft—with the heavy texture of smooth raw silk. Strands of it clung to her fingers as she buried them luxuriously, reciprocating his embrace so ardently that he finally groaned in frustration and lifted her bodily onto the prep table behind them.

Alicia gasped as he broke the kiss and pressed his face into the hollow at the base of her throat. His skin was hot, his mouth wet from her kisses, and Alicia arched her neck to give him greater access as his lips traveled inside the collar of her sleeveless blouse. He had one large hand splayed against her back at the base of her spine to hold her to him. With the other he undid the buttons of her blouse, fumbling in his haste but never taking his mouth from her skin. Alicia shrugged and let the blouse fall, staring at him as he finally raised his head and took in the wisp of strapless bra she had worn with the gown earlier. His lashes lifted and he met her gaze; his expression was hazy, needy, drugged, and she knew just how he felt. When he moved to kiss her again she opened her mouth expectantly and wrapped her legs around his hips.

This time he did not hesitate; he knew she wanted him as much as he wanted her and he acted accordingly. His mouth moved from her lips to her cheek and then to the curve of her shoulder as she lay back in his arms submissively. She sighed as he trailed his lips to the hollow between her breasts and then gasped as he covered one swollen nipple with his mouth, its heat beating through the silk as if the cloth barrier were not there. Impatient, he popped the front clasp of the fragile garment with his thumb and sent it sailing to the floor. In the next instant he had pulled her toward him again, lifting her up to brush his lips over her breasts as Alicia closed her eyes and held his head against her. His mouth was everywhere, laving and teasing, driving her finally to tug on his clothes in a frenzy, so hungry to feel his skin against hers that she pulled his shirt loose from his cummerbund and ran her hands up the smooth skin of his back.

He released her long enough to unbuckle his shoulder holster and drop his gun to the floor, then pulled the top stud from his shirt and yanked it over his head and dropped that too. As he stepped forward to embrace her again Alicia looked avidly at the strong line of his throat, the dense mat of black chest hair, the long, ropy muscles of his arms, the flat, ribbed abdomen. The overhead light glinted off his glossy black hair and brought out the hollows under his cheekbones. This man was gorgeous and decent and on fire with desire for her. She had wanted him, she now realized, from the moment she met him.

She reached up to smooth the raven hair back from his brow, and he turned his head to kiss her palm. Her throat closed with emotion and she flung her arms around his neck. He moaned as he felt her bare torso against his, pressing his lips to the back of her neck as she dropped her head to his shoulder. He ran his hands down her spine and then slipped them under her to lift her down to the floor again. She leaned into the cradle of his hips and felt him, ready, against her thighs.

"Where?" he said hoarsely, looking around the room. It was the first word he'd spoken since he kissed her.

Alicia lifted her head to direct him to the study next to the kitchen, then froze in his arms as they both heard a sound in the front hall.

Lafferty released Alicia immediately. He reacted faster than Alicia, bending down and retrieving her blouse and handing it to her. Alicia slipped into the top, buttoning it with shaking fingers, while Lafferty picked up his own shirt from the floor and fumbled into it. Seconds later Claire stood in the doorway staring at them, wide-eyed with surprise, barefoot and silent in her nightgown.

"Darling!" Alicia said, her voice sounding hollow in her own ears. "Did you want something?"

"I came down to get a glass of milk."

"I'll get it for you," Alicia said quickly, turning toward the refrigerator.

"I don't want it anymore."

"Is there something else you'd like?" Alicia asked, defeated.

"What is that policeman doing here again? I know he's been here before, I saw him from my window."

Alicia glanced at Lafferty, who was strapping his holster on again.

"And I know what that is," Claire added waspishly, nodding to the revolver.

"Claire," Alicia said evenly, striving for calm, "you can't possibly understand..."

"I understand that you're here with this cop in the middle of the night in my own house!"

"That's enough."

"How *could* you?" Claire demanded, as if her mother had not spoken. "Maybe you did kill daddy after all!" Claire whirled and raced down the hall and up the stairs.

Both adults stood flat-footed and listened to her door slam in the distant reaches of the house.

Alicia put the back of her hand to her mouth as her eyes filled with tears.

"I don't know what to say," she whispered.

"You don't have to say anything."

"I just told the children yesterday that I was accused of their father's murder. It was one thing for them to know that Joe was dead, but another to realize that the authorities thought I had killed him. Claire has taken it hard. She's old enough to have few illusions about Joe, but she has always leaned on me and looked to me, and she expects me to be perfect..."

"Don't explain. I understand." Lafferty brushed past her and into the hall, picking up his coat and tie.

"I should go," he said gruffly.

Alicia nodded numbly. "I'm so sorry," she said to him quietly, her expression miserable.

"No need for an apology. The kid did us both a favor. I never should have started something I had no business starting."

"You weren't alone."

Lafferty's hot blue gaze met hers, and for an instant

she was pulled toward him again, despite the incident in the kitchen. She closed her eyes, amazed at herself.

How could she still want him so badly in the face of what had just happened?

"I should go to Claire," Alicia said in a neutral tone, opening her eyes again.

He nodded.

"Good night," she said.

"Good night."

He went through the door.

Alicia closed it behind him, and then ran upstairs to her daughter.

Chapter 5

Lafferty slid into the driver's seat of the unmarked car and let his head rest against the seat. He closed his eyes and folded his still-shaking hands around the rim of the steering wheel.

Well, this was just great. He had never made a bigger fool of himself in his life, and that was saying something. No past humiliating experience compared to what he felt seeing the stunned look on that kid's face when she spotted him with her mother in the kitchen of her own home.

Lafferty sighed. What a mess. It was his job to help the district attorney convict Alicia Walker, and every time he saw her all he wanted to do was get her into bed. He had to put a stop to it, yet he felt helpless and unable to control what was happening, as if he were trapped in the path of an oncoming train. And worse than his personal interest in the murder suspect was his overwhelming desire to help her, which was going to make him about as popular with his superiors as a lion at a lamb picnic. This was all wrong in every way. He knew that, but he had to force himself to stay where he was and not run back into the house to pick up where he'd left off.

He opened his eyes, and the small spotlights along the drive to the Walker mansion blurred as he looked at them. He blinked and glanced away. He didn't think Alicia was guilty, but the facts of the case militated against his gut instinct, and as a police officer he was forced to go with the evidence. He should ask to be taken off the case. The captain would not be pleased, but he would be a lot more unhappy if this situation escalated and one of his detectives wound up sleeping with a murder suspect.

Lafferty sat up, peered out the windshield into the darkness and turned the key in the ignition. It was the darkest part of the night, just before the blackness would begin to lighten into dawn. He steered the car into the street and headed back to the city.

He knew what he had to do.

Alicia closed the door to Claire's room, hoping that the sleeping child would stay asleep. She went into the hall bathroom and splashed cold water on her tear-stained face, glancing at herself in the mirror and wondering briefly what Lafferty could possibly have found attractive about her on this occasion. She looked as if she hadn't slept in a week, and if things went on this way she might never sleep again. She knew she should be exhausted but she felt alert and wired, too anxious to rest. She glanced at the clock on the wall outside the bathroom and then headed for the phone in her bedroom. It was an ungodly hour to call anybody, but she was too needy to consider politeness. She sprawled on her bed and punched the buttons for Helen's number.

It rang several times before Helen's foggy voice mumbled, "H'lo?"

"Helen, it's Alicia."

It took a few seconds for that to register. Then, hoarsely, "Do you know what time it is?"

"I know what time it is," Alicia said calmly.

"Is something wrong? Are you okay?"

"I am okay, sort of."

There was a crash, followed by fumbling sounds.

Helen had dropped the phone.

"Helen, are you there?" Alicia asked, smiling in spite of her distressed state. Helen never woke up well, or easily.

"I'm here, I'm here," Helen said irritably. "If you are okay, can you tell me why you are calling me at this time? Have you been arrested again, has war been declared, is there a new world order?"

"I'm in trouble."

There was a heavy sigh from Helen's end of the phone line. "I know I'm half-asleep, sweetie, but didn't you just say that you were all right?"

"Lafferty was here tonight at the house. He stayed for a while after he brought me back from the benefit."

"Ah, the delicious detective," Helen said, and Alicia could tell that the mention of the policeman's name had improved Helen's attention span immediately.

"Yes, and something happened."

"Something? Animal, vegetable, mineral?"

Animal, Alicia thought, before saying, "Do you think you could come over here?"

"Now?" Helen asked.

"Well…"

"Can't it wait until morning?"

"I don't think so."

"Just what went on there tonight, Alicia?"

"Lafferty and I came close to…well, we were in a somewhat compromising position when Claire interrupted us. We heard her coming toward the kitchen or it would have been much worse. And if she had not arrived when she did…" Alicia left the sentence hanging.

There was a moment of stunned silence and then Helen said, "Wow."

"Exactly."

"I guess the man of steel really knows how to unwind when the mood strikes him."

"Helen, I am very upset and I don't want to be alone. It took me an hour to get Claire back to sleep and during that time I endured the most difficult conversation I have ever had with another human being. If I wake up Maizie and tell her this story she will just give me another lecture. You are the only person who won't be judgmental about it and who is capable of giving me objective advice. I know I should have waited until morning to call but I will be climbing the walls by then. Can you come over here now?"

"I'll be there as soon as I can," Helen said briskly, and hung up the phone.

Alicia replaced the receiver and rolled over on her bed, a sense of calm stealing over her as she realized that her friend would soon be with her. One part of her felt guilty for imposing on Helen this way and for being unable to handle this latest trauma on her own. But she was near the end of her rope—in a short time she had learned her husband was dead, then had been accused of his murder and now was dangerously attracted to the policeman who had arrested her. All this, following years of an unhappy marriage and the strain of acting the role of a devoted wife to a man who had privately ignored her, had left her depleted and without resources. She was simply unable to resist Lafferty's concern, not to mention his considerable attractiveness and low-key charm. She had no doubt about what would have happened if Claire had stayed asleep in her room, and the memory of the near lovemaking in the kitchen made her face grow warm.

Alicia got up and went into her closet to change clothes. Her blouse was rumpled, a reminder of the haste with which she had donned it, and the reason for that haste. She closed her eyes and sat dejectedly on a footstool. It was difficult to imagine how her life could be any more disastrous. If something happened to one of her children that would complete the nightmare, which was why she was so protective of them. No matter how this situation was resolved for her, the children must emerge from it as little damaged as possible. And so the image of Claire's blank face that night refused to fade from her mind. The child was calm now, and asleep; it was her mother who was agitated and awake.

Mike Lafferty leaned against the wall outside Captain Cramer's office, his arms folded, his expression grim. What he was about to say to his boss would not be easy.

"Back so soon?" Cramer said, balancing a foam coffee cup as he unlocked his office door. "How did the escort duty go?"

"Not so hot," Lafferty replied flatly. "Got a minute?"

Cramer glanced at him and then at his watch. He had twenty minutes before his first meeting, time he had planned to use to catch up on phone messages, but Lafferty had never needed individualized chitchats before this week. He was clearly troubled by the Walker case, and giving one of his best cops a little more reassurance would be time well spent.

"Come on in, Mike," he said.

Lafferty followed him into the office as the captain switched on the lights and said, "Sit down. Shelly will be here in a few minutes, and she'll make coffee."

"No coffee, thanks." Lafferty sat.

"So what's on your mind?" Cramer said, pushing a stack of papers aside on his desk.

"I want off the Walker case," Laffery said.

Cramer stared at him for a few seconds, then nodded. "Did you have a tiff with the lady last night?"

"Not exactly."

"Then what, Mike? Don't you think this request is a little drastic?"

"If I'm not excused then I'll wind up being suspended for misconduct."

Cramer eyed him thoughtfully, then sighed. "That bad?" he said.

"I almost slept with Alicia Walker last night. I won't be able to do an effective job in aiding the prosecution. I'm too involved with her."

Cramer exhaled. "Kind of sudden, isn't it?"

"No," Lafferty said.

Cramer stared.

"I felt it from the moment I met her, at her arrest. I felt drawn to her, didn't want her to be guilty. I did my job, but it got worse as time went on and the DA moved closer to a grand jury proceeding. Last night it crossed the line."

"Well, I can take you off the case and assign you to something else, but you will still have to answer a subpoena as the arresting and investigating officer, appear in court and give evidence."

"I know that. But I am not just asking for reassignment. I want to take a leave of absence, starting today."

Cramer said nothing.

"I know it will leave you shorthanded," Lafferty said hastily, "but it's not just a matter of getting off the case and no longer pursuing her as a suspect. I want to help her prove her innocence, which will be actively working against the interests of the department. Alicia is the prime suspect in a high-profile murder case, and as it stands now her conviction is likely. If I help her evade that conviction, the police department who mistakenly arrested her and the DA who prosecuted her will both look bad. I am trying to save you the embarrassment of explaining why the arresting officer is continuing to investigate the case, when the DA has already decided that he has enough evidence to take to a grand jury."

Cramer pursed his lips thoughtfully. "And that is what you plan to do?"

"Yes."

"I can't dissuade you?"

"No."

"Mike, I have to say this. This woman is in a tough spot, as you just said. Are you sure she isn't using you, leading you on to get you to help her? She's beautiful, quite capable of turning any man's head, and if she comes out of this all right she'll be Walker's legitimate heir, a widow worth a fortune."

"So you're asking if I am in cahoots with her? Whether she has promised to share the wealth if I put a monkey wrench in the prosecution and turn traitor to the department?"

Cramer's face reddened but his gaze did not waver. "Yes," Cramer said.

"Would I be here talking to you if that were true? Wouldn't I just stay on the Walker case and covertly do everything I possibly could to sabotage it?"

Cramer sighed and looked away.

Lafferty got up and began to pace before Cramer's desk. "Look, Captain. She has never said a word to me about helping her or offered me a thing. As far as she knows I escorted her last night and she won't see me again until I appear to give evidence against her in court. All of this is my doing. I feel in my gut that she is innocent, and I can't go forward and help to convict her."

"You realize that if you do dig up evidence that helps her you won't be presenting it as a police officer on the case but as a private citizen?"

"I realize that."

Cramer shook his head. "I don't like it, Mike. If I give you leave I have to justify it to the commissioner. What am I going to say, you have the hots for the suspect so it's all off, you aren't prepared to do your job anymore?"

"I think you will find a way to put it more delicately than that," Lafferty said dryly.

"Why should I?"

"Because I think it's necessary. I'm not naive, Captain, I've been around—you know that. It isn't just a sexual thing, I wouldn't turn my life upside down just to get this woman into bed. I feel more for her than I have felt for any woman I've ever known, including my ex-wife. I don't know why. I don't know what it means. I need time to figure it all out, and I can't be trying to put Alicia Walker behind bars while I'm pondering it. I only know that my reaction to her isn't passing or trivial, and it's a matter of conscience as well as emotions. I need time away from the job to sort through it and to help Alicia the way I want to, for myself as well as for her. That's all I can say."

Cramer sighed. "And what about your future? I have to tell you, this is a real career staller. Even after you return, that's *if* you return, the question about this leave is going to come up at every promotion hearing."

"Well, you just told me that my girlfriend is loaded," Lafferty said flatly. "If she avoids a conviction she should be able to set me up for life."

Cramer put his fingers to the bridge of his nose and rubbed. "All right. I guess I deserved that. I am just trying to make sure you understand that this is not a step to be taken lightly."

"I understand. I have been up all night thinking about it, and I don't know what else to do. I can't continue aiding the prosecution when I think Alicia Walker is innocent, and I won't sabotage the department's case by working at cross purposes to it while continuing in the role of detective. So this is the only thing I can do."

Cramer shrugged and folded his hands on his blotter. "I'll put the paperwork in today."

Lafferty stood. "Thanks, Captain. I owe you."

Cramer waved his hand dismissively. "You've given 110 percent to the department all the time you've worked here, and you've never asked for any special treatment, not so much as an extra coffee break. If this woman has such an effect on you, there may be something to what you say regarding her innocence. I haven't seen any evidence to support your feelings, but that doesn't mean you're wrong. As long as you know what you're risking by taking this walk, I'll go along with it."

Lafferty was silent.

"I'll assign Delgado to do the post work on the Walker case with Chandler, and Hanson is due back from that forensics course at the university next week so he can take over for you."

Lafferty nodded.

"Do you plan to tell Chandler?"

Lafferty sighed. "I'll tell him."

"He won't be happy."

"I know it."

"Good luck, and I mean that."

Shelly walked in from the hall and said, "Detective Lafferty. You're in early."

Lafferty nodded at her. "Hi, Shel. Just leaving." He brushed past her and strode out the door. He tried to focus his thoughts on the upcoming conversation with Chandler, but the image of Alicia Walker, half-undressed and eyes glazed with passion, filled his mind. Not yet, he told himself, and headed resolutely toward the squad room to start cleaning out his desk.

"Don't give me any more fluids, I'm floating already," Helen said, rejecting Alicia's offer of juice.

"It's breakfast time," Alicia said, replacing the carton in the refrigerator.

"Breakfast time for roosters, maybe, not for me," Helen groaned, closing one eye and peering through the kitchen curtains. "Is that the sun?"

"Large orange ball in a pale sky?" Alicia said.

"Looks like it," Helen sighed. "Thanks so much for routing me out of bed in the middle of the night. I'll look like Frankenstein's monster at lunch today."

Helen had been left very comfortable by a divorce from an older, wealthy investment banker, who was now engaged to wife number three. Helen worked as an assistant to a curator at the Museum of Modern Art, a job which paid a token salary but allowed her to mix with the social elite she cultivated and enjoyed.

"You have a lunch date?"

Helen sighed. "A pep talk for some possible donors. A museum employee's work is never done."

"You look fine," Alicia said.

"So you say, since you're responsible for my unfortunate condition."

"Scrambled eggs, toast?"

"No food, please. Let's see if I can walk." She stood up gingerly and then sank back slowly into her chair. "I guess not."

Alicia finally laughed. "Helen, if you are trying with these ridiculous dramatics to take my mind off my numerous troubles, you are not succeeding."

Helen made a comic, downcast face. "I thought I was doing pretty well."

"I'm still going to be tried for Joe's murder."

"And Mike Lafferty is still the object of your erotic obsession," Helen said.

"Thanks a lot, Helen. You've been listening to me unburdening myself about all of this for three solid hours and *that's* your conclusion?"

"Well, am I right?"

"No. I won't be seeing Lafferty again, except in court when he takes the witness stand against me, so that's the end of that. The police investigation is over, the detective is out of my life. I have enough to worry about now with the upcoming trial."

"If that's your opinion, why were you on the phone at three o'clock this morning in a semihysterical state begging me to come over here?"

Alicia shrugged. "I told you what happened with Lafferty last night. I didn't think myself capable of such a…"

"Lapse?" Helen supplied.

Alicia nodded. "Claire saw the aftermath of it. I don't think I will ever forgive myself for that."

"But it's all over now."

"Yes."

"And if Lafferty came back, looking at you so seriously with those pool-blue eyes?"

"He won't come back. When he left here he looked no happier than I was. He knows that his job puts him in an impossible position. He arrested me, for heaven's sake." Alicia sat down opposite Helen and put her hands over her face.

"I'm sorry," Helen said softly. "I think he really cares about you."

Alicia withdrew her hands. "Why do you say that? You haven't seen us together very often."

"I didn't have to see you often. He watches you so closely...so protectively...it's like he feels responsible for you." Helen stopped talking abruptly when she saw that Alicia's eyes were slowly filling with tears.

"I know," Alicia whispered. "That's what makes it so hard, not seeing him again." She wiped her eyes with the back of her hand. "How could this be any worse? For so long I felt dead, no man had looked at me with interest in what seemed like forever, and now this happens, under these horrendous circumstances." She shook her head. "I don't want him to disappear from my life, but how can I possibly—" She stopped, swallowing. "What am I going to do, *date* him? Date the cop who assembled the evidence against me while I'm out on bail? It's bizarre, grotesque—" Alicia sobbed once, then shook her head. "The whole thing was so horrible, Joe dying, then everyone thinking I did it, the effect on the kids." She got up and pulled a paper towel off the roll, blowing her nose. "The only bright spot was Lafferty. He was always polite, kind even, always looking out for me, and I know I seized on that. Maybe I made too much of it. I shouldn't have asked for him to escort me, what happened last night could have been prevented...."

Helen reached across the table and put her hand over Alicia's. "You didn't do anything wrong. Your situation would be impossibly difficult for anybody. But you have to get over this cop and concentrate on preparing your defense now. If you keep having these emotional breakdowns, you won't be able to focus on your case."

Alicia nodded vigorously. "You're right. And that's what I plan to do—focus on my case."

Helen glanced at the clock. "I should go. Won't Maizie be down soon? I guess the kids will sleep late."

"Yes. Joe always sleeps in, and Claire will be tired, considering what happened last night."

Helen hugged her friend. "Don't think about it. And call me if you need anything, anytime."

"Haven't I done that once already?" Alicia asked ruefully, smiling wanly.

"You can do it again, as often as you need. I mean that. Now try to relax and keep in touch." Helen picked up her purse and walked out of the kitchen.

Alicia sat back in her chair and watched the sun rise higher in the sky as the day began.

"Hey, Mike, what's this?" Chandler's voice boomed behind him as Lafferty dumped the contents of a drawer into a cardboard box. "Going somewhere?"

"You could say that," Lafferty replied neutrally, "I'm taking a leave."

"A leave?" Chandler echoed, his face blank.

"Leave of absence," Lafferty clarified, avoiding his partner's eyes.

"What are you talking about?" Chandler said, looking stunned. "What the hell for?"

"I want to be taken off the Joseph Walker case," Lafferty said shortly.

"Then ask for another assignment."

Lafferty looked around the squad room, which was filled with cops absorbed in various tasks, having conversations, drinking coffee. If Chandler got any louder they would begin to attract attention.

"Can we take this next door?" Lafferty asked, slamming a second drawer shut and picking up the box filled with his desk's former contents.

"I think we'd better," Chandler said testily as he marched into the hall and opened the door of an interrogation room a few steps away. Lafferty followed him inside and closed the door behind him.

"Mike, what are you doing here?" Chandler demanded. "You trying to scuttle your career?"

"I've already talked to the captain. He's agreed to grant me an indefinite leave."

Chandler shook his head wonderingly, his mouth tight with anger. "It's that dame, isn't it? Can't bring yourself to make a case against her?"

"I've already made the case, we did it together."

"Then why do this?"

"Because I think she's innocent, and now I want to help her prove it. That would be working against the best interest of the department, so I can't stay on the job while I do that."

"The best interest of the department? If the woman is guilty, it *is* in our best interest, in everyone's best interest, to bring her to conviction. *Your* problem is that she's guilty as hell but you don't want to believe it."

"Come on, Chandler, you know there's a big political push to get this woman convicted. The investigation is over, there's enough evidence to get an indictment. Nobody's going to turn over any rocks to find clues that point in the other direction."

"Except you, right, buddy? Except you." Chandler sighed heavily. "Michael, this dame is using you."

"I don't think so."

"Why not?"

"She doesn't know about me doing this."

"Oh, but she hoped you would, hmm? Maybe she can read your mind? Shouldn't be too hard. Since she was arrested you've been acting like she was as pure as the driven snow. All of us 'cop bullies' have just been *imposing* on her since this whole thing began, right? If she's got two brain cells to rub together she knew exactly how you would react. She's playing you, Mike. She thinks you can get her off the hook, and if you do, I guarantee she'll go back to the jet set once the case is closed."

Lafferty shifted the cardboard box and watched as stapler, tape dispenser, paper clip holder and a dozen other sundries cascaded into the right side of the container. Then he dropped the box on the floor and rubbed his eyes, trying to keep a lid on the temper that threatened to erupt with each new word Chandler spoke. Chandler was his friend, his partner and a loyal guy, but Lafferty was getting tired of hearing everyone tell him what a fool he was making of himself.

"I'm going, Charlie," he finally said wearily. "I won't be on the job, but I'll be in touch."

Chandler looked amazed. "Hell's bells, kid, I didn't think you were this stupid. This is your life, your pension, your whole future you're dumping here."

"Charlie, I can't work to get her convicted when I think she didn't do it, and that's the bottom line."

"*Can't?* You mean you *won't*."

"However you look at the situation it comes down to the same result."

"And why do you think she's innocent?" Chandler demanded. "Because she made cow eyes at you and asked to have you for her escort at that charity do? She was setting you up!"

"I know what you think, Charlie. You have made your opinion perfectly clear. Now will you help me lug this crap down to my car or will I have to call a uniform to do it? Hanson will be taking over in a few days."

Chandler stood staring, and then picked up the box at Lafferty's feet, grunting as he bent down to it. "You're making a big mistake," he muttered under his breath as Lafferty fell in behind him.

Lafferty reached for the ring of keys in his pocket that he had to leave with the duty sergeant.

Maybe he was sacrificing his career, but he felt as if a burden had been lifted from him, a burden he'd been carrying since he first looked into Alicia Walker's eyes and hoped she was innocent.

Alicia looked across the cherry desk at the venerable lawyer and said, "So the DA doesn't have to prove anything for the grand jury proceeding?"

"He merely has to show the grand jury probable cause that a crime occurred and that there is enough evidence to bring you to trial," Kirby said. "I would be astonished if they refused to return an indictment against you."

"So I will have to go through with the trial."

"Unless you want to plead guilty to a lesser charge, in which case I can most likely get you a deal. But your previous attorney offered you this advice while he was on the case and you rejected it."

"Yes," Alicia sighed. She had been closeted with Kirby for almost four hours. She had been trying to absorb the attorney's preparation for her testimony, but all she could think about was her two children, with their father murdered and their mother on trial for the crime.

"We should go over your statement at the time of your arrest again," Kirby said evenly.

Alicia nodded obediently. She did not want to deal with any of this; thank God the lawyer was a neutral party capable of rational consideration of her case.

All she really knew was that she had not killed Joe. After that, her life was in the hands of this paid expert.

The phone buzzed on Kirby's desk, and he pressed a button and picked up the receiver.

"Joan, I asked not to be disturbed during my session with Mrs. Walker," the lawyer said, mildly annoyed.

He listened for a few moments and then said thoughtfully, "I see."

Alicia searched his face anxiously.

"Thank you, Joan," Kirby said to his assistant, and hung up the phone.

"What is it?" Alicia asked.

Kirby looked back at her solemnly.

Alicia felt suddenly that her situation was about to get markedly worse.

"It appears that Detective Lafferty has removed himself from your case."

"Removed?" Alicia whispered. "You mean he asked for a transfer?"

"More than that. Detective Lafferty is taking a leave of absence."

Alicia felt a knot forming slowly in her stomach. "Why?" she asked quietly.

Kirby shrugged. "I have no further information."

"He'll still be called to testify about the evidence against me?"

"Most certainly. A leave of absence does not absolve

him from his subpoena obligation, so I don't know what he thinks he is accomplishing with this move. Frankly, it's puzzling. Putting you away could be a career maker for him.''

I know why he's doing it, Alicia thought despairingly, barely listening. He wants to get away from me. He wants to get away from the crazy woman who killed her husband and then threw herself at the cop in charge of investigating her case.

''Mrs. Walker?'' Kirby asked.

Alicia swallowed and looked at him.

''Are you all right? You look…shaken.''

''I'm fine,'' Alicia lied. ''Are we almost done here?''

The lawyer started to talk again, summing up, but Alicia was not listening.

Lafferty had abandoned her. He had taken a radical path to sever himself from her entirely. He might not have to see much more of her, anyway, since the arrest phase was over, but if he was totally removed from the case he would never have to deal with her again at all. So he had decided to be safe. He would just testify in court and then leave her to fate.

Alicia felt a dull weight at the pit of her stomach but was too drained to cry.

She had never felt more alone.

Chapter 6

The austere, paneled lobby of the New York Athletic Club at Seventh Avenue and Central Park South was filled with plaques and photos commemorating past sporting events and business fetes. Lafferty ignored them as he emerged into the dark, spacious, leather-smelling room. His sneakered feet made no sound on the parquet floor, which gave way to plush carpeting at the sides and back of the hall. His hair was still damp from his shower after the handball game with Steve Killian, whose wealthy father had been a member of the club for thirty years. He had met Killian in a forensics class at John Jay, and they had been playing together weekly ever since. Killian, a Department of Justice researcher with the New York Division who liked Lafferty because he lived the adventures Killian only read about, stopped short at the sight of a well-dressed young woman waiting nervously just inside the double doors to the street.

"Mike," he said carefully, nodding to the right, "is that who I think it is?"

Lafferty followed the direction of Killian's gaze curiously and then froze.

"Wait for me," Lafferty said to Killian, who stopped walking but remained riveted to the scene, his eyes wide behind his gray-tinted glasses.

"What are you doing here?" Lafferty greeted Alicia, taking in her stylish skirt and blouse. She was immaculate as always, even when working on her last reserve of strength.

"I know I shouldn't have come," Alicia replied hastily, as if she had rehearsed a speech, "but no one at the police department would tell me anything. The captain and that man Chandler, they wouldn't give me your address, and you're not listed in the phone book."

"Standard procedure for cops," Lafferty said shortly. "So how did you find me?"

"I finally got your address from my grandmother."

Alicia and the old lady going head to head. Lafferty would have bought a ticket to that.

"And when I went to your apartment house the super there told me that you play handball here at the club every Monday afternoon," Alicia continued.

Lafferty wondered what else chatty Mrs. Martinez, aka The Voice of New York, had told Alicia. The minimum most people escaped with was her recipe for *arroz con pollo* and a diatribe about the parking situation in Queens. He stared down at Alicia inquiringly and then reached out for her hand.

Alicia snatched her fingers from his. She bit her lip, and despite her best efforts at control her eyes filled with tears.

"I just wanted you to know that I understand your decision to take a leave of absence and get away from my mess," she said quietly. "It is obvious that your involvement with me could backfire badly for you, and the best way to steer clear of any possible scandal is to get off the case."

"Alicia, that's not why I did it...."

She held up her hand to interrupt him, determined to have her say. Lafferty fell silent.

"I will always be indebted to you for the help you gave me and for your willingness to keep an open mind when everyone else had me convicted. I understand of course that you still have your doubts and that's why—" She stopped and swallowed hard.

"Alicia..."

She closed her eyes and shook her head, unable to continue. Tears slipped from under her closed lids and ran down her cheeks.

"Please don't lie to me, Mike, I can't bear it," she whispered finally.

"Lie to you? What...?" He took her by the shoulders and pulled her toward him, and at his touch her resolve faltered. He enfolded her in his arms and she rested her head on his shoulder.

"Settle down. Stay and talk to me," he murmured. He needed time to explain what he had done, but the feel of her in his arms and the scent of her skin, her hair, her perfume drove the calming words from his mind. He felt as if he were back in the Scarsdale kitchen with her and looking for the nearest bed. His reaction to her was always the same—desire flooded his body and drove all other considerations into the dark.

Alicia drifted in the warmth of his embrace for several seconds, then recalled the purpose of her mission and wrestled herself away from him. Lafferty looked at her as she quickly straightened her clothes, as if dusting off his touch.

"You were kind to me and I'm grateful," she finished hastily. "I just wanted you to know that." She turned abruptly and ran out of the lobby, moving so rapidly that she left Lafferty staring after her.

Killian was at his side in a second. "Buddy, you got a problem there," Killian said sagely.

Lafferty picked up his gym bag and thrust it into Killian's arms, then dashed outside after Alicia, crashing into a woman walking her poodle past the club door.

"Watch where you're going!" she yelled after Lafferty, as he dodged another pedestrian and then ran into the path of a hansom cab heading into the park. The horse shied and the driver cursed him as he changed direction and dashed madly back the way he had come, his head turning wildly.

How could Alicia have disappeared so quickly? She had vanished into the crowd, as completely as if she had never been with him.

She was gone.

It was raining in Scarsdale later that evening when Lafferty knocked on the door of the Walker house. He was wearing jeans and a sweatshirt with a soaked navy anorak unzipped to his waist.

"Mrs. Walker is not here," Maizie said to him crisply as soon as she opened the door.

"Where is she?" he asked.

"She told me that you quit her case, Detective," Maizie informed him accusingly. "Is this official business? Because if you're not assigned to her case anymore I don't know if she should even be seeing you."

"It's personal. Did she go somewhere with the children?" Lafferty inquired patiently.

"The children are with their grandparents for the weekend. Her new lawyer, Mr. Kirby, said that she should let them go. He's afraid that the Walkers will want custody of the kids during the trial and that Mrs. Walker would not be able to take losing those children. So he said she should let them visit."

Lafferty nodded.

Maizie eyed him warily.

"I'm not here to bring Mrs. Walker more grief, Maizie. I actually think that what I have to say might make her feel a whole lot better. Please tell me where she is."

"Well if you're bringing good news I won't keep you from her," Maizie said finally. "She's at the grounds-keeper's cabin about a mile down the path. It starts at the servants' entrance, the door right around back, next to the kitchen."

Lafferty glanced past the side of the house but couldn't see anything but drenched foliage, shining wet paving stones and the silver curtain of driving rain. He turned to go.

"Detective, wait," Maizie said. "There's no lighting along that path, you could break a leg in this weather. Let me get you the lantern, it's right here. Come in a minute."

Lafferty stepped into the front hall and stood dripping on the mat while Maizie went into a closet next to the front door and emerged with a hooded glass lantern.

"It's battery operated and rechargeable, you just put this into the socket when you get there," Maizie said, handing him the device and showing him the plug. Lafferty examined the lantern as Maizie went back into the closet.

She appeared again seconds later with an oversize yellow rain slicker.

"Have this," she said.

"What else have you got in there? A flak suit?"

Maizie smiled. "If you'll make Mrs. Walker feel better I want to make sure you arrive safely."

"What is she doing down there?" he asked, glancing up at the black sky as he stood in the doorway pulling the slicker's hood up over his head.

"It's a private place...quiet. Mrs. Walker goes there sometimes to think. Mr. Walker expanded it and brought in electricity when the children were small, and they used it for a playhouse, had parties there."

"Alicia picked a bad night for solitary reverie," Lafferty said wryly.

Maizie shrugged. "I couldn't talk her out of it. She said she felt like she was rattling around in this big house with the kids gone, and she needed to think."

"So she just strolled off into this monsoon?"

"It wasn't raining when she left. She has been down there for hours, planned to stay the night."

A horrible thought flashed across Lafferty's mind and he glanced at the housekeeper sharply. "Maizie, you don't think she wanted to be alone because..."

Maizie shook her head firmly. "No. Not while those kids are alive. She would never leave them with no parents, not voluntarily."

Lafferty nodded. "I'm off, then."

"Good luck."

Lafferty hadn't gone very far from the house when he realized why Maizie had given him the lantern. Once away from the lights on the garage and the driveway he was in total darkness. He was able to stay on the gravel path by holding the light aloft and picking his way. The rain poured down as he walked, soaking his exposed face and hands, and errant branches whipped against his head and neck and jabbed his ankles. Several times he stopped to wipe his face and clear his vision, and he was beginning to worry that he had missed a turn Maizie forgot to mention when he saw a feeble light in the bleary distance. As he got closer he saw that it was candlelight showing through a window; either Alicia had chosen to "think" by candlelight, or the storm had knocked the power out in the cabin. He glanced back toward the house, but could see nothing but a thicket of blowing, sighing trees. It was impossible to say from this distance whether the power was out in the main house.

He stumbled in a puddle and paused to get his bearings; he could see the outline of the cabin and aimed for it, head down, lantern dangling from his hand. When he looked up again he was standing in front of the door.

He went to the window and looked inside. By the light of a candle on an end table he could see a figure covered with a blanket huddled on a sofa before the empty fireplace. It was Alicia, but he couldn't tell if she was asleep. He set the lantern on the ground outside the door and knocked.

There was no response. He wasn't sure if he could be heard above the din of the storm so he knocked again, then tried the door. It wasn't locked and swung open heavily.

Alicia jumped up, the blanket falling to the floor. She gasped and covered her mouth with both of her hands, her eyes wide and staring, her face white.

"Alicia, take it easy. It's me, Mike. Mike Lafferty." He pulled the hood back from his head and let her see him.

Alicia closed her eyes as her hands fell away from her

face. Lafferty suddenly realized that he was probably wearing her late husband's slicker, and she'd seen him appear suddenly before her when she was roused.

"I'm sorry I scared you," he said.

"That was Joe's coat," she whispered. She was wearing a slip and the blouse she'd had on at the Athletic Club; her discarded skirt and hose and shoes were on the oval, braided rug. She hadn't even paused to change her clothes before retreating in misery to this rustic womb in the rain.

"I'm sure Maizie didn't even think about that, she was just trying to keep me dry when she gave it to me. Did I wake you up?"

She shrugged. "Who sleeps?" she said. He saw her effort to compose herself; she put her shaking hand to the back of the sofa and swallowed, then said, "Are you lost or something? Did you take a wrong turn back into the Alicia Walker disaster? I think I already said everything that needed to be said today, and I was hoping to end it on that civil note."

"I didn't take a wrong turn," he said quietly, realizing that he would have to wait for her to wind down before he could talk to her. She was overstressed, and her recent ordeal was telling on her.

"You're out of my quicksand now, so you'd better run along and polish your badge," she added. "I am sure you'll be up for a promotion soon. That's all you care about anyway, isn't it?"

"No, that's not all."

Lafferty took off the dripping slicker and let it fall to the floor in a heap.

"Don't get too comfortable, Lafferty. You're not staying," she said.

He ignored her and pulled off the sweatshirt. He toweled his torso with it and dropped it when he was done.

Her eyes followed his every move but she said nothing further.

He had to admire her grit; she looked ready to drop but she was still able to berate him for turning his back on her. The polite facade and ladylike gratitude she had managed that afternoon were gone. Now the effort to put up the front, to play the role of gracious lady and say the right thing was too much for her. She was exhausted and defeated and spitting mad.

"Alicia, we have to talk."

"Oh, go to hell. Are we going to have a conversation now about why you had to distance yourself from the black widow? Isn't it a little late for that? Take off, your captain is calling you."

Lafferty crossed the room in two strides and took her arm. She yanked it away from him indignantly and then slapped him as hard as she could.

He was stunned. He stood staring at her as the impact of what she had done registered in her face.

"Oh, my God," she whispered, her lips pale. "Please go. I'm turning into someone I don't even recognize. Get out of here before I do something worse."

"Alicia..."

"I mean it. I can't seem to control myself, and I don't need a witness to my hysteria."

Lafferty was silent, watching her, the side of his face still tingling. She folded her hands and he could see she was making an effort to choose her words carefully.

"You have every right to do what's best for you, and it is not my place to judge you for it," she said slowly. "You made no promises and if I jumped to conclusions and read my own hopes into your actions that's my problem." She laughed shortly, bitterly, her fingers unsteady as she pushed back her hair. "The irony here is that you are one of the few people who has behaved decently to me through all of this and I am rewarding that by taking my frustrations out on you. I think the last time I slapped somebody I was twelve years old.''

Lafferty knew all too well the turmoil she was feeling. She was telling herself that logically he had done nothing to deserve her censure, but on an emotional level she felt betrayed by him.

And emotionally she was right.

Lafferty sighed heavily. ''Look, Alicia, you have to calm down now and listen to me. You've got it all wrong.''

''No, I think I've got it all right. And I understand. I really do. A little dalliance with a needy and desperate woman was entertaining, I am sure, but when it began to look like the situation might interfere with the all-important career path…''

Lafferty held up his hand, and the expression on his face convinced her to stop talking.

''I took a leave of absence from the force, but not to distance myself from your case,'' he said. ''I couldn't continue because the department wants a conviction, and I think you're innocent. I want to help you prove that, which would be a conflict of interest. So I'm suspending my job until your case is over and the real murderer is found.''

Alicia stared at him as if afraid to credit his little speech.

''Are you telling me the truth?'' she finally said slowly.

He realized that she was so spent she could barely process what he was saying.

''Yes. I felt I had to inform my captain first, but as soon as I did I called your house and got Maizie, who told me you were spending the day with Oswald Kirby. I called three times, Alicia. I didn't think I should leave a message on this subject, I wanted to talk to you directly about something so important. But before I could do that you obviously heard about my decision from somebody else.''

''Kirby told me.'' She sank to the sofa and gazed up at him. ''You really want to help me?''

Lafferty sat next to her and met her gaze. ''Yes.''

She put her head back against the sofa cushions and closed her eyes. He watched as her lashes moistened and then became wet, her throat working. He watched the anger drain from her and leave her without even the energy to speak. Finally she wrapped her arms around her torso and shivered.

''It's freezing in here,'' Laffety said, retrieving the blanket she had discarded and folding it around her. ''I'll build a fire.''

She watched him passively as he took kindling and paper from the box and placed a few logs in the fireplace. He lit the paper with a match from the mantel and ignited the kindling, dropping the match on top as the sticks blazed suddenly. When he had the fire going steadily he returned to the sofa and sat next to her.

''Better?'' he said.

She nodded.

He took her chin in his hand and turned her face to his. ''You're not alone anymore,'' he said softly. ''I promise.''

She pressed her lips together, then turned into his arms blindly like a child seeking comfort. He pulled the blanket over both of them and held her as she crawled into his lap. He heard her deep sigh as her head fell to his shoulder.

''I know things look bad for you right now,'' he said,

"but I sense that there will be a break in your case soon. I can feel it. I've had these premonitions before and I'm never wrong. I'm going to assemble all the evidence we have and go over it again from a fresh perspective, trying to anticipate what the prosecution will make of it. There has to be something I am missing, and I'll find it. You didn't kill Joe Walker and that means somebody else did. Who else would be motivated to do it? Who had a grudge against him, who might have hired a look-alike to impersonate you and take suspicion away from the real perp? Does anyone hate you enough to frame you? We'll find some answers soon. You just have to work with me. Can you do that?"

When she didn't answer, he looked down at her.

She was asleep.

The warmth of the fire and the drumming of the rain soon lulled Lafferty into slumber also, and it was near dawn when Alicia started awake, gasping and sitting up, her heart pounding.

"What is it?" Lafferty said drowsily, aroused by her abrupt movement.

"Nightmare," she said, shaking her head to clear it. She sighed and pulled the blanket up over her shoulders. "I haven't slept deeply enough to dream in so long." She settled back into his arms. "You make me feel so safe."

Lafferty was acutely conscious of her slim form pressed against him. He had been telling himself since she first collapsed in his arms that she was an exhausted and depleted woman and responding to her sexually was the worst thing he could do under the circumstances. Unfortunately his body was not listening to him, and as he felt her warm breath on his neck he pulled away from her.

"Where are you going?" she said.

"To rebuild the fire. It's getting chilly in here again."

She watched him fuss around with the logs and the poker until she couldn't stand it and said, "Will you come over here please?"

He returned to her side and stood looking down at her. She patted the seat next to her.

He sat. "Not mad at me anymore?" he said.

She put her arms around his neck and said, "I'm sorry. I didn't realize how much I had invested in you until I thought you had deserted my sinking ship."

"Not sinking," he said, tensing as she curled against him once more and sighed deeply. "Not now."

"I can't keep my eyes open," she murmured.

"Go back to sleep," he said. "You're making up for a lot of lost time."

He felt her body go slack and heavy in his arms, and her even breathing told him when she was asleep again. He sat holding her and staring into the fire as her fragrance filled his nostrils and her soft hair brushed his cheek. It was some time before he noticed that the sound of the rain was lessening and gray light was filling the room. He moved his arm, which was cradling Alicia's head, and glanced down at his wristwatch. Eight o'clock in the morning. Alicia had been sleeping for twelve hours.

He eased her down to the sofa and lifted her legs, covering her with the blanket. She stirred slightly and then became still again. He waited to make sure she was out and then went to explore their little hideaway. He grimaced as he turned and every muscle in his back protested; sleeping on narrow sofas was not for ex-football players. He straightened and headed for the kitchenette.

First results were disappointing: no coffee and no food. There was a cooking area that seemed to contain appliances but no edibles, and also a small bathroom that had obviously been added after the main cabin was built. Exploration there proved more fruitful. In a cabinet under the sink he found towels, bars of soap still in the wrappers and even shampoo. He turned the knobs in the bathtub and released the shower latch; he was rewarded with a cascade of tepid rusty water which became clear, then hot.

He unbuckled his belt and stepped out of his jeans. He might as well take advantage of the amenities.

Ten steamy minutes later he felt almost human again. There was no toothbrush and he couldn't shave, but at least he was clean. He dressed again in his jeans and put his sweatshirt on the fireplace hearth. He added a log to the lowering blaze and then stood over the sleeping woman who had changed his life.

The lines of tension in her face had relaxed, and she was sleeping deeply, sprawled loosely like a child. He flattered himself that his arrival had contributed to the end of her insomnia. Now if he could get her to eat he would feel like he was accomplishing something. Her cheeks had deep hollows and her collarbones were too prominent; her wrists were about as big around as a child's.

He walked over to the window and watched the rain, now a drizzle, enlarge a puddle on the muddy ground under a gnarled elm tree.

If anyone had told him how important Alicia would become to him in such a short time he would not have believed it. His job, which had been his world, had suddenly slipped into second place, and he had never wanted to make love to a woman so much in his life. He didn't understand it himself. She was hardly a statuesque goddess to inspire fantasies; if she weighed one hundred pounds at present he would be surprised. But from the moment he first saw her he had wanted her so badly that he could hardly think about anything else. Lafferty was a pragmatist; he didn't believe in fate, and romance had already let him down once. So the knowledge that he was acting for all the world like a heartsick teenager should have been alarming. And that, of course, was the worst part. He didn't care.

The only thing that mattered to him was Alicia.

Alicia opened her eyes, and it took her several seconds to remember where she was. Then she saw the figure standing near the window and she remembered everything.

It was a jest of fate that this man had come into her life at its lowest point. What should have been a source of joy was therefore a mixed blessing. She wanted him with her, her reaction when she thought he had departed her life permanently had taught her that. But she also feared to lose him. She was about to be indicted for capital murder, and Lafferty was young, handsome and available.

No matter what he felt at the moment, he would not wait for her forever.

She looked at his bare back, wide at the shoulders, narrow at the hips, the wavy black hair curling at his nape. His jeans fit him like a second skin, and the patch of down just above his belt made her mouth go dry with longing.

She wanted to touch him so badly.

Her one experience of intimacy with him was seared into her memory, fixed there immutably like a cotillion flower pressed into a keepsake album. She recalled his skin, how it felt and tasted and smelled, its satin texture covering the taut muscles just beneath the surface. After that night in her kitchen Alicia had tossed in bed, sleepless with the memory. She had relived many times how it had felt to have him hold her, kiss her, touch her, and wished that they had been together, really together.

Maybe that chance was not gone forever.

She sat up abruptly and swung her bare legs over the side of the couch.

It had been so long since she'd been with Joe, since she had been with anyone. She had assumed that those feelings were dead, or nearly so. Whenever she'd felt an attraction to a man during the years Joe was ignoring her she had viciously suppressed it, acutely aware of what would happen to her and her children if The Chairman's wife stepped out of line. Over time that suppression had become a habit, then a way of life. But now Joe was gone, and this policeman who had put himself on the line for her had fanned long-dormant flames. And Alicia was more nervous about being with him than she cared to admit. But she was also determined to hang on to the one good thing that had happened to her in the past fifteen years: Detective Michael Lafferty.

She crossed the room, slipping her arms around his waist from behind and placing her warm cheek against his smooth back.

"Good morning," she said.

He turned and faced her, holding her loosely, his hands on her shoulders. He was smiling slightly, and in the faint light his eyes looked very blue.

Lafferty stared. Her hair was hanging over one eye, and her blouse was buttoned wrong, but she looked so much better than she had the previous night that he was amazed. The dark circles under her hazel eyes had diminished, and the taut, drawn look around her mouth was almost gone.

"What is it?" she said, noticing his measuring gaze. "Do I look that bad?"

"You look beautiful."

"Oh, please. Remind me to show you that bridge over in Brooklyn I'd like you to buy."

"I mean it. The sleep did you good."

She reached up and touched the corner of his mouth, which was bruised slightly.

"Did I do that?" she asked softly.

"Nah, I cut myself shaving."

"Yesterday?"

"Alicia..."

"I smacked you pretty hard, Mike." She stood on tip-toe and kissed the mark. Her tongue came out, and she licked his lips as his grip tightened.

"I tried to forget what happened in my kitchen that night," she sighed.

"I tried, too," he murmured, closing his eyes as she moved her mouth to his shoulder. She dragged her lips along his collarbone.

Lafferty couldn't say anything. He was transfixed by the sensation of her mouth on his body. His hands moved to her hair, his fingers weaving through the silken strands.

"I love your hair," he murmured. "The softness, the scent, like lilies. I can smell it in my dreams." He bent his head and put his cheek against the silken mass, then turned her face up to kiss her.

His mouth was full and warm on hers, his touch gentle at first, then escalating until Alicia was hanging on him, barely able to stand without his support.

"I imagined what might have happened so many times," Alicia whispered when his mouth left hers to caress her cheek, her throat, the hollow of her neck. "I imagined what it would be like to feel the weight of your body on mine, to know that you wanted me that much. To feel you inside me..."

Lafferty groaned deeply and picked her up in one swift movement. He strode to the rug in front of the fireplace.

He had had enough of the sofa.

He let her down gently, putting one palm flat on the floor and lowering her with his other arm. As soon as she was down he enveloped her with his body; when she felt him hard against her she moaned and clutched him helplessly, instinctively pulling him into the cradle of her hips. He sought her mouth hungrily with his and she received him, sighing at his sound of satisfaction when his tongue found hers. Her fingers fluttered down his spine restlessly as he pressed her closer, kissing her deeply, evoking a wild response from her that she was not ashamed to give—this was what love *should* be like and never had been with Joe, even in the beginning.

Lafferty raised his head and released her long enough to reach for her blouse. His fingers fumbled, and he finally yanked on the cloth impatiently, spraying the floor with buttons. He shoved the material aside and drew his thumb along the line of her collarbone as she leaned toward him, eager for his touch. He stroked her throat and she arched back, exposing more of her flesh to his caress. With his forefinger he drew a line between her breasts, bending his head to lightly kiss each silk covered nipple. Alicia closed her eyes and sighed.

"So beautiful," he murmured, cupping one breast and stroking the nipple with his thumb, feeling it rise to fullness as she pressed back against his hand. He laved the valley between her breasts with a hot tongue, then mouthed her breasts through the thin veil of her slip. Alicia's eyes closed blissfully. He sucked gently at first, then more intensely, nipping and laving her until the silk was wet and she was whimpering, holding his head against her and sinking her fingers into his thick hair. When he finally raised his head to kiss her mouth again she met him with equal ardor, then sat and pulled the slip over her head.

Her hands fell away as he knelt and took it from her, tossing it onto the floor.

Alicia flung her arms around his neck, and he lifted her into his lap, his mouth going back to her breasts, bare now, the nipples still erect and swollen from his recent attention. Alicia looked down at him as he made love to her—his expression intent, his eyes closed. He took a rigid peak between his lips as he ran a caressing hand up her slim leg. She sobbed and her head fell into the cradle of his arm.

"I want you so much," she whispered, barely able to get the words out; in her entire life she had never felt so overwhelmed with longing.

She hid her hot face against his shoulder as he turned with her in his arms and let her sink back to the floor. His skin was like raw silk, redolent of soap and sweat, the blue veins in his upper arms heavy and prominent. She pressed her nose to his bicep and inhaled deeply, licking a line of freckles marching down his inner arm toward his elbow. He held himself up with one hand and watched as she moved her tongue to a flat nipple, then closed his eyes and bit his lip as she sucked gently, imitating what he had done to her. Her hair flowed over his free hand in a silken cascade as she used her mouth on him until he made a sound of frustration, pulling her under him in one swift movement.

She lay still as he kissed his way down her body to her navel and invaded it with his tongue. Then she ran her hands down his muscular arms, slick now with sweat, and gasped as he pressed his burning cheek to her belly.

Alicia abandoned herself to sensation, lifting her hips as he pulled off her panties and kissed her thighs. She tangled her fingers in his hair, seal-sleek and dark. His mouth moved everywhere, evoking sensations she had never felt so intensely, making her wonder how she had lived half a life with Joe Walker for so long.

She moaned in disappointment when Lafferty sat up, but when she saw him reach for his belt she watched as he unbuckled it and dropped it on the blanket. Flickering firelight fractured his movements as he unzipped his fly and pulled his jeans and shorts off, kicking them out of the way as soon as they hit the floor. She drank in every inch of him as he moved, studying the broad shoulders and slim hips, the carved ridges where his legs joined the trunk of his body, the flexing tendons in his legs and the flat panels of muscle in his abdomen. He caught her staring, and she held out her arms. He bent immediately and enfolded her again, lying down to press his full length against her.

Her breath escaped abruptly when she felt his bare skin next to hers and the impact of his full arousal without the barrier of clothing. Then his mouth found hers and she was awash in sensation once again. She strained against him, running her hands down his body, dewed now with perspiration, feeling the tension in his taut muscles. Lafferty twined his limbs with hers, grunting when she reached down to touch him; when she began to stroke him he moaned and lifted her tight against him. She wound her legs around his hips and dug her heels into the hard muscles at the back of his thighs.

"I want to get so deep inside of you," he said raggedly, his breath coming in harsh gasps against her ear, "that you won't know where I stop and you begin."

Alicia drew back to look at him. His eyes were heavy-lidded, smoky with sensual overload, gazing into hers. His mouth was swollen and very red from her kisses, the bruise she had given him a dark smudge on his lower lip.

His face was flushed, and his damp hair fell boyishly over his forehead.

"I have longed for you, Mike," she said. It came from her soul and it was true.

"And I've wanted you from the moment I first saw you," he replied huskily. He kissed her, his mouth open and inviting, then kissed her neck, her shoulder, the indentation at her waist, leaving a wet trail behind him as he moved down her slim frame. She held his head against her, her body lifting off the floor and her legs falling apart in anticipation as he drew the flat of his hand across her stomach, seeking the mound below. When he touched her she sighed with deep satisfaction. He stroked her, inching lower, as she writhed with pleasure, and by the time he lifted her to his mouth she was more than ready.

Alicia's nails dug into Lafferty's scalp, then his damp shoulders, as he lost himself in exploration, pausing only when she gasped, "Please!"

He looked up, his mouth wet, his eyes cloudy and his expression dazed.

"Now. I can't wait any longer."

He obeyed immediately, lifting himself up, his palms flat on the floor as she wound her limbs around him like a spider monkey. His skin was hot and slick, and her hands slid up to grasp his shoulders tightly as he entered her. She groaned and clutched him, her sound of gratification lost in his.

Outside the rain continued to fall, lightly now as the storm waned, feathering the drenched trees with droplets. Drizzle pattered against the windowpanes as the two figures intertwined on the cabin floor moved in a rhythm as old as time.

Alicia woke first to find that it was midday and the rain had stopped. She looked at Lafferty, who was sprawled across her, facedown in the boneless sleep of satiation. His hair had dried into finger width curls at the nape of his neck and his back was scraped lightly from the scoring of her fingernails. She touched one of the wounds gently and he stirred. She withdrew the pressure and tried to slide out from under him, but as she crawled up to a kneeling position his hand closed around her ankle.

"Going somewhere, lady?" he murmured sleepily, his eyes still closed.

"I thought maybe I would take a shower."

"Why? I've licked every inch of you clean."

When Alicia didn't answer, Lafferty opened one eye and saw that she was blushing furiously.

He grinned. "Oh, look. She's embarrassed."

Alicia picked up his jeans and threw them at him.

Lafferty ducked, then seized her and pulled her down with him. "Forgive me," he said contritely, kissing her nose. "I promise not to tease you. It's just that you take the bait so easily, and I love to see that look on your face."

"What look?"

"That innocent, confused, 'I'm not quite sure what's going on' look."

"You make me sound like a slow twelve-year-old," Alicia said disgustedly.

"In some ways you are twelve," he replied seriously. "Not slow, but definitely twelve. And it is a miracle that all those years with Walker did not kill the kid in you."

"Joe always said I was childish."

"That is not what I meant, and you know it." He put his tongue in her ear and his hand on her breast, but he was off balance and she slithered out of his grasp.

"Oh, no, you don't," she said firmly as he hit the floor,

wearing an expression of comic despair. He rolled over and propped his chin in his hand as he watched her don her flimsy slip and walk over to the kitchenette.

"What are you doing?" he inquired.

"Looking for food," she said.

"Forget it. I already checked, there's nothing."

Alicia shot him a superior smile. "That's what you think. You don't know about the breadbox drawer."

"What's that?"

"A stash for leftovers." She opened a large drawer lined with metal under the half refrigerator and extracted the bin's contents, ticking them off for Lafferty as he watched.

"One half bag of SuperSpuds potato chips, soggy," she announced. "One box of Whippersnappers graham crackers, three crackers left, also soggy. And a complete, intact, unopened can of Krazy Kids Superheroes ravioli."

"Great. That's quite a menu. Who was your last tenant? Dennis the Menace?"

"My kids used to bring their friends here for sleepovers. This must be the remains of what Maizie gave my son's group the last time they used the place."

"I think I'll pass."

"We could walk up to the house, and Maizie could make us breakfast." She glanced at the ship's clock on the fireplace mantel. "Lunch."

"No thanks," Lafferty said, sitting up and tossing the blanket aside. "I can just imagine the two of us sitting there munching omelettes under Maizie's watchful eye when she knows full well what we've been doing down here."

Alicia laughed delightedly. "Now who's embarrassed?" she demanded in an amused tone.

"Yeah, laugh it up. I'll tell you, she scares me. You

should have seen the look she gave me when she answered the door last night and saw who it was. Lafferty the cop, the heartless, good-for-nothing flatfoot who abandoned poor Mrs. Walker to her tragic fate.''

"I've seen that look. It's very effective with Joey," Alicia said, smiling.

"It was having a considerable effect on me." Lafferty stood and looked around for his pants.

"Well, something must have changed her mind. You arrived here in rain gear she supplied."

"I told her I had good news for you. That's when she broke out the slicker and the lantern."

Alicia held up the chips with an inquiring look.

Lafferty shook his head.

She bent to pitch the bag into a plastic trash can and Lafferty watched her slip ride up her thighs, saw the outline of her breasts against the light. He forgot the search for his pants and joined her in the kitchen.

"Got something for you," he said softly, as she turned into his arms. He lifted the slip above her waist and pulled her legs tightly around him.

The Whippersnappers fell from her hand.

"I really have to take a shower," she said weakly, not even pretending to protest as he picked her up and carried her toward the bathroom.

"We can do that," Lafferty said reasonably, setting her down in the stall and peeling off her slip.

"Am I going to like this?" Alicia asked, smiling slightly as he adjusted the shower head and played with the taps.

"Oh, I think so," Lafferty said, as a gush of warm water cascaded over them. He picked up a bar of soap and worked up a lather, rubbing the creamy foam on Alicia's breasts and upper arms, working his way down her body to her knees.

"Hot enough for you?" he asked, as Alicia watched him avidly through a cloud of steam.

"I can make you drop that soap," she whispered, reaching out and caressing him with slick, sudsy hands.

He dropped the soap.

"Told you," she purred.

Lafferty lifted her up, propping her back against the wall. She hooked her arms around his neck and wound her coltish legs around his thighs.

"Tell me what you want," Lafferty said into her ear, as water beaded on his hair and cascaded off his nose.

"You," Alicia whispered, kissing his wet shoulder and guiding him into her. "You, you."

He moaned as he felt her enclose him and he reached up blindly with one hand to shut off the water. Alicia clung to him, falling in with his cadence and feeling as complete as she had the last time he made love to her. They rushed headlong to a swift conclusion, winding up on the floor of the flooded shower stall in a puddle. The dripping of the shower head was the only sound except their steadily slowing breathing for about a minute.

"Well, this was mature," Alicia finally said, looking around at the flood they'd created on the floor as her pulse returned to normal. "Who's going to clean up this mess, I wonder?"

Lafferty gazed at her sidelong and raised his eyebrows inquiringly.

"Don't look at me, buddy," Alicia said darkly.

"Work, work, work," he muttered under his breath. "Slave, slave, slaving away twenty-four hours a day, seven days a week..." He sighed as he picked up a sodden towel and threw it in the sink.

"That's a big improvement," Alicia said dryly.

"Do you mind?" he asked archly. "I'm not finished yet." He picked up another towel and added it to the pile.

"I can't believe I did this," Alicia said musingly. "What's next? High noon in Macy's window?"

"I'm game," Lafferty said, standing and grabbing a dry towel and draping it around her shoulders. He took another for himself and wrapped it around his waist.

"I'll bet you are. Do any of the solid citizens who see you striding around in that straight blue suit, looking so capable, know what you're really like?"

"What *am* I really like?" he said, kissing her damp cheek and helping her out of the stall.

"Insatiable."

He eyed her narrowly.

"Not that I'm complaining, mind you," she added, and he grinned.

"It's really amazing," she continued.

"What is?" He dropped two more towels on the flooded floor and pulled the shower door closed.

"I am in the midst of the worst crisis of my life. I am about to be indicted for the murder of my husband. I should be miserable, and I was, until you showed up here last night looking like a drowned rat. Everything has changed since then. This morning I am the happiest I've ever been."

He enfolded her silently, and she felt the droplets still clinging to his shoulder dampen her face.

"You know we have to get started on your case," he said, his voice rumbling in his chest under her ear.

"I know."

"I would love to stay here and…" His voice trailed off into silence.

"Play?" Alicia suggested.

He kissed the top of her damp head.

"But we can't," he said. "We can't waste time, Woods is already issuing subpoenas. The hearing will be scheduled as soon as he can cut enough red tape to get an early court date."

"You mean my case will be pushed up on the calendar?"

"I'm sure Woods is trying."

"Do you think he'll succeed?"

"Yes."

"You sound pretty certain of that," she said warily.

"Woods is DA, he's been around for a while and he is owed a lot of favors. He'll be calling them in now. All of them. He'll find a favorable judge with an opening on his or her calendar, and if there isn't an opening he will create one."

"That easily?"

"I've seen him do it before with cases he didn't want to win as badly as he wants to win yours."

Alicia stood still within the protective circle of his arms. A sudden shiver overtook her, and his grip tightened.

"Okay," she whispered. "You're right." She stepped back from him and looked up into his eyes. "Where do we start?"

He met her gaze soberly. "I think we should begin with a little visit to your grandmother."

Chapter 7

Several hours later Alicia was sitting in the passenger seat of Lafferty's car, gazing out the window as they drove through the rolling farmlands of central New Jersey. She was wearing the jeans and sweater she had picked up at the main house before they left Scarsdale, and Lafferty had changed into fresh clothes when they stopped at his apartment. After a late lunch on the road they were nearing the country home of Alicia's grandmother, Hannah Campbell Green.

"I think you're right. I think my grandmother does know something," Alicia said suddenly.

He looked over at her. "Why?"

"Well, you've met her. Does she strike you as the type to give up information easily?"

Lafferty snorted. "In a word, no."

"But when I told her I wanted your address she didn't ask me why, she didn't play coy or inquire what I was planning to do with it or conduct any kind of interrogation. She just read it off to me like Dan Rather delivering the evening news.''

''Hmm.''

''It was weird—it was like she had been waiting for me to ask.''

''Well, when she came to see me she tried to make me feel personally responsible for you,'' Lafferty said, ''like I was your only hope, your only possible salvation.''

Alicia smiled at him. ''She was right.''

He shook his head. ''That's not my point. She thinks for some reason that I'll be able to pull a rabbit out of a hat, so she would certainly want me to continue working with you in some capacity. That's why she gave you my address.''

''I guess so.''

''She also thinks I have a major crush on you,'' Lafferty added, shooting Alicia a sidelong glance.

''She said that to you when she came to your apartment?'' Alicia asked, aghast.

''She implied as much. She kept dropping hints about how attractive you are.''

Alicia groaned. ''Hannah was never subtle.''

''I think she noticed that I wasn't arguing with her.'' Lafferty chuckled.

Alicia sighed. ''Well, she certainly agreed to this visit readily enough.''

''Is that unusual? Do you generally have to make appointments weeks in advance to see relatives?''

''You don't know Hannah. She kept the president of the Colonial National Bank waiting for two hours in her study because she wanted to judge a local flower show and the spring calla lilies were delivered late.''

''Imperious, huh? Yeah, I got that.''

"I just wonder why she hasn't come forward with what she knows," Alicia said thoughtfully.

"That's what I plan to find out today."

"That's the turn at the next corner," Alicia said.

"A private drive?"

"Yes."

Lafferty turned where she indicated and drove for several hundred yards before they encountered iron gates barring the road and a call box on the right side of the barrier. Alicia opened her door and went over to it, talking into the speaker to somebody at the house. Seconds later the gate buzzed and the two metal sections parted.

Alicia got back into the car.

"Where's the angel with the flaming sword?" Lafferty asked dryly.

"On a coffee break. This is nothing, believe me. When I was a kid there was a full-time security guard in that fieldstone hut over there. Armed."

"So Hannah's feeling a little more secure these days? She doesn't see the need for a mercenary anymore?"

"Now she's got the house wired like the Pentagon. More electronic surveillance, less manpower. It's the age of the microchip, haven't you heard?"

They were proceeding down a long drive lined with marble busts and overhung with ancient maple trees. At the end of it loomed a three-story brick mansion with six gables. Two wings flanked a central colonial edifice with wide steps leading up to double, leaded-glass doors. Extensive gardens fronted the house and swept around to the back on either side.

"And who are these people?" Lafferty asked, indicating the statues. "Ancestors?"

"Greek and Roman writers, philosophers, statesmen. My great grandfather was a student of the ancient world."

Lafferty looked over at her inquiringly. "No kidding?"

"No kidding. Rich people aren't necessarily stupid, Mike," Alicia said quietly.

"No, they just have a lot more time to pursue self-indulgent hobbies because they don't have to work," he answered.

"When I was thirteen I was given a trip to Paris when I learned all the names of the people represented here," Alicia said, trying to lighten his darkening mood. She should have known that bringing him into this cocoon of privilege was going to be a tricky process.

"A trip to Paris? When I won the ninth-grade algebra contest, I got a pass to a Mets game."

"That's Plato," Alicia said, ignoring the jibe as she pointed to a bearded figure on their left.

Lafferty followed her gaze.

"And that's Plato's pupil Aristotle. He tutored Alexander the Great."

"I know who Aristotle was, Alicia. I have a Master's degree. Didn't your grandmother tell you that? She did an extensive background check, she knows all about me."

Alicia reached over and covered his hand on the wheel with her own.

"Relax, Mike," she said. "Don't let all of this get to you. I know the atmosphere here is a bit intimidating."

He looked at her testily, then sighed. "I'm sorry. I knew your family had money, of course, but this…" He made a sweeping gesture to indicate the house, the grounds, the marble fountain in the circle at the end of the drive. "There must be thirty acres here."

"Thirty-five."

"And how many rooms in that house?"

Alicia shrugged. "Never counted." She studied his grim profile and added, "It has nothing to do with us."

"Like hell it doesn't. And how many other houses, condos, apartments, plantations and estates?"

"Hannah *likes* you," Alicia said, ignoring his question. "She wants you to work on my case, you said that yourself."

"She wants me to get you off the hook, Alicia. She thought she could use my attraction to you to persuade me to do that."

"She's a pragmatist," Alicia said lightly, trying to change the subject.

He didn't answer, slowing the car as they approached the front door. The fountain, a statue of Poseidon spewing water from his upturned mouth, sprayed droplets into the air as Lafferty parked next to a large puddle, a reminder of the storm which had just passed.

"It doesn't matter what Hannah thinks, Michael," Alicia said. "I know what I think."

He stopped the car and looked at her. "Do you?"

"What does that mean?"

"It means that I don't exactly fit in with the opera crowd, and I can't see you tossing back brewskis at the Queens County NYPD softball games."

"So?"

"You want me now because I can help you. I would not be your bedmate of choice if you weren't looking down the gun sights of a grand jury hearing."

She threw up her hands, exasperated. "I wanted you before I ever thought you would help me. I wanted you when you were putting me in jail!" She heaved a heavy sigh. "Michael, do we have to have this particular discussion right at this moment, on my grandmother's doorstep? I realize that this environment is making you feel insecure but…"

Lafferty closed his eyes and put his head back against the seat. "Don't psychoanalyze me, Alicia."

Alicia sighed. "You do choose your moments to get all macho and stubborn, don't you?"

"So, I am an extremely hard-headed man," he intoned levelly, without opening his eyes.

Alicia suppressed a grin. She edged over to his side of the car and kissed his nose. "I happen to be fond of your extremely hard head." She kissed his eyelids. She bent and kissed his right hand, which still rested on the wheel, then ran her hand up his thigh. "And your exquisitely hard…"

He grabbed her and wrestled her down on the seat. "I should wash your mouth out with soap," he said roughly, pinning her and slipping his hand under her sweater to find her skin.

"Didn't you already do that this morning?" Alicia asked innocently.

"I have other things in mind for these luscious lips," he murmured, pulling her with him as he sat up again and kissed her neck, her cheek and finally her mouth. Silence ensued until Lafferty suddenly said in a strangled voice, "Who is that?"

Alicia craned her neck to look over his shoulder. "Um, that's Gibbs."

"Gibbs?"

"My grandmother's butler."

"Her butler?" Lafferty released Alicia, and she straightened her clothes as he moved away from her. "What is he doing standing on the driveway?"

"He's come to escort us into the house."

"The house is twenty feet away."

"That's his job, Mike, and don't go all Karl Marx on

me again. Now come on, since he has seen us we'd better get going.''

"I wonder how long he was standing there," Lafferty muttered as he got out of the car and went around to open the passenger door for Alicia.

"Long enough. But he won't say anything, he's an old family retainer, and they don't talk unless tortured."

The butler walked toward them regally as he saw them leaving the car.

"What's that vest he's wearing?" Lafferty said in an aside to Alicia.

"A waistcoat in the family colors," Alicia replied.

"I see. Your grandmother has her own army?" Lafferty inquired darkly.

"It's a tartan, Michael, and I want you to stop it right now. I mean it," Alicia hissed.

Lafferty subsided as the butler paused before Alicia, who extended her hand and said, "Hello, Gibbs. It's nice to see you again so soon."

"Miss Alicia. A pleasure to see you also. Your grandmother is expecting you in the library."

"Gibbs, this is Detective Lafferty."

The butler nodded at Lafferty and then turned and led the way up the wide brick steps into the house. Lafferty didn't look at Alicia as they entered the dim, cool vestibule. The front hall was a large expanse of marble flooring with cherry wainscoting that rose halfway up the silk-covered walls, which were hung with gold-framed portraits. An oak staircase climbed to the upper floors, dividing into two on a wide landing. An oval Aubusson rug the size of a handball court hushed their steps as they walked across it and a Baccarat chandelier on its dimmest setting lit the silver accent pieces in the hall with a soft glow.

Alicia waited for Lafferty to make a sarcastic sotto voce remark as they were led past the equally opulent sitting room to the second set of oak sliding doors. But when she glanced at him she saw that he had slipped into detective mode as they entered the house.

He was all business now.

Gibbs knocked and waited for Hannah's voice before opening the doors and gesturing for them to precede him.

Hannah Green rose as her company arrived, and she held out her arms to Alicia.

"My dear," she said as Alicia returned her embrace and kissed the old lady's cheek.

The room was an old-fashioned library, which must have changed little since Hannah's husband died. Paisley drapes in a muted dark green silk swept across a large bay window with leaded panes. Tiffany and Stiffel lamps placed strategically on items of oak furniture cast pools of light on the parquet floor, even though it was still day outside. The walls were lined from floor to ceiling with books, heavy volumes encased in leather as well as more recent additions in paper covers. A ladder stood in a corner and two stepstools were positioned near the door to the hall. A dying fire in a brick fireplace with Dutch facing tiles and a marble mantel gave off warmth to ward off the spring chill. Hannah had been seated before the fire in a plush armchair reading a newspaper when they arrived.

Gibbs remained in the background as Hannah turned her steel-gray eyes on Lafferty. She set her glasses and her paper down on an end table.

"Detective," she said crisply, putting out her ringed fingers delicately. "Handsome as ever."

Lafferty shook her hand. "Mrs. Green."

Hannah was wearing a navy silk blouse with a long skirt. Her iron-gray hair was in a bun and marcasite diadems hung from her ears, matching the pendant around her neck.

"Please join me," she said, gesturing to the sofa that faced her chair. "Gibbs, tell Mary to bring the tea."

Gibbs bowed his head and left the room, closing the door behind him. Alicia and Lafferty sat on the burgundy leather sofa facing Hannah's deep upholstered chair before the fireplace.

"You don't know how happy I am to see you here with my granddaughter, Detective," Hannah said, sitting again herself.

Lafferty said nothing.

"When Alicia told me you had taken a leave of absence from the police force I was very concerned," Hannah added evenly, arranging her striped bombazine skirt over her legs. "I had been confident that with you on the job my granddaughter's case would at the very least be investigated fairly."

Lafferty looked at Alicia with raised brows and then back at Hannah. The old lady was laying it on thick; she was definitely up to something.

"I took a leave because the district attorney wants to convict Alicia and I think she is innocent," he replied. "Since the police force functions as the investigative arm of the prosecutorial system I thought it only fair to remove myself from the case. If I had stayed I would have been working at cross purposes to my superiors."

Hannah nodded sagely. "Nicely stated, Detective. I think what you meant to say is that you and Alicia are now an item and it would have been a conflict of interest for you to be sparking with the murder suspect while the case was pending."

Lafferty stared her down. "Exactly."

Hannah laughed delightedly. "I do like him, Alicia," she said, glancing at her granddaughter.

"So I have gathered," Alicia said dryly.

Hannah sat back in her comfortable chair and surveyed Lafferty measuringly.

"I am never wrong about people," she said, raising a forefinger for emphasis. "I knew in my heart that Joe Walker was the runt of that whole Walker litter, but I let his fortune and his family connections overrule my good judgment, to my regret and Alicia's. And I knew you, Detective Lafferty, were the genuine article the very first time I met you."

A knock sounded on the door

Hannah said, "Enter."

A uniformed maid arrived bearing a silver tray set with an elaborate teapot, china and an assortment of tiny pastries. She put the tray on a coffee table and waited.

"I'll serve the tea, Mary, you may go," Hannah said pleasantly to the girl.

"Yes, mum," the girl answered in a Cockney accent.

She curtsied to Hannah briefly, then left soundlessly.

Lafferty felt like he had entered an episode of *Masterpiece Theatre*.

"Mary is a good girl," Hannah said. "I have been using a British domestic service for several years now."

Lafferty hoped they were not going to have a conversation about the difficulty of getting good help nowadays. He leaned forward with his hands clasped.

"We came here today for a specific reason, Mrs. Green," he said briskly, trying to get the old lady on track. Hannah apparently liked company and seemed prepared to drag this interview out until the cookies on her tray had turned to stone.

"I am aware of that," Hannah replied. "If Alicia had

not called me earlier today I would have asked to see her, or both of you, very soon.''

Lafferty waited.

Hannah leaned forward and poured a cup of tea, filling the delicate Rosenthal china cup with a rosemary-scented brew. When Lafferty shook his head she handed it to Alicia and then poured another for herself.

"I'm happy you are here for more than one reason, Detective," Hannah said. "What I have to tell Alicia will be very difficult for her to hear.''

Alicia and Lafferty exchanged glances. Hannah's welcoming mood had changed with the sentence. She now looked sober and every minute of her age.

"Every family has secrets," she went on, sighing. "Wealthy families probably have more than most." She added cream to her tea from a Waterford crystal jug and sat back in her chair. "I was determined to take this one to my grave." She seemed to lose interest in her drink and held it untouched in her lap, staring straight ahead. Then she stirred. "I had hoped that I could see Alicia through this awful experience without breaking my silence. But it has become obvious to me that Sandler Woods intends to make an example of Alicia, and I cannot allow that to happen while I know something which may be pertinent to her case. I don't know if it will be helpful or not, but I can't keep it to myself any longer.''

Alicia was leaning forward, her eyes narrowing. Hannah finally took a sip of her tea and then set the cup down; the saucer rattled in her shaking hand.

"Come here, my dear," Hannah said to Alicia.

Alicia looked at Lafferty, then went to Hannah and sat on the leather ottoman at the old lady's feet.

"Do you recall how much your mother loved you?''

Hannah said gently, smoothing Alicia's hair back from her forehead.

Alicia nodded.

"From the moment she saw you, Margaret put you before everything and everybody," Hannah said. "I never knew a woman to dote on a child that way. She took you everywhere with her, did everything for you, and adored you immoderately. My son followed her lead, and you were a most cherished, most beloved little girl."

"I know that, Granny," Alicia whispered gently. "I know. I remember."

Hannah's eyes were filling with tears. "I feel it is a betrayal of my late daughter-in-law's dear memory to tell you this, because she never wanted you to know. But my son and his wife are dead, and I am the last person in this family who knows the truth."

The silence in the room was deafening as the old lady drew a trembling breath and took Alicia's hand.

"Alicia, you are not your mother's natural child. You were adopted when you were ten days old."

Alicia stared at Hannah as Lafferty tensed to rise and go to Alicia.

Alicia finally mumbled feebly the first fleeting thought that entered her head. "But I look just like Daddy..."

Hannah nodded, biting her lip. "Yes. My son, Daniel, was your father. You are the child of my son and a girl who worked for the family thirty-five years ago. It was a secret adoption. Your biological mother was underage, and my son would have been guilty of statutory rape for having relations with a teenager. Daniel paid a fortune in blackmail for the rest of his life to conceal these facts, something I discovered after he was killed. I never did know all the details—I never wanted to—but I arranged to continue the payments to the numbered account Daniel

had established. That was thirteen years ago and I have
heard nothing since, so I assume that arrangement is still
in place.''

''Blackmail to whom?'' Lafferty asked sharply, his
eyes on Alicia's white face.

Hannah shrugged.

''The girl, I assume. Alicia's birth mother, Deborah
Lassiter. I found papers after Dan was killed when Alicia
was in college. Apparently after some years the girl's own
mother, Nancy Lassiter, who had arranged the deal, died,
and Deborah was alone. The original lump sum was not
enough, and Deborah came back looking for more. Dan
worked out a schedule of twice-yearly payments to keep
her quiet. He did not want to go to jail, and he did not
want Alicia to find out she was not her mother's natural
child. So he paid that Lassiter girl and bought her silence.''

Lafferty noticed how she referred to Alicia's blood
mother as ''the girl.'' And that's all she was to Hannah,
a vessel who had provided her son with the commodity
he most desired.

As if she had read his mind Hannah said flatly, ''Daniel
and his wife bought his child with another woman, because Margaret was infertile and could not produce one.
It was not legal, there are no court papers and there is no
evidence of it today except for the memory of the survi-
vors. The whole matter was handled by Ambrose Kirkland, the lawyer, do you remember him?''

Alicia nodded numbly, in shock. Lafferty got up and
put his hand on her shoulder. She was the color of rice
and unable to look away from her grandmother. This, on
top of her recent experiences, might well be too much for
her. How much more could she be expected to take? But
despite his sympathy for his lover he felt a surge of ex-

citement, a leap of hope. This revelation opened up possibilities he had not considered. If Hannah was right, and nobody but the participants knew about Alicia's adoption, and there was blackmail and extortion involved, he had a whole new line of investigation to pursue. He wasn't sure how it might be tied to Joe Walker's murder, but like Hannah, he suspected strongly that it was relevant. Money was a powerful motivator. If Alicia hadn't killed Joe Walker somebody else had, and the reason could very well lie in the secret the old lady had kept for over a generation.

"Kirkland is still alive, though long retired. I have his address," Hannah added wearily. "He can fill in the sordid details. I don't have the full story. Daniel would never discuss it again after Alicia came to us, and truthfully I did not want to know. After Daniel was killed when Alicia was in college, I just authorized the money to continue." She sat back wearily and closed her eyes.

"How did it all happen?" Alicia asked.

Hannah sighed and opened her eyes again, wiping them with a forefinger decorated by a huge amethyst surrounded by diamonds. Her other hand was still wrapped around her granddaughter's.

"I will tell you what I know," Hannah said. She picked up her tepid tea and drank half of it. She looked exhausted, and Lafferty felt a flash of sympathy for her. She was an elitist old snob but she did love Alicia, and sitting on this secret for so many years could not have been easy. Now she was trying to do the right thing to save her granddaughter, but it was going against the habits of a lifetime for her to reveal the skeletons rattling in the Green closet.

"Daniel and Margaret had been married for several years before Margaret started seeing specialists about her

failure to become pregnant,'' Hannah said. ''Daniel
wanted an heir, we all did, and Margaret was young and
seemingly healthy. We were puzzled as month after
month went by and nothing happened. Well, this was a
long time ago and techniques were not what they are now,
but Margaret's trouble was not too difficult to fathom,
apparently. A malformation of the uterus prevented the
implantation of an egg. At that time there was nothing to
be done. So no Green heir and no grandchildren for me.
The marriage suffered as a result. Daniel began to cat
around, Margaret began to drink. About two years after
the infertility diagnosis Daniel told me he'd been bedding
the daughter of Nancy Lassiter, the cleaning woman, who
came here several times a week to do the floors. The
woman had brought the girl with her on several occasions
and Daniel had met her, then arranged to meet her elsewhere as the affair continued. By the time Daniel told me
about it, the girl, Deborah, was pregnant.''

''How old was Deborah?'' Lafferty asked.

''Fifteen.''

At the look on Lafferty's face Hannah added, ''I make
no excuses for my son. He was hopelessly spoiled, saw
the world as his playground and took everything that he
desired from it. Rich people are accustomed to buying
whatever they want, Detective, and when confronted with
a problem they can't solve with money some of them lose
control. Margaret's failure to become pregnant was a great
blow to Daniel and he reacted badly to it. He did not want
to divorce her and try again with someone else, as he
might have. He loved Margaret, so he stayed with her.
She drank and he looked elsewhere. He sought distrac-
tions. The girl was a distraction. She looked older, perhaps
he assumed she was older. I doubt very much that he

asked her age before he was confronted with the reality of her minority when she became pregnant.''

''Did 'the girl' have a father?'' Lafferty asked dryly.

''Her name was Lassiter but the girl's father was never mentioned. Daniel dealt solely with Nancy. I think the girl's parents were divorced. Or maybe Nancy had never been married, I don't know. They lived in Bridgehampton and Nancy came here to clean. They disappeared with the money, and I never heard about them again until my son was killed. At that time I learned that Nancy had died, and Deborah, Alicia's mother, who was at that time about thirty-seven, had come back to Daniel and demanded more money. He arranged the payments and she disappeared again.''

''We can find her,'' Lafferty said to Alicia quietly, squeezing her shoulder. ''We have a name to trace, and she has to be collecting and depositing the checks somewhere.''

Alicia nodded dumbly.

Hannah waved her hand in a resigned fashion.

''You can guess the rest,'' she said, as if Lafferty had not interrupted. ''Adopting the child seemed the perfect solution. Even I thought so at the time. Daniel and Margaret wanted a child, and Daniel would have been prosecuted for statutory rape at the very least if word of your true parentage had gotten out, Alicia. So Kirkland arranged it all. He paid off the Lassiters and we got the baby. Daniel and Margaret went to their place in Jamaica for a year and then came back with the child—you, Alicia. Margaret said she had been pregnant while she was in the islands. Nobody disputed her, no one suspected a ruse. And the most poignant part of this whole charade is that it worked. Margaret was thrilled with Alicia and sobered up as she made the baby the focus of her life. Daniel got the child he wanted, not a stranger's child but his blood, and they were able to patch things up between them and make Alicia their whole existence. It worked out for everybody.''

"Except for Deborah Lassiter, whose child was taken from her," Lafferty said flatly.

Hannah was silent.

"Well?"

"She gave up the child. She took the money," Hannah finally answered. "Then and later."

"What choice did she have?" Lafferty asked.

A tear slipped from Alicia's lashes and ran down her cheek, into her mouth.

Lafferty snorted derisively. "A teenager and her scared single mother up against the Green millions? That sounds to me like no choice at all."

"I can never make amends for what we did," Hannah said wearily. "I am merely reporting what happened then, in the hope that it will help Alicia now."

Lafferty produced a handkerchief and gave it to Alicia. The old lady got up and went to a sideboard, where she poured an inch of whisky into a crystal glass from an amber bottle.

"Have this, my dear," she said gently to Alicia, handing her the tumbler.

Alicia obediently swallowed half of the whisky and made a face.

"You'll feel better in a minute," Hannah said, patting Alicia's arm. Lafferty watched as Hannah went over to the fire and stirred it with a poker, her face pensive. It was easy to see that she was lost in the past.

"Do you want to go now?" Lafferty inquired in a low tone to Alicia.

Alicia nodded, putting the glass on the tea tray next to the silver pot.

Hannah turned and saw Alicia picking up her purse.

"Oh, please don't go," she said to her granddaughter. "Stay and have dinner with me."

Alicia looked pleadingly at Lafferty.

"I think Alicia has had enough, Mrs. Green," he said firmly. "This is a lot to take in, and I imagine she needs some time to digest it."

"You won't stay the night, then? Your old room is ready, Alicia. I include you in the invitation, Detective Lafferty, since you seem to be speaking for my granddaughter these days."

Alicia bristled at that, as Hannah had known she would.

"Don't get uppity, Granny, this is not the day to test my familial devotion," Alicia said sadly, sniffing and wiping her nose with Lafferty's handkerchief.

Hannah faced them down. "So you're a duo now," Hannah said. "As fast as that."

Lafferty took Alicia's hand and she curled her fingers around his.

Hannah nodded. "I see, and maybe that's a good thing. This is going to get a whole lot worse before it gets better," she said to Lafferty.

"I'm aware of that," he replied.

"You're going to track down every lead and expose every dark corner of our lives, aren't you, young man?"

"That's right. And it's exactly what you want me to do or you wouldn't have revealed this secret. We both know it's the only way to keep Alicia out of jail."

Hannah walked over to her granddaughter and kissed her cheek. "I'm sorry for the years and years of lies, my dear," she said softly. "I'm sorry for all the trouble a past deception may have brought you. Can you forgive an old woman for the mistakes of previous generations? Can you get past this and go on?''

Alicia looked at Hannah and then shook her head slowly, lifting her shoulders slightly.

''I don't know, Gran. I don't know. I have to think. I feel somehow that I should be angry or indignant or disgusted, and maybe some of those emotions will come later. Right now I have to deal with this new information and see how it fits in with Joe's death. You think it does or you would not have exposed this truth after thirty-five years, and Mike thinks it does, I can tell that much just from looking at him. So let me go and mull this over, and I'll call you in a few days.''

Hannah watched Alicia warily. ''You won't disappear, will you?'' the old lady finally said fearfully, and Lafferty saw the uncertainty and loneliness behind the matriarch's polished, controlled facade. She was afraid her last-remaining relative would desert her and leave her alone in her magnificent mansion with her guilty memories and her tattered conscience.

''We'll be back,'' he said, surprised at how much the old lady's fear touched him. He didn't much like her but he could feel sympathy for her, which surprised him.

Hannah met Lafferty's direct gaze and nodded. ''Thank you, Detective.''

''Don't thank me. Your granddaughter is the forgiving one,'' Lafferty said.

Hannah smiled sadly. ''Perhaps you'll be less judgmental when you need that forgiveness yourself someday.''

Lafferty looked at Alicia, who nodded and moved toward the door of the library.

''We'll say good-night, Mrs. Green,'' Lafferty said.

Gibbs was waiting for them in the hall and fell into line behind them.

"What is he, psychic?" Lafferty said in an undertone to Alicia as the butler opened the door for them.

"I'll take it from here, buddy, thanks," Lafferty said and shut the door in the butler's face.

Dusk was becoming night as they stepped out onto the portico and stood on the top step. An orange sun was disappearing below the horizon, night birds were calling, and the exotic scent from the spring lilacs in the garden filled the rain-washed air.

Lafferty glanced at Alicia standing next to him. He wasn't sure what to say to her.

"It's all right, Mike," Alicia said quietly. "I am not going to have hysterics. I feel more drained than anything. At this point it's just one more bombshell. So what else is new?"

He touched her hair gently, and she turned immediately into his arms.

"I know this is tough on you emotionally, but this could be a *good* bombshell, try to remember that," he said. "What we need for your case is an explanation of the unexplainable—how people could have seen you shoot your husband at the Plaza Hotel when you weren't even there. Anything previously unknown can help solve that puzzle, and what Hannah told us tonight is a lot of new information, the type of information people pay a lot of money for and commit crimes to keep quiet. I'm going to run this thread right back to its source, and see if maybe, just maybe, we're starting to get somewhere."

Alicia nodded against his shoulder. She had never known a haven as comforting as the circle of this man's arms.

Lafferty glanced over the top of her head at the house behind them.

"Now let's get out of here before Lurch reappears," he said, and took her arm, leading her back to the car. Alicia leaned on him heavily, content to let him take over as her mind drifted and childhood memories overwhelmed her. As he handed her into the car and started the motor she saw her mother as she had first known her, a smiling young woman filled with hope and promise, delighted with her little girl. Alicia's vision blurred as Lafferty negotiated the long drive and returned to the municipal road.

Oh, Mommy. Alicia was an adult herself and a mother, but she still missed the woman who had raised her, every minute of every day. And now to find out the secrets Margaret had lived with in order to keep her...it was too heartbreaking to absorb.

"Are you okay?" Lafferty asked.

"Yes," she replied. "I just...I loved my mother."

"I know. She must have been young when she died."

"Both my parents died young and tragically. Do you think people pay in the long run for the mistakes they make?"

"No," Lafferty said. "Stop talking that way. If there is one thing I learned on this job it's that there is good and bad in everybody, and anybody can take a wrong step."

Alicia was silent, staring out the window. In the sudden glow of oncoming headlights Lafferty saw the moisture on her cheeks.

"Where would you like to go?" he asked.

She put her head back against the seat. "I don't care. Back to Scarsdale."

"Alicia, you should eat something. You had half a slice of lettuce for lunch and nothing since then. There's an inn about two miles down this road with a restaurant. Let's stop there."

"The Inn at Fox Crossing? They know my grandmother there. They know me. I don't want to talk to anybody. I certainly don't want to explain to the staff why I am dining with a mystery man at a hotel a stone's throw from Hannah's house."

"All right. I'll book a suite and you can come up afterward. We'll order from room service. No one will see you. We should really stay the night, Alicia. You don't look ready for a long drive."

She shot him a sidelong glance. "That bad, huh?"

"Fishing for compliments?" he said, and grinned.

He was relieved to see that she smiled wanly in response. "Thanks for not asking a lot of questions," she said.

"No problem," he said evenly.

"I'm still so tired," she said. "I feel like I have climbed Mt. Everest in the last few days."

"It's emotional overload. Am I included in that great fatigue?" Lafferty said, turning into the Inn's parking lot.

"You're the sherpa who dug me out of the avalanche on the way to the summit," she said, and reached over to touch his hand.

"Count on it," he said, and she closed her eyes in gratitude.

Lafferty pulled into a space and stopped the car. "Stay here," he said to Alicia, and she nodded.

She waited, reliving the session with her grandmother in her mind until he returned and said, "It's done. I checked the place out, there's a secluded back entrance. We'll go in that way."

Alicia stepped out as he opened her door and put his arm around her, shielding her face against his shoulder.

They threaded their way through the guests arriving for dinner and slipped around to the rear of the building, where Lafferty had propped open a service door. They went inside and ascended to the second floor via a staff elevator, which was occupied by a bored housemaid with a cart of linens. She looked them over carefully and then devoted herself to staring at her damaged manicure.

"I'm afraid she recognized me," Alicia said nervously as they got off the elevator on the second floor and walked down a hall of guest rooms.

"Nah, she just thinks we're clandestine lovers," Lafferty said, stopping before a numbered door and sliding the plastic keycard into the slot.

"Well?" Alicia said, and he looked back at her and smiled as the metal guard lit up and the door opened.

He went inside and took off his jacket as Alicia looked around at the spacious room, which was done in the same rococo style as the lobby and restaurant, with a brocade spread on the king-size bed, matching drapes at the windows and cherry furniture.

"What do you want to eat?" he asked.

"Anything."

"Anything it is," he replied, unfolding a cardboard room service menu.

"As many times as I have been downstairs I've never seen one of these rooms," she said. She sat on the edge of the bed, and its softness was so inviting that she immediately lay down. She was dimly aware of Lafferty on the phone ordering food, and then he sat next to her and took her hand.

"How are you doing?" he asked quietly.

"Fine, as long as you're here."

"I'm not going anywhere."

He put his arm around her waist and pulled her into his arms. She didn't resist.

"Were you thinking about your mother?" he asked. "You must be looking at the past now with new eyes."

Alicia nodded. "She was my real mother, no matter what the biology books would say. Nobody will ever love me like that again. What she must have lived with all those years—the fear that I would be taken away from her, that my father would go to jail. Even the Green money would not have saved him on a charge like that if word of it got out."

Lafferty stroked her hair.

"When I was little she would put her arms around me and say, 'You are my girl, *my* girl.' I never knew how significant that was until now."

She reminisced for a while; he held her and let her talk. When she was quiet again he said, "Alicia, I want to talk to you about Ambrose Kirkland."

She sighed deeply. "I know we have to see him next."

"Yes."

"But tomorrow is a problem. It's the first day for the home tutoring I set up for the children and I should be there...."

"Alicia, I think I should see him alone."

Alicia drew back and looked at him.

"It's your life and your case and I will do what you want, but I think it's going to be a very unpleasant interview," he said.

"I expected that."

"No, I don't think you know what I mean." He paused, choosing his words carefully. "I have heard of this guy Kirkland. He was a hatchet man for the rich, he would do their dirty work for them for a price. Illegal abortions, illegal adoptions, bigamous marriages, questionable quickie island divorces…you name it. He was a fixer for the bluebloods and he did very well from it financially for forty years.''

''After what my grandmother said I didn't think he was Prince Charming.''

''Okay, let me put it this way. I think I would be more effective alone.''

Alicia closed her eyes. ''Mike, what are you going to do that you don't want me to see?''

''Whatever is necessary to get the truth out of him.''

''That's what I was afraid you were going to say,'' Alicia responded.

Lafferty pulled her back into his arms.

''If I have to hang him upside down by his heels and shake him until the information falls out of his mouth, I'll do it.''

''Michael, the man has to be eighty years old.''

''I don't care if he is Methuselah, if he blocks my path I'll mow him down.''

''How can you be so sure he'll help? He can only tell you about my adoption, right?'' she asked, her voice muffled by his shirt.

''There's a link here to who killed your husband. I can feel it. Instinct is involved in doing my job, it's what separates the good cops from the average joes.''

''And you're a good cop,'' Alicia said.

''Damn straight.''

''And you may never be a cop again.''

Lafferty was silent.

''Do you think I don't know that you've risked everything for me? If you can't turn this thing around and I'm convicted, your career is over at NYPD.''

''That's not going to happen, Alicia. Have a little faith in me, please.''

Alicia clutched him silently. She wanted to have faith in him, but it wasn't so easy. The social differences between them that bothered Lafferty didn't matter to her at all. But trusting him completely was still a stretch. Right now Lafferty wanted to help her and secure her release because he was caught up in the intoxicating infatuation that had consumed them both. But would it last after the novelty wore off and day-to-day life took its place? Would he get bored with her? Joe had. Would he cheat and stray like her father? It was possible. Would he even want to be with her once the crisis was over and the drama had subsided?

Even more important, what would his reaction be if his optimism was unfounded and she was convicted? Would he stay with her then?

"Woods isn't undefeatable," Lafferty added, interrupting her thoughts. "He's wrong about you and we're going to prove it."

Alicia sat up and blinked rapidly, wiping the back of her hand across her eyes.

"Some dame you hooked up with, eh?" she said, laughing lightly. "A sexy guy like you should be able to find a woman with a few less problems."

"Doesn't matter. I don't want anybody else."

He kissed her, tentatively at first to see if the time was right, then with certainty when she responded avidly. He pulled off his own sweater and then hers, answering her murmur of pleasure as skin met skin with a sharp intake of breath when she reached for his belt. A silence fell, broken only by slight sounds: the whisper of silk against flesh, the creak of the bed as they moved, the sigh of a woman's gratification.

"I can never get enough of you," he muttered as he entered her. "You're like a drug."

Alicia dug her heels into his hips and arched against him. He groaned.

"Are you addicted to me?" she whispered, running her hands down his back and pulling him deeper inside her.

"Hopelessly," he said hoarsely.

"Good." She rocked him and he rolled her over, leaving her sitting astride him, moving gently but persistently as he closed his eyes and beads of sweat broke out on his forehead.

Alicia fell forward and embraced him; their mouths met and connected avidly.

A knock sounded at the door. Neither heard it, wrapped as they were in their sensual dream.

It was quite some time before they claimed the meal from the cart room service had left against the wall outside their door.

Chapter 8

District attorney Woods was having a good day. The Walker murder case was falling into place nicely, and just that morning Judge Halperin had assigned the date for the preliminary hearing. As Woods had requested, the Walker case had been permitted to take precedence over other pending matters and been given a date just a month away. This would put pressure on the defense team as well as get the case into court while the headlines were still fresh.

He was confident that he couldn't lose.

He was whistling cheerfully when the telephone on his desk rang.

"Ya?" he said distractedly, thinking about his lunch with Councilman Paretsky. He listened for several moments and then said, "I know Lafferty is off the case. He took himself off it, took a voluntary leave of absence."

As he listened his pen stopped its motion and then fell from his fingers onto the desk. "What do you mean he is still investigating?'' Woods sat still in his chair, the folder he had been notating forgotten.

The tinny voice from the other end continued to deliver its message.

''You're saying there is a personal relationship with the Walker woman and now he's helping her?'' Woods asked, his expression getting darker.

Woods closed his eyes as his caller responded.

''Who is Ambrose Kirkland?'' Woods then demanded.

The answer did not please him.

''How could he figure into this?'' Woods asked, leaning forward in irritation.

The other phone on his desk buzzed, and he yanked the cord out of the wall.

''You don't know? You don't know!'' he yelled into the receiver. ''Is this what I am paying you to do? I don't want to hear 'I don't know'! Find out!'' He slammed the phone into its cradle and shoved his chair back from his desk. He got up and paced around the room several times, then picked up the receiver again, poised to dial.

Then he thought better of what he was about to do. He replaced the phone and left his office to get into his car and make the call from a pay phone a distance away.

His day had suddenly turned very bad.

''My, my, we're chipper, aren't we?'' Helen said, entering the Scarsdale kitchen as Alicia, humming to herself, chopped a stalk of celery for salad.

''Chipper for anyone? Or chipper for a person about to be indicted for murder?'' Alicia asked dryly.

''Chipper as befits a person who spent the weekend with the luscious Detective Michael Lafferty.''

Alicia looked at her.

"Maizie told me when I called yesterday," Helen said, dropping her purse on the counter.

"We went to visit Hannah," Alicia said.

"Oh? Is that *all* you did?"

"He's helping me with my case, Helen," Alicia said, blushing furiously.

"Is that what they call it now?" Helen asked, sitting on a kitchen chair and swinging one foot, shod in a David Evans pump, back and forth. She was grinning.

"Oh, go ahead. I know you're dying to speak your piece, so say it."

"Say what? This whole episode has turned out exactly as I had hoped. And anticipated."

Alicia looked at her. "You were telling me to stay away from him and concentrate on my case."

"Not exactly. I told you that if seeing him was making you upset and confused you should stop seeing him *in order to* concentrate on your case. But if he is now working with you that is another situation entirely. The situation I would much prefer, actually. So when is the wedding?"

"I think we'd better get through the trial first."

"Come on. Give me *all* the details."

"All of them? How much time do you have?" Alicia said, putting the salad in front of her friend and going into the dining room to get the bottle of wine she had brought up from the cellar. She waved to her son, who was being tutored at the dining room table while her daughter occupied the den with her teacher. Alicia returned and opened the wine while Helen nibbled on an olive.

"Don't let me have more than one glass of that," Helen said, gesturing toward the wine. "I have to be coherent this afternoon."

"Then eat something more than rabbit food," Alicia replied, handing Helen a crab cake on a Limoges plate.

Helen eyed it suspiciously and then said, "You are avoiding my question."

"Which one?"

"The details."

Alicia took her salad and sat across from Helen. "Well, it's a complicated story, full of family secrets and past misdeeds and payoffs made in the dark."

Helen eyed her narrowly. "I'd rather hear about Detective Lafferty in bed. That's what I've been looking forward to since I got your message asking me to come today."

"You'll have to wait for the book on that one."

Helen sighed. "I knew you were going to be a prude about it. So what's the big family secret?"

"I'm adopted," Alicia replied.

Helen's eyes widened. "Get out of town!"

Alicia nodded, picking apart her crab cake with a fork.

"Tell me," Helen said.

For the next hour Alicia filled Helen in on all the details she had learned about her past. Helen listened and stared, her meal forgotten.

"Hannah told you this?" Helen said, when Alicia was done. "After what team of forty horses dragged it from her?"

"I think by this time she really needed to get it off her chest. When Mike told her we wanted to talk to her she seemed ready to give up the information. She thinks it is related somehow to Joe's murder. Mike does too."

"How?"

Alicia shrugged. "I have no idea. He says that a history of criminal behavior connected to my past raises more possibilities about who might have shot Joe. Today he's going to see Ambrose Kirkland, the man who arranged my secret adoption.''

''Kirkland? That fossil? He's just going to open up and tell all, I suppose?''

Alicia sighed. ''I doubt it. Mike didn't want me to go with him so he expects it to be…difficult.''

Helen downed the rest of her wine in one swallow. ''Wow. How do you feel about this? How are you taking it? Your mother wasn't your mother, your father was paying blackmail to keep that quiet, your grandmother knew about it all along…good grief.''

''You mean how do I feel about all that in addition to being prosecuted for my husband's murder, a crime I didn't commit?'' Alicia asked, smiling thinly.

Helen nodded slowly.

''I must be numb. Maybe all of it hasn't registered yet.''

''How do you feel about Mike?'' Helen asked quietly.

''I can hardly think about anything else besides making love to him. And when I'm not thinking about it, I'm doing it.''

''Sounds like a happy fate.''

''For a murder suspect? I think we're both dancing in the dark.''

Helen raised her eyebrows. ''What does that mean?''

''Who knows what will happen once my legal crisis is over, one way or the other. We are not in normal circumstances and can hardly establish the basis for a future. It's as if this relationship is taking place outside of space and time, in some sort of a vacuum.''

''So you don't think it can last?''

Alicia looked down at her plate and speared a lump of stringy crab. ''I don't know. Even if I'm absolved of the murder charge, my experiences with my husband and my father have hardly set me up to trust a man. And Mike is divorced. We're not lambs in the woods skipping down the path toward happiness. I just don't know if there is anything between us to base a life on. We were thrown together by extraordinary circumstances—once those circumstances change what will happen?''

Helen surveyed her friend's downcast eyes, sighed and patted her hand. ''Don't worry about that right now. One step at a time. Let's just hope he can get Kirkland to talk.''

Lafferty got out of the taxi and glanced up at the tan brick facade of the brownstone. The neighborhood was in the east Eighties. Old money. Kirkland had done all right with his shady dealings if he could afford these digs. The old man lived with his daughter, who had initially maintained that an interview with her father was not possible. Lafferty had persuaded Captain Cramer to call her and throw a few phrases like ''obstruction of justice'' around until the daughter caved in. She finally had, adding in irritation that she would have a doctor's note waiting that would outline the conditions of the visit.

Neither Lafferty nor Cramer had mentioned that Lafferty was on a leave of absence.

The daughter answered the door.

''Mrs. Claiborne? I'm Detective Lafferty to see your father,'' Lafferty said smoothly.

She offered him a limp hand. ''Esther Claiborne.''

She was a stout woman in her fifties with gray hair, attired in a cashmere twin set and a tweed skirt. Lafferty was ready to present a dodge if she asked to see his badge but she merely stepped aside to let him enter the foyer and then handed him a folded prescription sheet ripped from a pad.

Lafferty opened it and read that Mr. Kirkland was not to be interviewed for longer than twenty minutes, was not to be upset since he was a cardiac patient, and was not to be interrogated about past business dealings without a nurse present. There was the usual scribbled illegible signature followed by "M.D."

Lafferty glanced at Mrs. Claiborne, whose narrow hazel eyes were glittering with triumph.

"Any questions?" she asked slyly.

"None. I think you'd better call the nurse, though, because I will be asking your father questions about his past business. As you know very well, that is the reason for my visit."

Esther's mouth popped open in shock. "How am I supposed to get a nurse here on such short notice?"

Lafferty produced a card from his suit pocket and handed it to her.

"Elise Carroll, R.N., who also happens to be my sister. She's in Brooklyn, she has the directions to get here, and she is waiting for your call. I can begin now or we can both wait until she gets here. It's up to you."

Esther's expression darkened as she realized she had been outwitted.

"I am going to talk to him, Mrs. Claiborne, now or tomorrow, sooner or later, if I have to get a court order to do it," Lafferty said. "You can get a team of doctors to say his health will not bear it. I will get a team of judges to sign papers to say that he will go to jail if he doesn't see me. We can play those games if you want to, but they will only delay me a few days. I did a lot of research on your father before I came here. I know how he made his money, how he bought this house, and I am going to ask him about all of it. The fate of an innocent young woman with two children, a young woman wrongfully accused of murder, may ride on what your father tells me. So you can produce notes, you can rattle blood pressure machines, you can call out the fire department. But this is going to happen, and we might as well do it now.''

Esther had been listening to him with her arms folded and an expression of extreme annoyance on her pinched face. When Lafferty finished talking she pulled open a door to their left and made a sweeping gesture.

''I'll be back in twenty minutes,'' she said flatly, and stalked off down the hall.

Lafferty was surprised by the room he entered, pulling the door closed quietly behind him. He had been expecting Victoriana like the bibelots which filled Hannah's house, but instead the sitting room was furnished with modern leather and glass, with Picasso reproductions on the walls. Ensconced in a deep brown studded-leather chair was a porcelain old man, watching him.

Ambrose Kirkland looked as if he had been sent over from Central Casting to play the kindly uncle in a kiddie movie. He had wispy white hair combed over a pink pate, and a thin white mustache. He was wearing a beige turtleneck sweater with trim dark pants and penny loafers with argyle socks. Lafferty found this a surprising outfit for a retired shyster, but sartorial choices were not his forte, so he said, ''Mr. Kirkland, I'm Michael Lafferty.''

The old man nodded. ''I heard you giving Esther a bad time in the hall. Not the words, just the tone. Esther is a drill sergeant who conspires to keep everybody away from me because she thinks if I never talk to anyone else I will be forced to leave her all of my money. Excuse me if I don't get up, my arthritis is particularly painful on a damp day like today.''

Lafferty nodded and sat in the Eames chair the old man indicated.

"Mr. Kirkland, I want to talk to you about the illegal adoption of Alicia Green Walker and the monetary deal that was made thirty-five years ago with her biological mother."

Kirkland surveyed him in silence for several seconds and then said, "I see you don't plan to beat around the bush, Detective."

"I only have twenty minutes."

Kirkland looked away from him. "You could have saved yourself the trip from Queens. I will not discuss the Alicia Green case, or any other, with you."

Lafferty nodded. "I see. You do realize that in refusing to cooperate with my investigation you could be liable for obstruction charges as well as open to subpoena."

Kirkland snorted. "*Your* investigation? You are on leave from the police force, Detective. I read the morning newspapers. Any investigation you are conducting is strictly on your own and without the sanction of any official body."

"Why didn't you tell your daughter that?"

Kirkland waved his hand dismissively. "Esther is a fusspot and I will determine who sees me and who does not. That doesn't change the fact that I won't tell you a damn thing."

Lafferty sighed. "You put me in a difficult position, Mr. Kirkland. I don't want to upset you, but one phone call to my captain will produce a search warrant which will have a team of detectives tearing apart your records going back to the Eisenhower administration."

Kirkland pointed to a teak desk against the wall to his left. "There's the phone."

Lafferty had to admire the old guy in a perverse way; he sure didn't rattle easily.

"Mr. Kirkland, it's four o'clock in the afternoon right now. I was at my precinct house very early this morning talking to a couple of old geezers who worked Manhattan when you were in your prime. They told me all about you. You were quite the fixer in your day."

"I helped my friends."

"Like Daniel Green?"

"His father was my best friend."

"Oh, why so noble? Your 'help' was not restricted to friends, was it? It was available to anyone who could pay for it, isn't that so, Mr. Kirkland?"

Kirkland picked up a magazine from the table at his side. "Young man, you're boring me. I believe your time is almost up."

"Okay, then I'll speed this up a little. Let's talk about blackmail, and extortion, and the facilitation of both."

Kirkland sighed. "In connection with a thirty-five-year-old adoption? The statute of limitations has run out on those felonies a long time ago, my boy. You should review your math, you'll have to do better than that."

"How about murder, accessory after the fact. The statute never runs out on murder, pal."

"I know nothing about a murder."

"Joe Walker's murder? You just told me you read the papers. Alicia Green Walker is accused of killing him, the same Alicia Green who was sold as an infant to your buddy's son Daniel Green and his wife Margaret."

"I fail to see a connection between the events of thirty-five years ago and the fit of insanity which led Alicia to shoot her husband down in cold blood."

"Well, Mr. Kirkland, that's what I am here to establish. And if you don't start talking pretty quick I'll have to call your daughter in here and tell her everything I know about Harmony House.''

The old man didn't move but the tightening of his lips told Lafferty that his thrust had reached its target.

"You did come prepared, Detective Lafferty."

"The precinct captain who protected you on that one is just a memory—retired, dead, gone. There's a new group in power now and they wouldn't mind dredging up that old chestnut if you refuse to play ball. I have their word on it. If you cooperate with me they will continue to let bygones be bygones. If not, your daughter, the pillar of Holy Cross Church, whose favorite charity is Mercy Foundling Hospital, will learn in the papers about the illegal abortion mill for the well-heeled and discreet, run quite profitably some decades ago on referrals from one Ambrose T. Kirkland.''

Kirkland looked like a man who had been unexpectedly checkmated.

"You didn't think anybody still cared about that, did you, Kirkland? Thought everybody had forgotten? Cops have long memories, especially one cop who lost his sister to a butcher you set her up with in 1960.''

Kirkland was silent.

"You're pretty much dependent on your daughter now, aren't you? Wife dead, son living in Europe, arthritis ready to put you in a wheelchair. What do you think would happen to you if I told your daughter how you paid for this house, her pony, her private school, her piano lessons? Funny, Ambrose, she doesn't seem like the type to forgive and forget to me.''

Kirkland eyed him malevolently.

"Let me help you out. That's how you got involved with the Green adoption, right? The Lassiter girl wanted to have an abortion at Harmony House but Green wanted to keep the baby. You paid her off to have the baby and give it to the Greens and keep her mouth shut about it. You arranged for the payments to continue after Daniel Green died, and in all likelihood they continue to this very day. How am I doing so far?''

Kirkland coughed delicately. ''I don't see why you need me, Detective. You seem to know it all already.''

''Not all. There's something missing, something I can't quite reach. And you're going to tell me what it is or so help me God when your daughter walks in here, which she is scheduled to do in about three minutes, I am going to give her chapter and verse on the doings at Harmony House Convalescent Home circa 1955-1970.''

Kirkland stared at Lafferty, as if weighing carefully what to say.

Lafferty looked at his watch pointedly. ''Now you have two minutes and forty seconds.''

Kirkland closed his eyes. ''There were two children,'' he said flatly.

''Two children?''

''Alicia and another. Two little girls exactly alike. The Greens took Alicia and the other...''

''Alicia has an identical twin?'' Lafferty whispered.

''Yes.''

''Does her grandmother Hannah know this?''

''No.'' Kirkland closed his eyes and shook his head. ''Nobody knew there was a second baby except the Lassiters. And me. Daniel was not there when the children were born, and the Lassiter girl's mother, Nancy, wanted to keep one of the children. Deborah just wanted it to be over, and Daniel was expecting only one child so Nancy Lassiter kept the second baby. As far as I know she raised the child. She probably used the payoff money to do it.''

Lafferty's mind was spinning with the implications of

what Kirkland had just told him. "You knew Alicia had a twin and you said nothing when she was arrested on eyewitness testimony? You know there is somebody else out there who looks just like her and you did *nothing* when the entire case against her is based on identifying her as the killer? You're a lawyer, man, an officer of the court! Didn't you feel any obligation to come forward and tell what you know?"

Kirkland avoided his gaze, saying nothing.

Lafferty threw up his hands. "No, of course you didn't. It was much more important to keep the secret of Harmony House and enjoy a peaceful old age."

"I would not have let her go to jail," Kirkland finally said quietly.

Mike could hardly contain his anger. The thought of what Alicia had gone through while this smug senior citizen sat on his laurels made him want to throttle the old man. Kirkland could have alleviated her pain with a single phone call.

"Oh, bully for you!" Mike exploded. "What about what she is going through right now, the fear, the uncertainty, the worry about her children? You were going to come forward only if she was convicted, right? You were going to wait it out, see what happened, see if maybe she might get off and then you wouldn't have to blow the whistle on yourself. You're a piece of work, Kirkland, a real credit to your profession."

There was a knock at the door to the hall.

"Time's up," Esther announced spitefully, pulling open the door smartly.

"Mr. Kirkland, tell your daughter that you need a few more minutes," Lafferty said evenly.

"Go away, Esther," Kirkland said. "I'll call you if and when I need you."

Esther looked from one man to the other and then hauled the door shut with a bang.

"Tell me everything you know about the Lassiters, the people who kept the other baby. Where they were living then, how they picked up the money, any mailing addresses you may have, any subsequent information—everything."

"The only survivor at this point may be Alicia's twin, and I have no idea where she is."

"What happened to Alicia's biological mother, Deborah, and the grandmother, Nancy?"

"Nancy died around the time Daniel Green was killed. I made arrangements to continue paying Deborah and Alicia's twin, who were still living together then. That's all I know. The checks were drawn on a trust account set up by Daniel Green and sent to a PO Box and were always cashed about three days after mailing."

"And this went on for all the years since Alicia was born? It never stopped?"

Kirkland smiled thinly. "You must understand about banks, Detective Kirkland. If you set up a trust account and make a bank officer the trustee, the bank will keep sending out checks as long as the money lasts or until the Creator arrives in person and tells the bank to stop. And then the bank will ask Him if He has a certified letter from the trust establisher to that effect."

"I see. And somebody picked the checks up right away. Somebody was waiting for them."

Kirkland nodded. "I assume so."

"Give me the addresses."

Lafferty scribbled down what Kirkland told him and then rose quickly, tucking his notebook under his arm.

"I assume you will be taking this information to the district attorney?" Kirkland asked.

"Yes, as you should have done."

"Remember our bargain and keep my involvement out of it, Detective."

"I won't bring your name into it. But if Woods is as sharp as I think he is, he'll figure it out eventually."

"You're sleeping with the Walker woman, aren't you?" Kirkland asked as Lafferty turned to go.

"I am not going to discuss Alicia with you," Lafferty replied, not even looking at the older man. "She managed to turn out just fine despite the machinations of people like you and a marriage that would have driven most people insane."

"Margaret Green was a good woman. I am sure she made a fine mother," Kirkland said.

Lafferty glanced at him then. "You were concerned about that?"

"We can't all be self-righteous heroes, Detective Lafferty. I did what I could. I knew Margaret Green wanted a child desperately and could not have one herself. Children given to such people rarely come to any harm."

"And what about the other child, the twin? Did you think the baby the Lassiters kept would not come to any harm?"

Kirkland shrugged slightly. "It is very difficult to take a child away from its biological mother."

"It sounds like it was the grandmother, Nancy, who really wanted to keep the baby."

"Even the grandmother would have had rights to her before a stranger," Kirkland replied.

"You have an answer for all of it, don't you? It must be nice to be able to justify everything in your mind."

"To tell you the truth, Detective, I rarely think of those days anymore. It was all such a long time ago."

"Not for Alicia, pal, not for Alicia," Lafferty muttered

under his breath and pushed open the door of the study abruptly. Esther Claiborne was standing two inches from it and jumped back, startled.

"It was a pleasure meeting you, Mrs. Claiborne," Lafferty said as he brushed past her. She opened her mouth soundlessly as he made his escape, saluting her with his fingers as she stared at him through the glass panel of the front door.

He could hardly conceal his elation as he ran down the brownstone's brick steps and stepped into the street to hail a passing cab.

Alicia had a twin. There was a woman out there who looked exactly like her, and this must be, had to be, the person who had murdered Joe Walker.

For the moment he was not concerned with how or why. The existence of a known double should be enough to reopen the investigation in light of Alicia's insistence that she was innocent. Where the twin sister was or why she might have wanted to kill Joe Walker was a mystery he would solve presently. His immediate task was to postpone Alicia's indictment hearing and to tell her this good news as soon as possible.

He hailed a cab and gave his Queens address. Alicia was coming to his apartment to have dinner that evening and discuss what he had learned from Kirkland. He had not expected to be this lucky. He knew that the existence of a sibling would be another shock for her, especially since it seemed likely that the sister was the killer. But nothing surpassed the feelings of relief and joy surging through him. He might finally be able to save Alicia from the horrible juggernaut that had overtaken her life.

He got out at his building and paid the fare, overtipping the cabbie and bounding into his building. The hall outside his door was empty and as he paused to pull his keys from his pocket a blow fell on the back of his head that knocked him to his knees. He turned to face his assailant and then suddenly realized there were several men in the narrow hallway, all coming at him. In the few seconds of consciousness he had as he struggled to return the punches and kicks raining down on him, he heard a harsh voice say, "Stay out of the Walker case!"

Then everything went black.

Chapter 9

Alicia balanced the grocery bag in the crook of her arm as she fished in her bag for her keys. Lafferty had given her a duplicate key to his apartment, but the ring had sunk to the bottom of her purse, into the morass of receipts, used lipsticks, crumpled tissues, assorted coins and lint-covered breath mints which abided there like the loose pieces of a child's board game. She rummaged in frustration for several seconds and then noticed that Lafferty's door could not possibly be locked. It was not even closed. It stood ajar, and she let the grocery bag fall when she noticed the drops of blood on the floor.

Lafferty was sprawled on the couch that used to grace his sister's living room before his nephew spilled day-glo paint on it. He was still wearing his jacket, and one hand trailed to the floor; his face was a mass of cuts and lumps, one eye was swollen half closed, his shirt was ripped across his chest, revealing a large purpling bruise across his ribs, and a gash on his lower lip ran all the way to his chin.

Alicia gasped and threw her purse and coat on the floor as she ran to the couch.

"Michael?" she whispered in a shaky voice, afraid that he wouldn't answer her.

His good eye opened. "Alicia," he said thickly.

"Oh, my God, what happened to you?" she said, wanting to touch him but leery of doing more damage.

"Got jumped. Get Charlie Chandler on the phone," he said, trying to sit up.

Alicia pushed him back down again. "You're going to the hospital," she said.

"No hospital," he said in as strong a voice as he could muster. "Listen to me. This is a good sign."

"A good sign?" she repeated, horrified.

He closed his eyes and nodded. "Means I'm getting close, and whoever is railroading you is getting scared."

"Michael, let me call Dr. Spaulding. He is Hannah's personal physician and he will come right over here…"

"Be fine. My sister can come over later, she's patched me up before."

"Your sister is not a doctor!"

He closed his eyes and clenched his fists. When he opened them again his expression was grim. "Are you going to flip out over this after everything else you've been through?" he demanded, pushing her hands away when she tried to hold him down. "I'm okay, I've had worse done to me by a junkie on angel dust. Now are you going to call Charlie or do I have to do it?"

Alicia stared at him for a few seconds and then got up to get the groceries from the hall and shut the door.

"What's the number?" she asked quietly when she returned, picking up the cell phone from his coffee table.

He recited it for her, and when she heard the ringing begin she handed him the phone.

He propped it under his chin, wincing when the top of it brushed the cut on his face. He listened impatiently and then said, "Hi, Annie, it's Mike Lafferty. Charlie there?" There was another pause and then Lafferty said, "Charlie, I need you to get over to my place right now, and bring all your notes on the Walker case."

He closed his eyes, and Alicia could hear the buzz of Charlie's annoyed reply.

Lafferty inhaled sharply and then grimaced. "Now get this, Charlie. I am reaching out to you here, do you understand me? I just got jumped by several upstanding citizens who did a tap dance on my face, and I have a strong feeling they were in the employ of whoever wants Alicia to take the fall for her husband's murder. The last thing one of them said to me before landing a final kick was, "Stay out of the Walker case." Now why would anybody care about keeping me out of the case if the real killer was already heading for indictment? Hmm? Can you answer me that? I don't want to hear any lectures. You get over here, pronto, and bring those files. You owe me, partner, and I am cashing in right now." Lafferty threw the phone down in anger and put his head back against the sofa. Beads of sweat stood out on his forehead and his lips were pale. The angry speech had all but exhausted him.

"Do you think Chandler will do as you asked?" Alicia inquired in a small voice.

"He will." Lafferty looked at her as if he had forgotten she was there. "Come here," he said.

She went to him and sat on the edge of the couch. He put his arm around her and kissed her cheek. "I'm sorry I barked at you," he said. "I just need you to help me now because I am finally getting somewhere and that's when you have to be really careful, when you are closing in at the end.''

"Can I at least clean you up?'' Alicia asked.

He smiled, licking his split lip. "Not a pretty picture, eh?''

"No.''

"Help me stand.''

Alicia helped to get him on his feet and walked him into the bathroom. She switched on the overhead light, and they both looked at him in the mirror.

"Not too bad,'' he said, turning his head from side to side. "Still got all my teeth.''

"Those ribs could be cracked,'' Alicia said, pulling his jacket and shirt off and throwing them in the tub.

"Don't think so. I can breathe okay, no stabbing pain when I inhale.''

"I see you've been here before,'' Alicia said dryly, running water into the basin and soaking a washcloth.

"A few times.''

"Sit on the edge of the tub,'' she said.

He sat.

He let her minister to him for several minutes, until the blood was washed away and the damage could be assessed.

"How do I look?'' he asked, grinning lopsidedly when she was done.

"Grotesque,'' she said crisply, breaking out the iodine she found in the medicine chest.

"I guess it's all over then,'' he said sadly. "I always knew you just wanted me for my beauty.''

She palmed the bottle and took his battered face between her hands.

"Idiot," she said tenderly.

He pulled her onto his lap, grunting when her weight fell against his chest.

"I'll bet I can make you drop that bottle," he muttered, nuzzling her breasts and pulling her skirt up her thighs.

Alicia was leaning into him, her eyes closing, when she glimpsed his ruptured lip. It slammed her back to reality. She levered herself off him and unscrewed the cap on the iodine.

His eyes opened. "Hey, where'd you go?"

"One of us has to remain sane," Alicia said acidly. "You're two steps out of the emergency room and I am not going to—" She stopped short.

"Going to what?" he inquired, his eyebrows raised, enjoying her discomfiture. "What aren't you going to do?"

"Oh, shut up," she muttered, shooting him a sidelong glance. "You're in a hilarious mood for a near stretcher case."

"That's because I have something wonderful to tell you. At least I hope you think it is wonderful. It's probably the solution to the mystery of who killed your husband." He gingerly pushed himself up from the tub and stood towering over her in the close quarters of the bathroom. His bruised face and torso were lurid in the ghostly lighting, his expression serious now.

"What did Kirkland say?" Alicia asked warily.

"Among other things, he said that you have a twin sister. An identical twin sister."

Alicia absorbed that in stunned silence. Then she said, softly, "Two babies?"

"Yes."

"My parents got one and the Lassiters kept the other?" Lafferty nodded.

Alicia's breath escaped slowly as she thought about what he had said.

"And you think the person who shot Joe was my... sister?"

"Identical twins often can't be told apart. If she was prepared to look like you and was wearing your clothes, even people like Smithson and that guard, Moresby—all of the witnesses who swear you were there when Joe was killed—could be fooled."

"But why? *Why?*"

"That's what we have to find out. First we have to prove to the DA's office that this person exists, and then we have to prove that she had motive, means and opportunity to kill Joe. I've got a P.I. friend tracking the Lassiter name in central Jersey and checking the post office box and bank records. Your sister had to be picking up the checks and cashing them somewhere. We'll find her."

"My sister," Alicia murmured softly. "How strange that sounds after spending an entire life as an only child." As she thought about it, all the emotions connected with her hidden past welled up in her and she started to cry.

"I always wanted a sister," she whispered.

Mike embraced her and stood holding her while she sobbed. They both heard the loud knocking on the apartment door a couple of minutes later.

"That will be Charlie," Lafferty said.

"Should I go?" Alicia asked, pulling a tissue from a box on his bathroom shelf. "I don't want to leave you, but I know how your partner feels about me."

"How does Charlie feel about you?" Lafferty asked as they walked into the living room.

"He thinks that I'm a spoiled rich tart who finally got fed up with my husband's philandering and plugged him," Alicia replied, sniffling loudly.

Lafferty chuckled, grimacing when the activity hurt his ribs. "You stay, Alicia. You are more than capable of handling Charlie, and you can help with this."

"With what?"

"Piecing together where and how your husband might have met your sister."

"You think that they knew each other?" Alicia asked him, shocked.

"People are rarely murdered by strangers, Alicia. Outside of the occasional bank robbery, mugging and random acts of violence, the victims usually get it from somebody they know."

She looked at him skeptically.

"It's the truth. The overwhelming proportion of murders are committed by the friends, relatives, business partners of the deceased. So if you don't know otherwise from the start, the assumption is that the victim and the perpetrator knew each other."

Lafferty pulled open the door of his apartment.

"Hi, Charlie," he said.

Chandler, who was dressed in gray sweats and carried a large briefcase, looked at his partner appraisingly.

"You don't look too bad, kid," he said. "I've seen you take it on the chin a lot worse."

He glanced nervously at Alicia's tear-stained face.

She nodded at him.

"Alicia, would you get me a shirt from the bedroom?" Lafferty asked. "There are some clean ones stacked on the lower shelf in the closet."

Alicia left and Chandler said in a low tone, "You didn't tell me she would be here."

"It's her skin we're trying to save, Charlie, so would you give me a break here? She might just be able to help us."

"You're trying to save her, boyo, I'm not," Chandler replied darkly.

"So who beat me up then, Charlie? Huh? The local Brownie troop? Somebody wants Alicia to go to prison, and from their point of view I guess I'm the only thing standing in the way of that happening."

Alicia returned with a shirt, and Lafferty tensed as he bent to ease himself into it.

"I'll get you some aspirin and make coffee. Would you like something to eat, too?" she asked, and Lafferty nodded.

The two men watched her leave the room.

"Let me see what you brought," Lafferty said.

"You've still got Lise's furniture," Chandler said, nodding at the couch.

"I'm waiting until the millennium to redecorate," Lafferty said shortly. He dumped the compendium of files, notebooks and computer disks on the cushions and began to sort through it.

"Cramer will string me up if he finds out I took all this," Chandler said.

"He'll be a lot more unhappy if we help to convict the wrong perp," Lafferty said. "I went to see Ambrose Kirkland today."

"Kirkland? That old fixer from Doyle's stable? I thought he was dead."

"He's alive. He told me some interesting things about Alicia's family background that you should hear before we delve into the rest of this."

Alicia listened to the men's voices going back and forth in the living room as she worked in the kitchen, crying in fits and starts. She didn't know why the discovery of a sibling should affect her so deeply; she supposed it was the enduring loneliness of being an only child. She had missed out on all those years of having a companion, a compatriot, a friend. She resented it and at the same time felt compassion for the baby who had been turned over to the venal Lassiters. What a mess it all was. She felt like a stranger in her own skin. Very little about her past was what she'd thought it was, and she felt disconnected, isolated. Why hadn't her sister made her existence known to Alicia? What possible motive could she have for killing Joe? In what context would she even have met him?

She heard Lafferty bark something at Chandler, and Chandler's querulous reply. She wondered how on earth these two men, a diffident, lonely detective, with whom she had fallen suddenly and desperately into a sensual affair, and a sixtyish world-weary cop, who thought she was guilty, had wound up in charge of her fate. It was only Chandler's loyalty to his partner that had brought him there, but she was grateful he had come.

She could use all the help she could get.

Three hours later the two men were surrounded by piles of notes, plates, cups and trays of Chandler's cigarette butts. Lafferty's sister had come and then left after examining her brother, leaving a bottle of pills for him and favoring Alicia with a few knowing glances. Alicia entered with the latest pot of coffee and found them going over the list of telephone calls Joe had made in the last months of his life for the tenth time.

"And what's this one again, Charlie? It appears here over and over, several times a week."

"It's a Chinese takeout place on the Upper East Side. That aide, Smithson, said it was Walker's favorite. Ramirez and I checked it out together."

Lafferty's brow wrinkled as he studied the handwritten sheet of paper. His black eye was already turning colors and promised to blossom into a tequila sunrise in a couple of days.

"I don't know, Charlie, this is an awful lot of shrimp lo mein. Did you and Jose go there yourselves?"

Chandler stared at him indignantly. "Of course we went there. It's a Chinese restaurant, Mike, the Howloon Dragon. Chinese people running it, Chinese signs in the window, Chinese noodles on the plates. Chopsticks, fringed lamp shades, red menus with tassels. Get the picture?"

"And this Smithson said Walker ordered from there all the time?"

Chandler nodded.

Lafferty looked at Alicia. "You know anything about this?" he asked.

She shrugged. "I didn't know about a lot in Joe's life."

Lafferty tapped the paper with tip of his pencil. "I want to see Smithson again. Call him."

Chandler stared at him. "The investigation is officially closed, Mike."

"Tell him we're just tying up a few loose ends."

Chandler rubbed his forehead with nicotine stained fingertips. "Don't do this to me, kid."

"I can't call him, Charlie, you know that. I'm on an official leave of absence."

"Mike, I can't bring him into the station, Cramer will have a stroke."

"Then tell Smithson to meet me at the coffee shop downstairs in an hour."

"You're dreaming. He's got to come in from the suburbs somewhere, and he doesn't even have to talk to you!"

Lafferty glanced at Alicia and then back at Chandler. "Didn't you get the feeling all along that this guy Smithson was hiding something? Something we nosed around but never nailed and that he didn't volunteer?''

Chandler was silent.

"He always seemed bewildered to me, like he couldn't believe Alicia had done it but he'd *seen* her do it so what else could he believe?'' Lafferty went on.

Chandler sighed and looked away, shaking his head.

"Charlie, he knows something, and I think I can get him to spill it. Get him on the phone.''

Chandler snatched the scrap of paper from Lafferty's overloaded coffee table and stalked into the bedroom. They could hear him punching the buttons on the cell phone.

"He does everything you tell him. Did you save his life once or something?'' Alicia asked.

"Yes.''

Alicia was nonplussed. "I was kidding.''

Lafferty shrugged. "I'm his partner. When we were working narcotics together, some crack dealer up in Spanish Harlem was drawing a bead on him and I took the sleazeball out with one shot to the temple. Charlie's been my slave ever since.''

Alicia narrowed her eyes. "Are you making that up?''

Lafferty smiled, his handsome face distorted by the half-closed eye and the split lip.

"You're making it up,'' she repeated.

He winked. "Coming down the home stretch, darlin'. I can feel it. I'll have Charlie take the information about your sister to Captain Cramer just as soon as I see what Smithson has to say. That should be enough to throw a monkey wrench into the Woodpecker's immediate plans to indict you, and then we'll work on finding your twin.''

"Oh, Mike, if only it could be as easy as that,'' Alicia said, afraid to hope.

"I'm on a lucky streak," he said.

She burst out laughing. "Yes, I can tell that just by looking at you."

He touched his mangled mouth lightly. "Occupational hazard," he said, shrugging.

Chandler came back into the room and announced, "Smithson will be downstairs at the coffee shop at 10:00 p.m. I told him you were taking over for me as a favor because I had a funeral to go to in the morning, and that was not a lie because the funeral will be my own. I also told him you would be looking a little raggedy and that did not seem to surprise him at all."

Lafferty smiled at Alicia.

"I am not so sure Drew will help you, Mike," Alicia said. "He was very intimidated by Joe and might still cover for him. The party still exists, he still needs to make a living."

"You let me worry about him," Lafferty said.

Chandler started shoveling some of the records he had brought with him back into the bag and said, "I am going home to tell my wife that I will be out of work soon and might need to ask her brother, the used-tire king, for a job. I didn't plan on spending my golden years capping retreads for my brother-in-law but it's shaping up that way. Do not call me, Mike. Repeat, do *not* call me." He tossed the last of the computer disks into the bag, zipped it shut and stalked out of the apartment.

Lafferty grinned. "I told you he loves me," he said to Alicia. "Now come over here and help me get presentable enough to be seen in public."

"Do you want me to go to meet Drew with you?" Alicia asked him.

He nodded. "If he is feeling the slightest bit guilty

about the way you've been railroaded, seeing you again tonight just might do the trick.''

''What trick?''

''Make him give up what else he knows.''

They did what they could to make Lafferty's injuries look a little less shocking, but he still attracted some stares as they descended to the coffee shop that occupied the ground floor of his building. Despite the hour and the trip in from Larchmont, Smithson was waiting for them in a booth. He was wearing jeans and a windbreaker. Without the obligatory dark suit he wore for work Alicia almost didn't recognize him.

He did not look happy.

He stood as they approached and nodded at Alicia.

''You're looking well, Alicia,'' he said.

''Considering the circumstances?'' Alicia replied lightly.

Smithson's gaze shifted to Lafferty. ''I wish I could say the same for you, Lafferty. Looks like somebody worked you over pretty good. I guess whoever did it hasn't heard about your leave of absence.''

''Guess not,'' Lafferty said. ''Or they didn't care. Whether I'm officially on the force or not, I want to help Alicia, and that seems to be the problem.''

''That's quite a shiner,'' Smithson said, sitting again as they slid onto the padded seat across from him. ''Funny what life brings you sometimes, isn't it?''

''Yeah, life's a riot,'' Lafferty said. ''Look, Smithson, I have a few more questions to ask about this Chinese place where Walker ordered takeout all the time.''

''The Howloon Dragon?'' Smithson said warily.

''Yeah.''

Smithson shrugged. ''I guess he liked the food.'' He did not sound very convincing.

"No chance anybody was running a prostitution ring out of there?" Lafferty asked.

The waitress stopped and took their order for coffee and they waited until she had gone before resuming the conversation.

Smithson shook his head. "Look, man, that place is spanking clean. Check with your vice people. No girls smuggled in from the northern provinces to work the streets here, no drugs, no illegal immigration of any kind."

"I did check. They say there's nothing going on there but food service, with all licenses and permits up to date."

Smithson opened his hands.

"Let's try this. We know Joe liked call girls, and we know he used a number of escort services."

Smithson glanced at Alicia and then away from her. "Right," he said.

"Did he have a particular girl that he used more often than the others, maybe one that he persuaded to go indy for him, that he supported?"

Smithson looked uncomfortable. "Your partner asked me that," he said.

"I know. I'm asking you again."

Smithson hesitated.

"Look, Smithson, if you know something more than you've already said, now is the time to come clean with it. This lady is about to go on trial for something she didn't do."

Smithson sighed. "I didn't lie to your partner," he said. "I told him I didn't know one particular person, and I don't. I don't know who it is, or was. But I knew Joe had to have a steady thing on the side because he was leaving messages for somebody to meet him at the Manhattan town house several times a month, and there would be bills sent to the office for food and liquor and then a housecleaning service would come in the next day.''

"How do you know it was the same person all the time?"

"It was always the same phone number," Smithson said, his eyes sliding away from Lafferty's.

"The Howloon Dragon," Lafferty said.

Smithson nodded resignedly.

The waitress returned with three coffees and deposited them at their table.

"You think Joe was seeing one of the employees there?" Alicia asked incredulously when she left.

Smithson closed his eyes. "I don't know. With Joe anything was possible. I'm sorry, Alicia, but that's the truth.''

"I know," she said, not meeting his eyes.

"Anything else?" Lafferty asked.

"I assume you're going to try to postpone the grand jury hearing on the basis of new evidence?" Smithson asked.

Lafferty nodded.

"Whatever you find out, make sure that your captain knows about it as well as other people in the DA's office when you take it to Woods. Put it in the newspapers if you have to, but get the word out there. Don't give it to him alone.''

"Are you telling me that you think Woods would try to bury it?" Lafferty asked.

Smithson held up his hand. "Just a word of warning. Woods wants to win the upcoming election, big-time. And he wants Alicia to be convicted because it fits his campaign profile of conservatives as lowlife hypocrites. Joe Walker's murder was a gift from God in his view, a golden apple that fell into his lap at the right time. He will not be happy if somebody other than The Chairman's wife turns out to be the guilty party.''

Lafferty looked at Alicia, who was turning pale.

"There's a new ADA in the office, very sharp, Althea Bransford,'' Smithson added. "She's ambitious and she is not in Woods' pocket. She has a reputation to establish and nothing to lose. I'd make sure she gets the same evidence Woods does. She'll buck him if she has to—she'll go right over his head to a judge.''

"Thanks for the tip,'' Lafferty said.

Smithson nodded and rose. "So who do you think sent the greeting party?'' Smithson asked, gesturing to Lafferty's pummeled appearance.

"Hard to say. After fifteen years on the force I have made so many friends,'' Lafferty retorted, smiling.

"Cui bono?'' Smithson said. "Did they teach you that at John Jay?''

Lafferty nodded. When Smithson reached out, Lafferty took his hand and shook it.

"Think about that in light of what I just said,'' Smithson advised. He looked at Alicia. "Goodbye, Alicia. And good luck to you. I mean that.''

"Thanks. Goodbye, Drew.''

They watched him walk away as the waitress refilled their cups.

"What was that he said to you?'' Alicia asked. "Latin, wasn't it?''

"Yes. *Cui bono?* Literally, *to whom the good?* In other words, who benefits?''

"And?''

"I think he was telling me that our esteemed district attorney sent the welcome wagon that rearranged my face.''

Alicia stared at him.

"He must have gotten wind that I was close to something and decided I needed a discouraging word."

"I can't believe that," Alicia murmured.

"Why not? Was your husband what he appeared to be to the millions of people who would have voted for him?"

She closed her eyes and said, "What next?"

"I think we take a little trip to the Howloon Dragon."

"What do you expect to see?"

"Won't know until we get there."

"Even Charlie says the operation is legitimate, and whoever Joe was involved with is hardly going to jump up and yell, 'Yoo-hoo, here I am!' And even if we do find the person Joe was calling, I don't see how it is going to help us track down my sister. There is probably no connection at all."

"Detective work is tedious, Alicia," Lafferty said gently. "You have to be patient."

"Patient!" she said disgustedly. "Thanks a lot, I'll remember that when I'm answering roll call in the prison yard."

Lafferty gave her a long, measuring glance and said, "It upset you to see Smithson again, didn't it?"

Alicia didn't reply.

"Look, he was your husband's sidekick, but he's trying to do the right thing now."

Alicia sighed. "I know. But he's such a powerful reminder of Joe and that charade I lived for so long."

Lafferty reached across the table and took her hand. "It's over, Alicia. That life died when Joe did. Try to put it aside and concentrate on your future."

Her future? Alicia noticed that he didn't include himself in that picture.

"The one I'm going to have in lockup?" she responded.

''The one you're going to have once we find the real killer.''

Alicia could feel the tightness of tears growing in her throat again and pushed them back. She nodded.

''Now let's go,'' he said, and she stood with him.

By the time they got to Manhattan the Howloon Dragon was closing. It was a tiny hole-in-the-wall on the ground floor of a walkup with six tables jammed into a narrow space and a take-out desk where the phone was still ringing as they entered. The sole waiter was refilling sugar jars, and the older woman answering the phone was turning the Open sign to Closed in the window when she looked up and waved and smiled at Alicia.

Lafferty and Alicia exchanged glances.

''Is she waving at me?'' Alicia asked.

''Looks like it,'' Lafferty replied.

They approached the counter and the woman said to Alicia, ''How you been, Miss Amy? No messages for you for some weeks. I answer phone all the time, I know. You away on trip?''

Chapter 10

"Miss Amy?" Alicia said, puzzled, but Lafferty was way ahead of her.

"Do you know this lady?" he asked the woman sharply, silencing Alicia with a gesture.

She nodded. "Why, sure. Miss Amy, she live upstairs." She narrowed her eyes at Alicia. "You do your hair darker while you were gone? I like it."

Alicia's heart began to bang in her chest. Who was the Miss Amy who lived upstairs?

"Have you seen this lady on TV?" Lafferty asked tersely, his attention focused on the Chinese woman.

"On TV? No, no, I no watch TV. Don't like it."

"Let me commend your taste. Did you see her picture in the newspapers?"

"Newspapers no. I can't read, I only speak. Three years this country."

"Then you speak very well." He took Alicia aside and said, "Keep on acting casual, I don't want to alarm her.

There's an apartment on the second floor and I'm going up there. From what she says I don't think she recognized you from the news blitz when Joe died—I have an idea she isn't terribly interested in American politics. She thinks you're your sister.''

"Oh, Mike." Alicia could barely talk.

He squeezed her shoulder. "There's a pay phone in the corner there. Call the precinct and tell the desk sergeant the message is from me. They need to send a car over here ASAP. *I* can't question this woman officially. Now keep smiling while I go upstairs."

Lafferty nodded at the woman, who was looking concerned by their whispered conversation.

"Something wrong, Miss Amy?" she asked.

"Nothing at all," Alicia replied, smiling, her pulse racing, as Lafferty went out the interior door to ascend the dusty wooden staircase they had seen on their way in from the street. "I just need to make a phone call."

"Phone not working upstairs? You turn it off?"

"Yes, while I was gone," Alicia replied, feeling like a criminal for lying but more concerned about getting through to the police. She got an alert response when she mentioned Lafferty's name, and then for good measure called Charlie Chandler, too, who sounded as if he was going to burst into tears when he heard her voice. But when she informed him of the details he said, "I'll be right over there," and hung up the phone in her ear.

Alicia turned to find the Chinese lady staring at her. "We closing, Miss Amy," she said.

"Yes, I know," Alicia replied, wondering how she could stall for time. Just then Lafferty returned.

"She's gone," he said, and Alicia knew how Chandler felt when she called him. Hysteria was just around the corner.

"The door is locked, I can't break in without a warrant. Charlie will have to search the place later. But nobody has been there for a while, there was dust on the floor mat and the mail slot. No mail piled up, I guess she stopped it, but I found this trapped under the mat. She must have missed it when she left."

It was a postcard from a video store alerting Amy Lester of an overdue rental, dated a month earlier.

"That's the name she was using here," Alicia said, and he nodded.

"Joe must have left messages at the number down here when he wanted to see her. Then she would meet him at the town house and generate the bills Drew Smithson saw. It was a good system, the perfect cover. Anyone seeing the phone number on his records would just assume he patronized the restaurant."

Alicia leaned back against the wall and closed her eyes. "We came so close. Now we'll never find her."

"Yes, we will. Now that she can be connected to this place, and to Joe calling this place, there's probable cause for an arrest warrant to be issued. We'll put an APB out on her. Joe is dead. The Greens' money isn't enough for her tastes, so chances are she'll go back to doing what she knows best. If she met him through an escort service she'll turn up with one somewhere else, and we know them all. If she killed him she planned the whole thing, and she had a job lined up to go to when she left here, you can bet on it."

Alicia shook her head. "It just doesn't make any sense to me. Why would she kill the golden goose? With Joe dead, her income from him stopped."

Lafferty shrugged. "Maybe he cut her off. Revenge is a powerful motive for murder."

They both realized at the same moment that their audience had grown. The cashier had been joined by the waiter and the cook, and all three were staring at them.

A police cruiser pulled to the curb outside the restaurant and all three then looked scared.

"We don't want no trouble," the waiter said.

"There won't be any trouble," Lafferty said shortly. "The police just want to ask you some questions about the lady who was living upstairs."

"This is lady," the cashier said, nodding at Alicia.

"No," Lafferty said. "This is her twin."

Two uniformed cops entered with Chandler right behind them, a notebook in his hand.

"What are you doing here?" Lafferty asked him.

"She called me," Chandler answered, nodding toward Alicia, who gestured helplessly.

Chandler whipped out his badge and showed it to the trio, who looked at it warily. Lafferty and Chandler conferred briefly and then Chandler said to the cashier, "Your name is?"

"Ling Ming Na."

"Mrs. Ling?"

She nodded.

"You took messages for the lady upstairs when she was not at home?"

"When she was at home, too. The phone ring here and I write it down, tell her when she comes into Dragon."

"So Walker never called her apartment," Lafferty said, and Chandler nodded.

"You just told me that you can't read English," Lafferty interjected.

"I write down in Chinese, say to her in English," Mrs. Ling replied.

"Very nice," Chandler observed. "No pesky evidence scraps lying around written in English for the curious to read.'' He looked at the cashier. ''How often did the lady come in for her messages?''

''Everyday she check. That's why when she no come for a while I was worry, so glad to see—'' She gestured at Alicia, then threw up her hands.

''Was it always the same man who called her?''

''From the voice, yes.''

''Did the lady pay you to take the messages?''

The cashier nodded.

''How much?''

''Two hundred dollar a month.''

''Two hundred dollars a month to take an occasional phone message? Didn't that strike you as a lot of money?''

Mrs. Ling shrugged. ''Land of opportunity,'' she said.

Lafferty and Chandler exchanged glances.

''Who is the landlord here, who owns the building?'' Lafferty asked.

''Big Apple,'' the cook said.

''Big Apple?'' Chandler repeated.

The cook nodded and had a quick conversation with the waiter, who went behind the counter and emerged with a payment book with some of the stubs ripped out. He handed it to Chandler, who read aloud, ''Big Apple Triangle Trust.''

''What's that?'' Alicia asked.

Chandler snorted. ''Snot-nosed yuppies running all the real estate companies.'' He handed the book to one of the uniformed officers and said, ''Make a note of that. We may be able to track this dame through her rent checks.''

''I doubt it,'' Lafferty said. ''She probably operated on a cash basis as much as possible.''

The cell phone in Lafferty's pocket rang and he answered it. He listened for a minute and then said, ''Thanks a lot, Roy. Good job. I'll be in touch with you later.'' He depressed the aerial smartly and replaced the phone.

Alicia and Chandler looked at him expectantly.

''Amy Lester was picking up her checks from the trust the Greens set up at a PO box in Fort Lee, New Jersey, just across the state line,'' Lafferty said. ''She cashed them in a bank in the same town where she had a checking account, which was used very little, drawn upon mostly for cash. There has been no activity on that account since the day before Joe Walker was killed.''

Chandler sighed. ''Some little racket she had going. Grifting on the Greens in the wake of a thirty-five-year-old peccadillo and playing hootchie mama for The Chairman whenever he dropped some coins in a pay phone. Nice work if you can get it.''

''So what blew it out of the water?'' Lafferty asked. ''She had a tiff with Walker?''

''Most likely. If they met by chance through an escort service and Walker got a kick out of the fact that this Amy looked just like his wife, but was willing to, uh, cooperate with certain activities his wife might have refused, that could have been something unique for him. We know he was attracted to Alicia's type, he married Alicia. So suppose he comes across a hooker who physically is his wife's double but who, for a hefty price, will do anything he wants. And I mean *anything*. I think from what we know about him a guy like Joe Walker would be interested, don't you?''

''Do you think Joe knew she was my sister?'' Alicia asked quietly.

''If he did, that probably contributed to his fascination, made his jollies even jollier, if you know what I mean.''

Alicia didn't want to think about it.

''Get the rest of the names and addresses here,'' Chandler said to one of the uniformed policemen, who nodded and took out a notebook. He gestured for the other two to follow him.

"We've got to get moving on this," he said to Lafferty. "We need an arrest warrant for Amy Lester, a search warrant for the apartment upstairs and a stay of the grand jury hearing Woods has on the calendar. Time to wake up some judges."

"Okay, Charlie, take it away," Lafferty said. "This is what you do best."

Chandler looked at Alicia. "I owe you an apology," he said stiffly. "I was wrong about you, and I'm very sorry."

Alicia glanced at Lafferty, who winked at her.

"Thank you, Charlie," she said.

Chandler cleared his throat. "Come on, you two," he said to the cops. "Let's get this show on the road and let these people close up the store."

Chandler apologized to Mrs. Ling and her companions for the inconvenience and thanked them for their cooperation. Alicia and Lafferty followed him out to the squad car, where he jumped into the back as the two cops got into the front.

"I'll call you," he informed Lafferty from the window, as the cruiser pulled away from the curb.

"We're almost there," Lafferty said to Alicia, who stepped into his enclosing arms.

Lafferty was up the rest of the night on the phone. Alicia called Maizie to check on her children and pass on the latest news, then tried to nap on the bed. The linens smelled of Mike, and she kept burying her face in the fragrant pillow as she heard his voice murmuring in the next room. It was the sound of her salvation; she could listen to its pleasing masculine cadence forever. At dawn she finally got up and went to sit next to Lafferty on the couch.

He smiled at her and put his arm around her shoulders. His injured eye was swollen almost shut, and the cut on his chin was dark with dried blood.

"Check the Virginia and Maryland suburbs. She seems to like politicians," Lafferty said into the phone. "That's Lassiter, Lester, maybe some variation of that. Get back with me when you have something. Thanks."

He put the phone down and kissed Alicia on the forehead.

"Get any sleep?" he asked.

She shook her head wearily. "Mike, you look terrible. Will you go to a doctor today?"

"I promise I will. As soon as we get some kind of a lead on your sister."

"What if she's left the country?"

"She hasn't. She can't get too far from those trust fund checks she has to cash at an instate bank, preferably one where she has an account if she doesn't want to elicit undue interest. I think she's still within a day's drive of New Jersey."

Alicia sighed. "I don't understand how she could have been going around New York all this time and never attracted attention if she looks that much like me."

"Mrs. Ling told Mainardi, one of the uniformed cops with Charlie, that she was always wearing scarves, dark glasses, even wigs, when she came in from the street. Apparently she felt comfortable enough to dispense with the accessories when she just came downstairs to check for messages, maybe because she knew the Lings had no interest in the social-political scene."

"Thank God she let them see what she really looks like or else Mrs. Ling would never have recognized me."

Lafferty nodded.

"Michael, this whole thing is so bizarre," Alicia began, then stopped when Lafferty pointed at the TV set and picked up the television remote. He released the mute button and the visual images moving on the screen acquired sound. Alicia followed the direction of his gaze and saw District Attorney Sandler Woods surrounded by a gaggle of reporters, all of whom were jockeying for position and jamming microphones in his face.

"You'll enjoy this," Lafferty said to Alicia. He looked at his watch. "Right on time."

"I've called you here to announce some late-breaking developments in the Joseph Walker murder case," Woods began soberly, using his best "meet the press" demeanor. "Due to the unflagging efforts of this city's excellent police force, another viable suspect has been uncovered and is being pursued with all of the means at our disposal."

Woods looked tired and his tie was askew.

"Good boy," Lafferty said softly. "Now sit up and beg. Woof, woof."

"You mean the wife didn't do it?" one of the reporters yelled while Woods was still talking.

Woods looked pained. "Uh, it appears that more than one person in this case had the motive and means to kill the victim, and we are on the trail of another such person. And that's all I am prepared to say at this time."

"Good doggie," Lafferty said. "Arf."

Woods tried to escape but the reporters closed in on him like a wolf pack on fresh meat.

"Are you saying that Mrs. Walker will be released?"

"When can we expect a new arrest?"

"Will the indictment hearing be postponed?"

"Who is the new suspect?"

"Will Commissioner Newly be making an announcement regarding this case?"

Reporters shouted questions as Woods's mouth became a thin line, and the scene shifted back to the anchor desk.

"And there you have it," the morning anchorwoman said in clipped tones. "With a second arrest possibly imminent in the Joseph Walker murder case, you may recall that Joseph Walker's wife, the socially prominent Alicia Green Walker, has been accused of that crime and—"

Lafferty clicked off the TV.

"I take it you had something to do with that performance," Alicia said to Lafferty dryly.

"I sent Charlie to get Woods out of bed and tell him that I was expecting an announcement on the morning news. Charlie also told him that Althea Bransford had already received a file outlining your twin's relevance to the Walker case. He added that if the media announcement I was expecting did not materialize then Commissioner Newly would hear about the tactics the DA was using to intimidate police officers in the performance of their duty."

"You're not a police officer at the moment," Alicia replied. "Technically."

"I think Woods got the message, anyway."

"Thank you for that. I know you understand that it is important to me to clear my name, but won't putting it on the television give a warning to my...sister? I mean, right now she thinks she got away with it."

Lafferty shook his head. "I agree it's a gamble, but I'm hoping it will have the opposite effect and flush her out if she sees it. Which she should, because we gave the bulletin to the wire services. There's a pattern to deviant behavior, and an experienced criminal would not be rattled by a news announcement, he or she would take it in stride and change plans accordingly. But I am banking on our assumption that Joe Walker was your sister's first murder, motivated by her desire for revenge. In that case she should just be calming down, convinced that you will take the fall she set up, and then if she suddenly realizes she was wrong, she may go into a panic. We're watching all the transportation routes and if she tries to make a move anywhere we'll nail her.''

"You said she wouldn't leave the country."

"She won't, but she should try to hole up until the time comes for her next trip to the bank. That could mean suddenly leaving whatever job she has set up for herself, packing up and bolting from her new apartment, whatever. This is just an attempt to accelerate the process, Alicia. We'll get her. Tonight or tomorrow, next week or next month. We'll get her.''

Alicia nodded. "I just want it to be over, you know? I just want to go home and tell my kids and my grandmother that it is over.''

"It will be. Soon."

Alicia closed her eyes. "And I can't even begin to think about how to rebuild our lives. Claire and Joey will need therapy and God knows what else…''

"And they're bound to resent my role in this," Lafferty said.

Alicia looked at him.

"Claire already does," Lafferty said.

"Oh, Mike, she'll get over that. She's so young, she misses her father even though on some level she knows what he was like. He could be very charming when it served his purpose, and she remembers those times and gets confused. She knows that…''

Lafferty held up his hand. Alicia stopped.

"She found me in her kitchen with her mother a short time after her father was murdered," Lafferty said quietly. "I think more than a few kids would have a problem with a widowed parent entering into a new relationship so quickly."

Alicia sighed. "Let's not talk about this now. One thing at a time. My sister has not been found yet, which means that I'm still the prime suspect in Joe's murder. If and when this is over, we can worry about the impact of our relationship on my kids, okay?"

Lafferty was silent, but the expression on his face indicated that for him the subject was far from closed. He realized Alicia was at the end of her rope and couldn't handle a domestic discussion while her fate still hung in the balance, but her insistence that all would be well with her children once her legal troubles were over confounded him.

He knew she was not that naive.

His cell phone chirped, and he grabbed it while Alicia's heart climbed into her throat.

"Yeah?" he barked. He listened intently for some seconds and said, "Good work. Keep me posted." He put down the phone as Alicia looked at him inquiringly.

"They found somebody matching your sister's general description who just signed up for an escort service in Richmond, Virginia, a few weeks ago."

Alicia clasped her hands together prayerfully, but he said, "Now don't get excited. That's all we know at the moment. Richmond is a little far from D.C. to be viable, but we'll see. This could be just a coincidence, I've seen it happen many times."

"When will we know?"

"Not too long. Virginia police are checking it out right

now and we should know something by the end of the day.''

Alicia bit her lower lip. "I don't know if I can stand this," she said.

"You'll stand it. We both will, because the end is in sight. You'll be off the hook as soon as we grab her."

"I still can't believe that you will. I must have gotten used to thinking of my situation as hopeless."

"Come here," Lafferty said, and she moved closer to him. He pulled her into his lap, and she heard him gasp softly as she brushed against his ribs. She stood up.

"Hey," he said.

"You are coming with me to that walk-in medical care place right now," she said firmly. "It's only two blocks away."

"All right," he said meekly, which indicated to Alicia that he was in more pain than he would admit.

"Do you want me to call ahead?" she asked.

He sighed and rose stiffly, wincing and putting his hand to the back of the sofa for support.

"Not necessary," he answered. "They know me there."

"Why am I not surprised?" Alicia observed wryly.

"Now, now, no sarcasm. It's too early."

Alicia watched him unfold until he was standing upright.

"See?" he said, grinning. "Nothing to it."

She pointed toward the door. "March."

"I'm okay as long as I'm walking around," he observed. "When I sit down I sort of seize up or something."

"Anybody else but you would be in a hospital bed," Alicia said, opening the door for him. "How would the commissioner feel if he knew that Captain Cramer was letting you run this investigation from your apartment sofa in your present condition?''

Lafferty didn't answer, but she hadn't expected a reply. He and his police colleagues seemed to operate in a universe of their own, where ordinary rules did not apply and standard procedures could be suspended as long as the greater good was served.

Alicia shut the apartment door behind them and used the key Mike had given her to lock it.

Alicia's sister was not apprehended for another three days. Alicia spent that time with her children, trying to follow their activities and keep them calm as her own heart leaped every time the telephone rang. The kids were aware that the police were pursuing another suspect, but not that the person was their mother's long-lost sister.

When the call finally came, Alicia was playing a board game with Joey and Maizie called her into the kitchen.

"Is it Michael?" Alicia asked.

Maizie nodded as she handed Alicia the phone.

"I think he has something," Maizie added, her eyes wide with excitement.

Alicia took the receiver with a shaking hand. "Michael?"

"Nobody else. We got her."

Alicia closed her eyes and nodded. Maizie let out a whoop and then started to cry.

"Are you sure?" Alicia whispered into the phone.

"She's your double. She cut off her hair and dyed it black, but I just saw a wire-service photo, and the resemblance is uncanny. So far she hasn't confessed to anything, but she will. The evidence has been piling up since we got the break about the Chinese restaurant."

"Where was she?" Alicia's children came in from the den, drawn by the sound of Maizie's weeping.

"A Virginia suburb. She was installed in a condo complex and lining up work. The arresting officer down there told me she went with him without protest, almost as if she had been waiting for him."

"Mike, I'm going to call Oswald Kirby and get him to represent her. I'll pay for it."

There was a pause from the other end as Maizie conveyed the good news to Alicia's children in a low tone.

"Alicia, are you sure? This woman may be your blood sister but you don't know her. She's a criminal. She set you up to take the fall for a murder she committed."

"There but for the grace of God go I. It was just chance that I got the good life with the Greens and she was left impoverished with a grandmother who died too young and a mother who apparently didn't want her."

"I don't know if Kirby will want to take her case after representing you," Lafferty said doubtfully.

"I have to try. He's very skilled, he can present her history sympathetically to a jury. Maybe if they hear the details of her background and childhood they will be able to understand why she did what she did."

"Do *you* understand it?"

Alicia hesitated. "I'm trying," she finally said, as Joey erupted into cheers and Claire put her arm around her mother.

"I take it the kids have heard the news," Lafferty said dryly on his end.

"Maizie told them." Alicia hesitated. "There's something else. I'd like to meet her, Mike. Talk to her."

"Are you sure that's a good idea?"

"I want to do it. Would that be allowed?"

"I think that under the current circumstances DA

Woods can be persuaded,'' Lafferty said with a smile in his voice. ''In the presence of counsel, of course.''

''Mike, I don't know what to say,'' Alicia murmured, suddenly overcome with emotion. ''You saved my life. If not for you I would have left my children parentless and gone to jail for a long time. Thank you.''

Claire moved away from her mother and went back into the den. Maizie, wiping her eyes with a tissue, shooed Joey in the same direction.

''No need to thank me,'' Lafferty said, his own voice low and filled with feeling. ''Just doing my job, ma'am.''

''Much more than your job, sir.''

''I'll call you tonight,'' he added quickly, and then hung up the phone.

Alicia stood in a daze, trying to absorb how that call had changed her life.

She would soon be free.

The dark world had become bright again.

Chapter 11

The office of the district attorney was an austere place, as befitted an institution supported by taxpayers' money and dedicated to dispensing justice to those who had violated the law. Alicia and Lafferty were shuttled by an aide into a room which contained a long refectory table and scattered chairs, where Oswald Kirby was already waiting for them.

Kirby rose and shook hands with Alicia. "Mrs. Walker. Allow me to congratulate you on your recent good fortune. The district attorney has supplied me with a copy of Amy Lassiter's full confession, since I am now her attorney of record."

"Thank you for taking the case," Alicia said.

"Not at all. It is always gratifying to see the innocent go free and the guilty apprehended. I promise you that your...ah... Miss Lassiter will get the very best representation I have to offer. If she agrees to accept my help, of course."

"Why did she confess so readily, Mr. Kirby? She seemed to be doing everything to evade capture, and then suddenly she caves in as soon as she is picked up? It doesn't make sense."

"It's a phenomenon we see occasionally with first-time murderers. Before the act the murderer is fueled by anger or desperation or whatever emotion causes him or her to commit the crime. But once the victim is dead, the situation calms down and the perpetrator begins to think about what he or she did. The murderer may go through the motions of eluding the police, but guilt and remorse and anxiety begin to take over the murderer's thoughts. By the time this person is arrested the primary emotion he or she is feeling, believe it or not, is relief."

All three looked around as Sandler Woods entered the room, followed by two uniformed policemen who were escorting a woman between them. She was handcuffed and wore leg irons with the gray scrubs that were Manhattan Prison issue.

Alicia looked at Woods and then met her sister's eyes.

Alicia had expected to confront her own image, but even with the dyed hair and unattractive clothing, the resemblance was astonishing.

Amy had cropped her hair to chin length and colored it very dark, perhaps in an effort to disguise herself, but the facial structure, full lips, hazel eyes, and body type were all Alicia's. Amy looked a little heavier, but perhaps it was just the jailhouse garb. Woods waited until she had seated herself, chains clanking, then glanced once covertly at Lafferty and left.

Alicia stared.

"Quite a shock to find out about me, wasn't it?" Amy addressed her dryly. "I have had the advantage all these years. I've always known about you."

"Miss Lassiter, as your legal representative I must remind you again of what we discussed last evening. You have already confessed to the crime of which you are accused, but anything you say here—" Kirby began smoothly.

"Save it, buddy," Amy interjected, cutting him off abruptly. "I've decided I don't want anything from goody two-shoes here, including you as my lawyer."

Kirby glanced at Alicia, who made a placating gesture. "Please stay," she said to him.

"Oh, isn't this nice?" Amy asked rhetorically. "The princess is determined to do the right thing. It warms my heart."

"Why did you do it?" Alicia asked quietly. "Why did you kill my husband?"

"Your husband!" Amy replied, laughing. "That's a good one. I saw more of him than you did. While you were running charity balls and taking modern jazz classes I was keeping him very happy."

"How did you meet him?"

Amy shrugged. "Purely by chance. He liked working girls, he booked me for a night, and once he saw me he was thrilled that he could hire me to do in bed what you wouldn't. It was a mutually beneficial arrangement, we both got what we wanted out of it."

"You haven't answered the question," Lafferty said, speaking for the first time. "Why did you kill him?"

Amy looked Lafferty over with a practiced eye. "This must be the boyfriend," she said, amusement in her tone. "Not bad. Not bad at all. Looks like you met with an accident recently, handsome."

"Something like that."

"I understand I have you to thank for my current incarceration. So jacked up about the princess you just couldn't stand to see her go up the river, huh?''

''Not for something she didn't do,'' Lafferty replied quietly, in an even tone.

''Oh, she did it,'' Amy said bitterly. ''She and all those other Greens who made her the apple of their eyes while I was jettisoned like so much garbage.''

''The circumstances of your birth and subsequent raising were not Alicia's fault,'' Kirby said.

''Oh, shut up, gramps,'' Amy shot back at him. ''I told you I don't want you here.''

Kirby rose and said to Alicia, ''I'll call you,'' then left the room.

''You really should let him help you,'' Alicia said. ''He can explain your situation so that a jury would treat you sympathetically, possibly even influence a judge to give you a lighter sentence.''

''My situation?'' Amy said, with a bark of derisive laughter. ''And what is that? Walker's whore, secret sister to Walker's wife? I was raised on stories of your wonderful life, my mother would cry when she saw you on the news or in the papers. *You* were the one she always wanted, the one she missed. I was the slightly less respectable and undesirable duplicate.''

''I didn't know!'' Alicia said.

''Oh, and you would have embraced the streetwalker sibling if you *had* known?''

''I don't know what I would have done. But I was never given the chance to decide.''

''Yeah, my heart bleeds for you. Such a tough life. I've been in your houses, seen your antique furniture, your designer clothes. I had to live on pills and salads for a month to fit into that Adolfo suit I wore when I shot Joe.''

"He brought you into my house?" Alicia asked her, aghast at the idea.

"Oh—shocking, isn't it? Of course not. He would not consider me good enough to walk on your carpets. I took his keys when he was sleeping and had them duplicated, that's how I got the clothes and the gun. I checked his schedule from that appointment book he kept in his brief-case. I knew when he would be appearing somewhere out of town and you would go with him. It was easy with the town house, since you were never there, but to get the clothes and replace them I had to go to Scarsdale and get past the servants. The day I shot Joe I sent a phony message to get the housekeeper to leave. I dressed up as you and made some excuse to the gardener when I ran into him. He just thought I was you and tipped his hat to me." She laughed.

"Why didn't you ever contact me?" Alicia asked quietly.

"Ah, well, that wasn't part of the deal, you see. In order to keep collecting those checks, mama was supposed to keep quiet and never say a word about you or the Greens. I wasn't supposed to know about you. But when she saw the news pictures of the gorgeous princess at the debutante balls and coming out parties she just could not contain herself. She sort of…slipped."

"And you never contacted Alicia because you wanted the money to keep coming," Lafferty said.

"Why not?" Amy demanded angrily. "She owed me! Her whole highfalutin' family owes me! I am as much a Green as she is."

One of the uniformed officers shifted position and Alicia glanced at him.

She had been so absorbed in Amy's story she had forgotten he was there.

"But why did you kill Joe?" Alicia asked, going back again to the central question. "Why?"

"Because he thought he could dump me! Just like the Greens dumped me when I was born. He used me as long as I was docile and played house with him for a price, but when I started getting ambitious he wanted to cut me off without a dime."

Alicia glanced at Lafferty.

"What happened?" Lafferty asked. "How did you start getting ambitious?"

Amy looked down at the scarred table and sighed. "There's a longevity problem in my business. You start getting a little older, the top services won't take you on, you have to take bigger risks with new clients, the johns want younger girls.... I had just about reached the limit of my marketability, so to speak."

"And so?" Lafferty asked.

"I wanted to start my own business. I'm good with clothes and fashion, I really am. I wanted to open a store. I know what appeals to the upper crust, I have been servicing their husbands long enough. I could have done it."

Alicia felt the sting of tears in her eyes. The plaintive tone in her sister's voice was painful to hear.

"And you hit Walker up for a loan?" Lafferty asked.

"He laughed at me!" Amy said, the outrage in her face explaining what had motivated her to kill her lover. "He told me to peddle it elsewhere if I wanted a nest egg, I was getting a little long in the tooth for him, anyway."

The silence in the room was deafening. The two cops looked at each other and then looked away.

"I would have paid him back, I wasn't grifting. It was a sound business investment! He wouldn't even consider it."

"And so you decided to kill him," Alicia said.

"Not then. It took a while. I saw you on the news with him about a month later and realized that if I nailed him and framed you for it I would be in the clear. I could pay you back for having the life I should have had and get back at him at the same time. It was perfect."

"Life with Joe was no picnic," Alicia said quietly. "You of all people should know that."

"Oh, yeah, that must have been tough. I sympathize. But you survived it, didn't you? With heirloom pearls intact. And now you have Mel Gibson here to console you."

The door to the hall opened, and Woods stuck his head into the room.

"Time's up," he said briskly. "Miss Lassiter is due back in lockup now."

"We'll need just a few more minutes," Lafferty said to him coolly.

Woods looked at him and flushed slightly. He shut the door with a bang.

Lafferty glanced at Alicia and winked.

"Are you sure you won't have Mr. Kirby as your lawyer?" Alicia asked Amy.

"No dice, honey. Take your guilt somewhere else," Amy replied shortly.

"I would like to come and visit you," Alicia said.

"Why? So you can thank me for getting rid of Joe for you and paving the way for cutie blue eyes here?"

"We're sisters," Alicia said awkwardly.

Amy snorted. "What? You think you're going to do old-home week with me now? It's a little late."

"I'd like to know about my biological mother, Deborah Lassiter."

"No, you wouldn't. Trust me."

"Will you at least put me on your visitors' list?"

Amy looked at her hard and then turned her head. "I'll think about it," she said.

The door to the hall opened again.

Alicia rose, shooting Lafferty a look that warned him not to bait Woods anymore.

"I'm ready to go," she said quietly. She looked at Amy. "I'll be back," she said.

Woods was watching as they closed the door behind them, and then he walked away without a word.

"I wish you would stop antagonizing him," Alicia said.

"Don't worry about it. He won't do anything. Having my unfortunate incident to hold over his head is like having money in the bank."

"I feel sorry for her," Alicia said. "I know she's done terrible things, but you can tell she's intelligent just by listening to her. I'm sure she would have been kind, too, if life had treated her better. What a waste."

"Alicia, lots of people have hard lives, much worse than your sister's. They don't collect blackmail money and become call girls and murder their clients. Or frame their sisters for their crimes."

"You don't understand. I do feel partly responsible for what happened to her, whether it makes sense or not. Do you know if her bail has been set?"

"Honey, she isn't going to make bail. She confessed to first-degree murder last night. There won't even be a hearing, trust me. She isn't going anywhere."

"So, I'll see her in jail," Alicia said.

Lafferty pulled her into his arms and kissed her, startling a legal clerk who was walking past them with a stack of folders. "Forget about your sister for a moment. I have some good news."

"Oh, tell me," Alicia said, sighing, resting her head

against his shoulder. "After the last hour I could use some good news."

"I'm going back to work in two weeks."

Alicia drew back and looked at him. "Oh, Mike, that's wonderful. I am so relieved. I was afraid that your career would suffer because of me."

"So let's go out and celebrate. What do you say?"

Alicia glanced back at the room that contained her sister, who would not be celebrating anything anytime soon.

Then she smiled at her lover.

"Sure," she said. "Let's go."

A week later Alicia was discussing Claire's lessons with her tutor when Maizie tapped on the door of the den and said, "Mrs. Walker, may I see you for a moment?"

Alicia excused herself and went into the hall.

"What is it?" she said to Maizie, who was standing by the ormolu table near the door. "You look worried."

Maizie handed her an envelope. "This was just delivered by messenger," she said.

Alicia glanced at it. "This is Michael's handwriting," she said, puzzled.

Maizie nodded.

"Why would he do this, send something by messenger? Why wouldn't he call me?"

"I don't know, but I think you had better read it."

Alicia turned the envelope over in her hands. "Maizie, please tell Mrs. Delahanty to return to Claire's lessons. Make my excuses and tell her I will get back to her."

Maizie left, and Alicia ripped open the envelope, scanning the handwritten lines anxiously.

"I wanted to wait until the charges against you had been dropped and I knew you were in the clear," Mike began. He went on to say that he needed her to think about their relationship and make sure she wanted it to continue now that she was free. It was understandable that she had grown dependent on him during her recent troubles, but now that she could return to her old life he wanted her to consider whether he was right for her. He had tried to talk to her about this subject the day they visited her grandmother, but after Alicia's negative reaction then, he had decided to put it off until her life was not complicated by an impending indictment. It was obvious that her children were her primary concern and it might be better for them… Alicia stopped reading in the middle of the page and skipped down to the bottom. She saw the last line, "so I will be taking some time away from you to let you consider what you want to do. I'll be gone until I start work again. Think about this, Alicia. It's the rest of your life."

It was signed simply, "Mike."

Alicia crumpled the note in her hand and stuffed it in her jeans pocket. Her expression was sad and thoughtful as she sat on the maple bench in the hall.

So Mike had doubts, he had just suppressed them after his outburst about their differing backgrounds at Hannah's house. He had focused on obtaining Alicia's freedom and allowed her to concentrate on the same objective without bothering her with sensitive discussions about their lifestyles or her family.

But obviously he had not forgotten, or changed his mind.

Alicia had concerns, too, but they weren't about how much money Mike earned as a cop or how many houses her family owned.

She was worried about her kids.

Claire had been traumatized by what little she'd seen the night she walked in on her mother and the policeman in her kitchen. Alicia needed time to talk to both Claire and Joey about her desire to continue her relationship with Lafferty, now that she was free and their official connection was at an end.

Apparently, Lafferty was giving her that time.

Maizie walked into the hall and saw Alicia's troubled face.

"I knew that note wasn't good news," Maizie said wearily. "What's wrong now?"

"I don't know. Maybe everything, maybe nothing. Maizie, what's the name of the child psychologist who saw your nephew when he was acting up in school?"

"Mary Phelps, she's in Midtown. I'll get the number for you from my sister."

"Thanks. I think it's important for the three of us to get in to see her as soon as possible."

As Maizie walked toward the telephone, Alicia glanced at the instrument sitting silently on the teak desk.

If it rang now, she knew it would not be Mike.

Ten days passed with agonizing slowness, during which Alicia and her children had three sessions with Dr. Phelps. Claire was resentful, Joey was confused, and Alicia was stymied. The therapist insisted that Alicia should not sacrifice her own happiness with Lafferty because her children would have a difficult adjustment to make; the purpose of the sessions was to help them make the adjustment, over time. Alicia did as Mike asked and did not contact him, but she missed him so terribly that his absence was like a physical pain. She missed him in her mind, she missed him in her bed, she missed him in her world. She was still afraid to trust him, to trust anybody, but decided finally that getting hurt again was just a chance she would have to take. The alternative, a life without Lafferty, the life she was currently living, was just too painful. By the time she was ready to accept that Phelps was right and maybe she could have both—the man she wanted *and* stable children—she was almost wild with longing for him.

Finally she could take the separation no longer. On the tenth day she awoke filled with resolve. She waited until the kids were busy with their tutors, then took the station wagon because the gas tank was full and floored the accelerator all the way into the city. It was a miracle she didn't get a speeding ticket. She left the car double-parked and ran up to the squad room, where she jogged past a bunch of staring cops and found Charlie Chandler at his desk eating a tuna fish sandwich.

"Early lunch?" she said to him.

Charlie did not respond. He was frozen with his sandwich in midair, a look of stunned amazement on his face.

"Tell me where he is," Alicia said.

"Uh, I, uh…what?" Charlie said, then swallowed.

"Lafferty. Where has he gone? I know that you know where he is, so don't try to bluff me."

Chandler glanced around the room, where Alicia's entrance was still the subject of intense interest. He didn't reply.

"Charlie, I am going to plant my feet here and scream bloody murder until either you tell me where he is, or the guys in the white coats come and cart me off to Bellevue. Now which is it going to be?"

"You're tracking him down again, aren't you?" Chandler said to her. "Why is that?"

"Because he's running away again. He has some idea that we're not right for each other for the long haul, or that our relationship will harm my kids. I had some doubts, too, but now I've cast them to the winds. I'm not going to have a chance like this again, and I won't throw this one away.''

"He thinks a lot," Chandler said, nodding. "You got to know that about him."

Alicia closed her eyes. "Is it something else, Charlie? Is he trying to let me down gently by telling me that it's because he's concerned for me? Is he trying to get rid of me?"

Chandler stared at her and put his sandwich down. "Lady, that is the last thing he is trying to do. Trust me. He's completely crazy about you."

"Then tell me where he is."

Chandler shook his head. "He'll kill me."

"I doubt it. He hasn't killed you yet."

Charlie rolled his eyes. "He's on my brother-in-law's houseboat over in Jersey—Weehawken. I'll give you the directions."

Charlie ripped a sheet of paper from the pad on his desk and scribbled a few lines, then stood up and read them aloud to her, looking at her inquiringly.

"I'll find it," Alicia said, taking the slip. She threw her arms around his neck impulsively. "Thank you so much, Charlie. I won't forget this."

"Neither will Mike. I'll pay for it when he gets back." Chandler was turning crimson.

Alicia grinned at him and ran past the onlookers who were observing her exit. When she got back to her car it was still there, wedged in behind a yellow cab, but if it had been towed she would have hired one.

Nothing was going to keep her away from Lafferty this day.

Chandler's directions were easy to follow. She went through the Holland Tunnel and found the marina with no trouble. The boat, Easy Money, was bobbing at anchor in the correct slip number, but Lafferty was nowhere to be seen. Alicia checked the boat and its environs, then was dusting off a deck chair to sit and wait when she saw him coming down the dock with a coil of rope in his hands. He was already sporting an early-spring tan, and his forearms were deeply sunburned.

He stopped short when he saw her.

"Not expecting company?" she said.

"No."

"I hope I'm a pleasant surprise," she said lightly.

"How did you find me?"

"Charlie told me where you were."

Lafferty nodded wearily. "It figures." He knelt to fasten a piece of canvas that had come loose from the hold.

"Don't blame him. I beat it out of him."

"I wish I could have seen that."

"It wasn't pretty."

Lafferty dropped the rope on the deck and turned to face her. He was wearing jeans with a navy T-shirt and leather boat shoes.

He looked delicious.

"So," he said. He looked apprehensive, as if he wasn't sure what she was going to say.

"Mike, if you want out of this, just say so," Alicia said without preliminary. "I will understand. A relationship has to be mutual. But if you love me, don't run away. You gave me time, I used it well. I've made my decision. I love you."

He swallowed. "I love you, too."

Alicia walked over to him and put her arms around his waist. He embraced her, and she inhaled deeply, feeling surrounded by his masculine scent and muscular protection.

"Then what are we waiting for?" she whispered. "Is there a bunk down inside that cabin?"

"There is," he said huskily, already pulling her blouse out of her jeans. He bent his knees and swept her up into his arms.

"Look out below," he said, and carried her down the stairs.

"Is anyone down there?" Alicia asked.

"Charlie's cat. Let's see if we can shock him." Lafferty drew open the curtain to the sleeping area and revealed a recessed bunk under the stern. It had a tiny window out to the dock and a foam mattress covered with material matching the miniature curtain, as well as a shelf containing a small television.

"A doll's den," Alicia murmured. "Is this where you've been sleeping?"

"This is where I've been lying awake and missing you," Lafferty replied, sliding her onto the bed and then flinging himself down next to her. The activity flushed the cat down from the shelf, where he had been hiding behind the TV.

"There he is, that rascal," Lafferty said. "He'll run outside and terrorize the local birds."

"I guess he feels you're invading his territory," Alicia said, as Lafferty began to unbutton her blouse.

"He has no territory, he's a nomad, a gypsy, passed around by Charlie's relatives like a tin pot. Charlie left him here with me, and we've been staying out of each other's way."

Alicia smiled. "So you don't feed him?"

"He's a scavenger."

"So who's been eating the Li'l Friskies?" Alicia asked airily, pointing to the box on the counter across from them. "Have you developed a taste for tuna-flavored snacks?"

"May we please concentrate on what's important here?" Lafferty asked uncomfortably, unzipping her fly.

"Certainly. Far be it from me to point out what a pushover you are," Alicia said, and then fell silent as he kissed her. He had not said much since she arrived, but now his mouth moved everywhere urgently, telling her without words how much he had missed her. Alicia clutched him, her hands at his waist, then at the back of his head, caressing his hair. He pulled off her jeans and panties and tossed them on the bunk as she clung to him, inhaling his unique fragrance of soap, sun and sweat. When he sat up to strip she let him go reluctantly, watching him pull the shirt over his head, the muscles in his arms working with the effort. Then he bent to peel off her bra and lifted her bodily onto him.

"I can't wait," he said huskily into her ear as she wound herself around him. "It's been too long."

Alicia closed her eyes slowly as she was impaled blissfully as he entered her; she moaned aloud and let her head fall to his shoulder.

"I missed you so much," he said hoarsely.

Alicia kissed the satiny expanse of skin next to her cheek.

She would make sure he never missed her again.

"So whose idea was this little separation?" Lafferty asked drowsily, and Alicia smiled. They were curled together on the bunk, the sound of the water lapping at the boat a counterpoint to their less rapid breathing.

"I believe it was yours, Detective. 'She has too much money, she'll never stay with me when she no longer needs me for her court case.'"

He opened one eye and looked down at her. "Worst idea I ever had," he observed. "But I don't think I was entirely alone. Who was worried that her kids would never accept me?"

"We're working on that. I hope you'll be part of it and participate in the counseling."

Lafferty traced the slope of her nose with a large forefinger. "I will do anything for you, Alicia. Anything. But I can't convince Claire of my undying devotion to her mother if she refuses to see it."

"One step at a time. Claire will eventually understand that I'm allowed to be happy. I don't expect miracles, but I have faith in her basic goodness and generosity of spirit. She loves me, and she will come to see that I need you."

"I hope you're right. I don't know what I'll do if she sets up a situation in which you have to choose."

Alicia put her hand over his mouth. "Both of my children will one day love you, as I do."

He kissed the fingers which sealed his lips but did not reply.

"Still worried?" Alicia asked him.

"A little."

Alicia sighed. "Claire's problem is her age as well as her father's death and how he died. She is on the verge of adolescence and she senses that our relationship is charged with—" She stopped.

"Lust?" he suggested.

"Physical attraction," Alicia amended. "Of course Claire recognizes that, and at a time when her own sexuality is just budding, seeing her mother so besotted with a handsome man is bound to be difficult for her. But we'll all work on it together and I have to hope for the best. That's all I can do."

"Besotted? I like that," Lafferty said, smiling. "Are you besotted with me?"

"You know I am," she said, kissing him.

"Would you care to demonstrate that fact?"

"Certainly."

And she did.

Epilogue

The living room of Helen's town house was banked with flowers. Baskets of lilies framed the fireplace, the mantel was draped with fragrant garlands, and the shelf in the bay window was filled with gladioli and flaming hibiscus in large standing vases. A white carpet runner extended from the front hall up the stairs and into the master bedroom, where Alicia was getting dressed. The staircase newel posts were graced with huge satin bows tied with bunches of baby's breath and golden pots of daisies and ivy stood at the foot of the steps. A caterer's truck was double-parked in the street below, and the staff was setting up noisily in the kitchen and dining room.

Helen, dressed in a cocktail-length silk dress in pearl gray, came flying in from the pantry and exclaimed, "No, no, no! I told you to put the caviar with the water crackers in the kitchen, then the pâté on the silver platter in the dining room. How many times do I have to say the same thing?"

The caterer's assistant threw Helen a dirty look but switched the trays.

Helen sighed and bolted up the stairs, moving as fast as her gray kidskin three-inch heels could carry her. She tapped on the bedroom door and then pulled it open when she heard Alicia's voice calling, "Come in."

Helen entered and found Alicia, fully dressed, pinning miniature carnations in Claire's hair. Claire's dress was a duplicate of Helen's, in a slightly darker shade. Matching bouquets of ivory orchids and white roses for the attendants sat on the brocade settee under the window.

"My dears, you both look lovely," Helen said breathlessly, taking in Alicia's candlelight satin suit and Claire's gown, which reflected her own. "Now if I can just refrain from throttling these idiots I hired to do the food, all will be well."

"Helen, you were shooting the florist this morning," Alicia said, kissing Claire on the cheek and patting her on the shoulder to indicate that she was ready. Claire smiled and slipped into the adjoining dressing room as Maizie and her four-year-old granddaughter emerged from it. Helen clasped her hands together and squealed with delight.

"Isn't she the most precious thing you've ever seen?" she said, gesturing to the preschooler, who was attired in an ivory brocade dress with a lace-trimmed capelet and matching lace-trimmed shoes.

"Have to go potty," the child announced.

Helen looked at Maizie, who raised her eyebrows. Helen pointed in the direction of the bathroom. Maizie took the child by the hand and led her out of the room.

Alicia glanced at herself in the gilt-edged mirror and was rewarded by a reflection of pure joy. She had never looked happier in all her years, and she knew it. The tea roses and baby's breath woven into her hair contrasted beautifully with her amber tresses, and the pearls at her ears and around her neck were her mother's. It was impossible to believe that this episode of her life, which had begun so badly, was about to end so well. And the next phase would be better. Her life with Michael was about to start, and she couldn't wait.

Alicia turned back to Helen, who was still fussing about details.

"Take it easy," Alicia said.

"Now the flower girl answers a call of nature. This morning the florist arrived with *red* roses, not white, and I had to have all the bouquets redone. Then the caterer arrived with the wrong kind of caviar." She picked up a piece of florist's paper from the bed and began to fan herself with it.

"Calm down, Helen. Everything is lovely and these little glitches always happen."

"Little glitch? Red roses at a wedding? I almost had heart failure."

They both heard Claire humming in the dressing room, and Helen added in a low tone, "How is she doing? I mean, with you getting married and all? We haven't talked about that for a while."

Alicia nodded. "She's fine. I think selling the house and moving helped a lot. A new place and going to the local school meant a different group of kids, putting aside the bad memories."

"And the counseling?"

"We're all still going. Mike has been marvelous. It's taken a while, but I think Claire realizes now that my meeting Mike right after her father died was just a coincidence, not a sinister plot or the end of the world. It was a tough thing for her but a good thing for me, and sometimes life just happens that way. It was a lot of work and a lot of tears but we got through it.''

"She seems to have accepted Mike now.''

"That wasn't the case in the beginning. Joey was younger, he was easier, but it took a while for Claire to stop throwing dirty looks and making snide remarks.''

Helen nodded. "I remember.''

"She has a little too much of her mother in her to keep her opinions to herself,'' Alicia said wryly

Helen grinned. "Good for her.''

"It wasn't until her own life became happier that she was willing to let me get on with mine.''

"Ain't that always the way?'' Helen said, then paused. "Maizie told me that you saw your sister last week.''

"Yes.''

"How is she doing?''

"As well as can be expected for somebody who will spend the next fifteen years of her life in prison.''

"She was lucky to get that. Thank God she finally listened to you and let Kirby represent her.''

They both looked up as Maizie and her small companion rejoined them.

"You look so pretty, Sara,'' Alicia said, addressing the fancily attired little girl.

"Thank you,'' she said, and curtsied.

Alicia and Helen burst out laughing.

"My daughter-in-law's influence.'' Maizie sniffed. "She gives the child airs.''

"Well, you do look scrumptious, cupcake, but not half as delicious as the groom,'' Helen said mysteriously, rising.

"Did you see him?'' Alicia asked, smiling.

"Of course. Last time I looked he was out on the terrace with his partner, his brother and Joey. Joey had a carnation in his buttonhole and was doing his best to look very adult. Mike's brother is pretty cute, too.''

"He's married with four kids," Alicia replied.

Helen sighed dramatically. "Well, back to older men with large bank accounts for me," she said wistfully. "Not all of us can have the real thing." Helen walked over to Alicia and hugged her. "When I think of where you were this time last year…" she whispered.

"Don't think about it," Alicia said. "One thing I've learned how to do is leave the past where it belongs."

Helen drew back, and the two women looked at each other.

Helen blinked rapidly and said, "I'd better go fuss over the seating arrangements before I start crying." She hurried toward the hall.

Alicia followed her and looked over the balcony. Mike, his brother, his partner and her son were all standing in the living room, looking very large and male in the middle of Helen's gilded antiques and fussy flower arrangements. Mike's brother resembled Mike but was less handsome—in Alicia's considered opinion—somewhat shorter and stockier than Mike with lighter hair. Charlie Chandler was wearing his Sunday best and looking a nervous wreck, sipping continuously from a tumbler containing amber liquid and wiping his brow with a crumpled handkerchief. Joey was almost as tall as Chandler and made her heart swell with pride. Alicia shut the door quickly and put her back against it, closing her eyes.

Could she be this lucky, after spending such a long time on the debit side of life? Could it all turn around so completely, due to one police detective?

"Mom, Helen says the minister is here. Are you ready?" Claire asked, entering the room.

Alicia opened her eyes and smiled at her daughter.

She was.

* * *

"Maybe we should just stay here for the rest of our lives," Lafferty said, polishing off the last of the room service dessert. "I could get used to this."

Alicia rolled over on the bed and took his plate out of his hand. "Oh, so you're accepting my corrupt offer to lead a life of indolence on inherited money?"

"I'd like to, really, but what would poor Charlie do without me? You know how he depends on my insights and perceptions to solve all his cases." Lafferty seized her shoulders and pulled her into his lap as the plate fell to the floor and then rolled over onto the flowered carpet.

"Michael, for heaven's sake, watch what you're doing!" Alicia protested, laughing.

"Why? Why should I watch what I am doing? This is the honeymoon suite, and we are on our honeymoon, and we had to go through hell and back to get here. If I want to break some plates I am going to break some plates. Champagne?"

Alicia sat up, shaking her head.

"Why not? Come on, dear wife of mine, I'm celebrating alone here." He handed her a glass. "Hannah looked pleased with herself at the ceremony, didn't she?"

"So she should. She was trying to fix us up from the moment she met you." Alicia pulled the glass back as he uncorked the bottle.

"Michael, there's something I have to tell you."

Lafferty turned to look at her, his smile wavering at the serious tone of her voice.

"What is it?" he asked. He put the wine bottle down and tied the belt of his robe. "Is something wrong?"

"No, something is right. At least, I hope you'll think it is very right."

Lafferty raised his brows. "I'm not drunk, am I?"

"No, I don't think so."

"Then why aren't you making any sense?"

"Mike, stop fooling around and listen to me."

He gazed at her soberly.

"I'm pregnant."

He stared at her for a long moment, then slowly a delighted smile spread across his face.

"Hot damn," he said.

"Really?" Alicia said. "I mean, I know we talked about having children and we planned on doing it soon, but...*this* soon? Are you okay with it?"

He put one arm around her and lifted her hair off the back of her neck with his other hand, kissing her nape. "Are you kidding? I'm thrilled. I can't wait to be a father, I have to make up for lost time. My brother has four kids and my sister has three. I'm a laggard."

Alicia smiled. "That can't be said about too many areas of your life."

He closed his eyes and pulled her head down onto his shoulder. "Now we'll have everything," he said.

"I want you to help me tell the children," she said, her words muffled by the nubby cotton of his robe.

"Sure. How do you think they'll take it?" he asked.

"I think they've accepted that you and I will have a new life together," she replied, sitting up and gazing at him. "They know that I'm still young enough to have more children and that children can be expected from a new marriage. But I'll talk to them, and if either one of them has trouble with it we'll discuss it in counseling."

"More counseling?" Lafferty said, looking at the ceiling. "I think Dr. Phelps funded her new Mercedes with the income we brought her last year."

"Michael..."

"Yes, I know. I'll look upon it as an opportunity to demonstrate, once again, how enlightened I am."

Alicia threw her arms around his neck. "I love you."

"I should hope so," he answered, embracing her tightly. "And when is the blessed event?"

"Around Thanksgiving."

"Plenty for us to be thankful for this year. So, counting back, was it the time on the kitchen table at my place after the St. Patty's Day party?"

"Probably," Alicia replied, blushing.

"You ravished me shamelessly, if I recall correctly," he said, laughing.

"Please don't remind me. I think your landlady heard us. She has been looking at me sidelong ever since."

"She looks sidelong at everybody. It's part of her job description. If she asks me one more time when I will be vacating my apartment I am going to bind her hands and gag her and chain her in the cellar."

"Well, she knows we don't need two places, and you told her about the new house."

"I should have kept my mouth shut." He peeled her satin dressing gown off her shoulder and kissed her collarbone. "So I assume that we can still, uh... I mean, it will be some time before the baby comes."

"We can," Alicia replied.

"Do we have to be careful?"

"Not really. Not yet."

He was very gentle, anyway, treating her as if she were made of porcelain, holding her to him as if she might break. When they fell to the bed together there were tears in her eyes.

"Why are you crying?" he asked, catching a welling tear on his fingertip.

"I am so happy, so lucky. I have everything I ever wanted. It scares me. I am so afraid of losing you."

He pulled her back into his arms. "You aren't going to lose me. I am not going anywhere."

"Your job is so dangerous, Mike. You could be killed."

He was silent, tightening his grip on her.

"Don't worry, I'm not going to ask you to look for another career," Alicia added. "I know that you love your work and you would not be the same man, the man I fell in love with, if you were willing to change. But I have nightmares about your being killed on the job. It haunts me, I can't help it."

"I understand that," Lafferty said quietly. "But I am always careful, and I will be even more careful now that I have so much to live for, with a new wife and a child on the way."

"I'll have to talk to Charlie and tell him to take care of you," Alicia said, smiling and brushing away tears.

"You'll have to wait until he sobers up," Lafferty replied dryly. "He was putting the scotch away as if *he* was getting married."

"He was getting emotional when I spoke to him, reminiscing about when you first started as partners. I think he is very attached to you."

Lafferty snorted.

"I mean it. His wife said that when you took that beating he was very upset."

"Not nearly as upset as I was," Lafferty said darkly, and Alicia laughed.

"That's better," Laffety said. "No more tears."

"No more."

He lifted her into his lap and said, "When will we know if the baby is a boy or a girl?"

"At four months. Amniocentesis will reveal the sex of the baby. Do you care?"

"Not at all. I'd like a son, but a girl as gorgeous as you would be just as nice. We'll have to have at least two."

"Please. One at a time."

"What about names?"

"If it's a girl I'd like to name her after my mother and call her Margaret," Alicia said.

"Fine."

"And for a boy Michael junior? Same name as yours?"

"Uh, not entirely the same. My middle name is Chester."

Alicia grinned. "Chester?"

"Don't ask. My mother's brother. He hates it, too."

"We have plenty of time to decide on a name," Alicia said.

He nodded and gestured toward the bathroom. "Want to take a shower with me?"

"I know what happens in your shower stall, Detective Lafferty."

"So are you game?"

She was.

* * * * *

If you enjoyed what you just read,
then we've got an offer you can't resist!

Take 2 bestselling
love stories FREE!

Plus get a FREE surprise gift!

Don't miss Silhouette's newest cross-line promotion,

Four royal sisters find their own Prince Charmings as they embark on separate journeys to find their missing brother, the Crown Prince!

Royally Wed

The search begins in October 1999 and continues through February 2000:

On sale October 1999: **A ROYAL BABY ON THE WAY** by award-winning author **Susan Mallery** (Special Edition)

On sale November 1999: **UNDERCOVER PRINCESS** by bestselling author **Suzanne Brockmann** (Intimate Moments)

On sale December 1999: **THE PRINCESS'S WHITE KNIGHT** by popular author **Carla Cassidy** (Romance)

On sale January 2000: **THE PREGNANT PRINCESS** by rising star **Anne Marie Winston** (Desire)

On sale February 2000: **MAN...MERCENARY...MONARCH** by top-notch talent **Joan Elliott Pickart** (Special Edition)

ROYALLY WED
Only in—
SILHOUETTE BOOKS

Available at your favorite retail outlet.

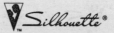

Silhouette®

Visit us at www.romance.net

SSERW

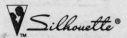

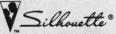

THE FORTUNES OF TEXAS

*Membership in this family has
its privileges...and its price.
But what a fortune can't buy,
a true-bred Texas love is sure to bring!*

Coming in November 1999...

Expecting...
In Texas
by

MARIE
FERRARELLA

Wrangler Cruz Perez's night of passion with Savannah Clark
had left the beauty pregnant with his child. Cruz's cowboy
code of honor demanded he do right by the expectant
mother, but could he convince Savannah—and himself—
that his offer of marriage was inspired by true love?

THE FORTUNES OF TEXAS continues with
A Willing Wife by Jackie Merritt,
available in December 1999 from
Silhouette Books.

Available at your favorite retail outlet.